Out of Bounds

It was too dark for me to see him, but I didn't need eyes to feel how strong he was; how easily he could overpower me. Then, just for a second, I felt his tongue lick my throat. I gasped with shock as his unshaven jaw grazed my chest and his tongue flicked up my neck.

His action had been incredibly carnal, and yet totally primitive. It was as if he wanted to taste me; to savour the sweat that was running down my neck. It was like some age-old ritual. He was making his mark on me. He was telling me that he was the predator and I was the prey. He must have tasted my fear.

Out of Bounds

MANDY DICKINSON

Black Lace novels contain sexual fantasies.
In real life, make sure you practise safe sex.

First published in 1999 by
Black Lace
Thames Wharf Studios,
Rainville Road, London W6 9HT

Typeset by SetSystems Ltd, Saffron Walden, Essex
Printed and bound by Mackays of Chatham PLC

ISBN 0 352 33431 2

All characters in this publication are fictitious and any resemblance to real persons, living or dead, is purely coincidental.

Prologue

Something had disturbed my sleep. I opened my eyes and listened with bated breath. There was definitely someone inside my cabin.

I reached up my hand, groped for the night light just above my bunk, then switched it on quickly. I gasped when I saw a man standing over me, completely naked.

My eyes took in every detail of his handsome features. His long black hair; his tall muscular physique; and his dark eyes, laden with sexual intent. I didn't scream, but my heart was pounding with a mixture of fear and excitement.

Without a word, he drew back the covers and climbed on top of me. He took my wrists in his hands and lifted them high above my head. Then he dropped his head down and kissed me.

He manoeuvred himself so that his legs forced mine apart and I felt his erect cock, pushing against my pelvis, wanting a way in. Still holding my wrists in his hands, he moved down a little and put his mouth on my nipple. He sucked then nipped it with his teeth, alternately, until my pussy was actually throbbing with lust for him.

Suddenly he stopped what he was doing and looked

at me. 'I've been looking for you, since I saw you last night in the restaurant. You're so beautiful.

'Now I'm going to fuck you.'

His brusque voice only added to my desire. I wanted him to do what he would with me.

He transferred my wrists to one hand, then, with the other, he guided his prick inside me. My pussy gave him a warm wet welcome.

He started to move in and out of me, going deeper and harder with every thrust. He put his mouth on mine and, as he plunged into me down below, his tongue plunged into my mouth.

The waves of the oncoming orgasm washed over me. I was drowning in his sensuality. In the distance I heard a woman speaking French; the sounds were muffled and distorted beneath the surface of the warm water. I lifted my head up, everything becoming clearer as I surfaced. I was alone in my cabin.

The announcement came again; this time in English. We would be docking at St Malo in fifteen minutes. Sighing with disappointment as the reality emerged, I sat up.

I had been fast asleep, buried underneath the duvet on my bunk, despite the fact that I was fully dressed. I felt hot and sweaty and now wished that I had something to change into; I had left all my stuff in the car.

I suddenly became aware of my pussy, throbbing inside my damp knickers, desperate for some attention.

Well, I still had a few minutes before the ferry was due to dock. And I was halfway there already.

Almost unconsciously, I slid my fingers in my mouth to moisten them, before slipping them inside my knickers.

Quickly and quietly, I took myself the rest of the way.

Chapter One

The moment I put my key in the door and opened it, I realised that something was not quite right. It was the smell of the place.

I hadn't been there for years and I would have expected it to smell musty, maybe damp, but not the aromas I was greeted with. Stale cigarette smoke filled the air, together with the unmistakable smell of half-empty beer cans. I even detected faint cooking smells. Somebody had obviously been here fairly recently; stayed here even.

Having checked the room to make sure that I was, in fact, alone, I sat down on the nearest chair.

I was exhausted; I had been travelling since yesterday. All I wanted to do was sleep. Looking about me, I could see that I had my work cut out: the place was filthy. Overflowing ashtrays, old magazines, plates with half-eaten food were scattered everywhere. It was obvious that someone had broken in, stayed here for a time, then buggered off leaving all this mess behind.

I was really cross. I was expecting to contend with a three-year layer of dust, not to mention spiders and perhaps the odd fieldmouse, but this was something else entirely – having to clean up someone else's shit.

I wandered through into the kitchen; it looked like a bomb had gone off in it. The dining room, on the other hand, was immaculate, as my grandfather had left it, apart from a thick layer of dust.

Thankfully the place had not been robbed. If whoever had been here had been that way inclined, they would have helped themselves to some of the things that were scattered around. My grandfather had been an avid collector and much of his stuff was antique.

I didn't really know where to start so I decided to unload the car first, bringing everything inside, before I ventured upstairs to see what further chaos awaited me.

It was nearly midday and I could feel the heat building up outside as I unloaded the car. It was going to be scorching in the afternoon.

I left my bags in the salon and tentatively climbed the stairs.

I felt sick when I saw the bathroom. The scum line round the old cast-iron bath; the built-up grime in the sink; the once white towels, now a disgusting shade of grey.

I just assumed that it had been a man staying here; I guess I found it hard to imagine a woman leaving things in such a state, even if she was a squatter. It then occurred to me that I had not seen any signs of breaking and entering. I would have to look into that later.

Originally the property had been a cluster of outbuildings and little farm cottages joined on to each other, but over the years they had all been knocked through. As a child, I had found it strange that my grandfather had all these big rambling rooms downstairs, yet upstairs was like a tiny cottage with only one bedroom.

When I used to visit, I slept in this room. Upstairs was so quaint, not much bigger than a children's playhouse, and I had loved it; my grandfather prefered to sleep in the barn, where he had his studio. He had virtually lived out there anyway, only coming in to get washed and to eat.

As I was remembering these things, I opened the bedroom door. I then got the shock of my life when I realised that I wasn't alone.

Almost immediately my shock turned to surprise when I understood what was before me. I was not in the least bit frightened, because the picture was actually beautiful and the last thing that I would have ever expected to see. It seemed somehow unearthly.

There were two men lying naked on the bed. Both of them young; both of them handsome; and both of them fast asleep. I stood there for several minutes just watching them; admiring them in their unconscious state.

They were both tanned, but one was as dark as the other was blond. The dark one was lying on his back with his arms behind his head. Either he had a very short beard or several days' growth on his chin; I was not sure which. He had a covering of dark hair all over his brown body.

My eyes automatically went to his cock, taking in every detail of this rare privilege. It was very large, although not erect, and lay in its bed of thick dark pubic hair. He was beautiful; like a Greek god in a painting.

I imagined he could be anything between 25 and 35 years of age.

My eyes went back to his face. From what I could see of it under his shoulder-length mane of black hair, he was extremely good-looking; a romantic Latin-lover type.

The blond one also had long hair, but tied back in a ponytail. He was lying on one side facing his partner. I could see that he was clean-shaven and probably very attractive, but in a less dramatic way than his partner. And maybe younger. He was definitely under 25 at any rate.

His arm was draped across the other's chest almost possessively; obviously they were lovers. And I felt a pang of regret, that two such beautiful men should be out of bounds to a woman.

I had to photograph them. I had to capture the intimacy between these two naked men, fast asleep and oblivious to their spectator. I rationalised my desire on the basis that it would empower me in a situation that was hardly tolerable – given that they were squatters. But I knew, deep down, it was more than that.

I slipped out of the room, ran downstairs and grabbed my favourite camera, my Contax automatic, with the film ready loaded – as always. I tiptoed back into the bedroom, held the camera to my eye and clicked.

It was only in that moment that it occurred to me that they might not take kindly to my photographing them in a scenario that, although undoubtedly erotic, was nonetheless compromising. And as I was thinking this, the blond one rolled on to his back. He opened his eyes, saw me and leapt up.

I had dropped my little camera on the chair behind me; thankfully he hadn't seen it. But his reaction had startled me and I felt like a voyeur; yet they were lying in my bed, in my house.

The blond one looked furious, cursing in French, words I couldn't translate, and started rummaging around in the bedside cabinet. As I opened my mouth to speak, he pulled out a gun. My words became a scream.

The dark man, so rudely awakened, leapt up and, immediately seeing the situation, pulled the gun out of his partner's hand. Speaking in French, his voice angry, he said, 'For fuck's sake, what's the matter with you? Put the gun away – she's on her own.'

'Miguel, how do you know she's on her own? There could be someone else downstairs –'

At last finding my voice, I cut in in French: 'I am on my own. And this is my house. What are you doing here?'

I was shaking with fear, but felt a little better knowing that the gun was no longer being pointed at me.

The dark one, Miguel, got off the bed and came

towards me. He grabbed me by the nape of the neck and walked me to the window.

'Is that your car?' he asked in a deep voice.

I nodded my head, overwhelmed by his strength, his height and, most of all, his nakedness. It made me feel vulnerable; it obviously didn't have the same effect on him.

'Well, don't be frightened. As long as you don't do anything stupid, you won't come to any harm. Now that you've seen us, I'll have to decide what I'm going to do with you.'

The blond one leapt off the bed and walked up to his partner. 'This is crazy, Miguel. I don't like it. Either we'll go or you get rid of her. The bitch will cause trouble if she stays with us and –'

All Miguel did was raise a finger. Coupled with the glare in his eyes, it was extremely threatening.

'Shut the fuck up!' he said quietly, as if to reinforce the point. And even I, who didn't know him, felt his aggressiveness bubbling away, just beneath the surface.

But it was enough to silence the younger one. He walked back to the bed, shaking his head, frustration written all over his face.

'You can't get rid of me. People know where I am. If my family don't hear from me, they'll come looking for me,' I said, forcing myself to speak.

Miguel looked as if he were surprised that I'd spoken. But a moment later, he released his hold on my neck.

I stood, frozen to the spot, while he strode across the room, picked up a pair of jeans from the floor and pulled them on.

Taking me roughly by the arm, he pulled me out of the room and down the stairs. I noticed, with relief, that the gun had been left in the bedroom.

He walked into the salon and saw my bags piled up in a corner. He picked up my handbag and emptied the contents on to a table. He found my purse and picked it up. I watched helplessly, while he looked through my credit cards and my money.

I was surprised when he just closed the purse and put it down again. It contained all the money I had with me; if he had taken it from me, I would have been really stuck.

He caught sight of my passport. He picked it up and glanced through it. 'You're English. Why is your French so fluent?'

'My mother's French,' I snapped. 'So now would you mind telling me what the fuck you're doing in my house?'

I felt a little more confident in his company than I did in his partner's. I guessed that, of the two, the blond one was the loose cannon.

He looked up at me briefly, but he didn't answer me.

Even though I knew I was in a precarious situation, I couldn't help noticing his beautiful brooding eyes and fantastic physique. Again, I thought what a waste it was that this man didn't like women. And he was a man in comparison to his partner, who appeared to be little more than a highly strung boy.

His fingers continued to rummage through the contents of my handbag. He smiled mockingly as he pushed aside make-up, tampons, a couple of photos and other rubbish that I kept in my almost bottomless pit.

'Is this really necessary?' I asked him, in a weary voice.

He looked up at me again, but this time his eyes bored into mine. In those moments, he made me feel so vulnerable, so uncomfortable, that I wished I'd held my tongue. When he dropped his head down again and continued to look through my things, I almost sighed with relief.

I felt embarrassed; my privacy was being invaded and I hated every minute of it. But I supposed that he would learn a lot by just looking through these things. He would see that I was a fairly innocuous character; completely harmless; certainly not an undercover police-woman, if that was what he was worried about. He was obviously being cautious for a reason.

At last he found what he was looking for – my car keys. Picking them up and slipping them into the pocket of his jeans, he said, 'Just in case you get any bright ideas.'

'Please give me back my keys. I won't cause any trouble. I'll go away and not mention anything to anyone . . . I can't stay here. If my mother doesn't hear from me she'll be worried.'

Even I could hear the panic in my voice.

'Katie, why did you come here?' he asked in a softer voice, probably picking up my fear. And he had addressed me by my first name, which took me aback. Of course, he'd seen it in my passport.

I decided that it wasn't in my best interests to tell him that I was actually intent on living here, so I replied, 'My grandfather used to live here. I've just come down here for a holiday.'

Then, just thinking about this untenable situation, where I was having to lie to protect myself, I suddenly snapped. 'Although some kind of fucking holiday this is turning out to be, with –'

He raised a hand, shook his head and tutted.

There were no words, but something told me that I was treading on very thin ice. I immediately shut my mouth.

'And there will be no one else coming to join you?' he demanded, a frown now playing on his dark brow.

I told myself to stay calm and think this one out before I answered him. If I told him that someone else was coming down – a boyfriend or a brother – would it make my situation worse or better? I decided that it would probably make it worse, so I decided to tell the truth. 'No. Nobody else will be coming to join me.'

'And how did you think to get in touch with your family? There are no phones here and I'm damn sure there's no reception for a mobile phone – if you've got one.'

'No, I don't have one. I intended to drive to a town and ring from there.They know I'm in France so they won't expect to hear from me for a day or two,' I answered, not daring to meet his eyes.

This was, in fact, another lie. My mobile was stashed away in the car's glove compartment. But after I had given him this latest, misleading piece of information, I wondered at the wisdom of it. Basically I had informed him that they could do whatever they liked with me, for the next day or two at least.

'Well then,' he said, with a flourish of his hand, 'make yourself at home.'

'How can I stay here – with you two – like this?'

He gave me a Gallic shrug, before he answered me. 'You came here for a holiday, didn't you? Just relax.'

He looked me up and down dispassionately, then he added, his tone heavy with innuendo, 'You never know: you might even enjoy yourself.'

He abruptly turned on his heel and walked into the kitchen, leaving me standing there, gaping like an idiot.

I did not know what to make of my situation; or my weird gut reaction to this man I had never seen before. I should have felt threatened, but instead I felt drawn to him. I found him incredibly attractive. No man had ever made this kind of impact on me, let alone a total stranger.

I wondered whether I was a prisoner or a hostage. He was treating me in a nonchalant, relaxed way, but I knew that I couldn't leave. Perhaps he was allowing me freedom because he knew that, without my car keys, there was nowhere for me to go. There were no other cottages for miles around; we were alone on this pine-clad hill and the nearest town was a good fifteen miles away. Not a distance I would have even contemplated walking in this heat.

But, of course, the remoteness of the place was exactly

why my grandfather had chosen to live here. And possibly why these two people had come here too.

The other one came down the stairs into the salon. He threw me a look of hatred out of his piercing blue eyes.

Now he, I decided, was dangerous. The less I had to do with him the better. He was now dressed, wearing torn jeans and a T-shirt. Again, a very attractive physique, but altogether slighter than Miguel's.

'I've made you some coffee,' Miguel said, wandering into the salon with two cups of steaming coffee in his hands.

Just for a moment, I thought he was going to pass one to me. But I thought wrong. He watched me, almost speculatively, while he passed one cup to his partner, then proceeded to take a swig of coffee out of the other.

I threw him a look of contempt, then marched into the kitchen. For some reason, I was most put out by his lack of courtesy. But, honestly, what did I expect, I asked myself. He was a loser ... a criminal, for Christ's sake. Of course he was going to be a wanker.

I didn't know what to do; the whole thing was bizarre. I felt like a visitor in my own home, yet they were the unwelcome house guests. But I decided to play along with them for the time being, doing nothing to irritate or alarm them; at least, then, I would be safe. As and when the opportunity arose for me to escape, and I was sure there would be one, I would seize it.

Thank God I had two cards up my sleeve. The photograph that I had taken earlier; luckily they hadn't noticed my camera upstairs on the chair. And my mobile phone. The reception was bound to be crap at the house, as Miguel had already pointed out, but if I could, at some point, get closer to a town, then I might just be able to call the police.

On the filthy kitchen worktop was my coffee. I took it, at the same time thinking that, if I had to stay here for any amount of time, I would have to clean up. I couldn't eat with all this mess around me: it was unhygienic.

Miguel and his partner were sitting in the salon when I walked back in. The blond one had been talking to him in a low ardent voice, but stopped in mid-sentence when he saw me. Miguel seemed to have an irritated, even bored expression on his face.

I had no idea what the boy had been saying but it must have concerned me; and it was painfully obvious that he thought I should have been 'disposed' of. My mind boggled at what he could be capable of doing.

Addressing Miguel, I said, 'I want to clean up this place; I can't stay here with all this shit around me. But I need to change my clothes; I'm too hot like this. I'd also like a bath.' I quickly added, 'After I've cleaned the bathroom.'

'You can of course change your clothes – after I've checked your bags. You can take a bath; we shan't bother you; but you've got to leave the door open. That way, if you get the idea to climb out of a window or something, we'll hear you. I suppose you know there is only cold water? I've been buying canisters for the cooker, but the gas tank was empty when we got here.'

'Well, there was no point in getting gas delivered, or reconnecting the electricity, if there was no one here to use it,' I answered dryly.

'Then maybe you should sort all that out. People might suspect something's wrong with you if you don't.'

Miguel picked up all my bags and carried them into the dining room. I followed him in and watched while he opened one at a time and tipped the contents out on to the dining-room table. When he was satisfied that there was nothing to be concerned about, being mainly summer clothes, he stuffed them back in. So much for me packing with care.

'What's the problem? Nothing in your size?' I quipped sarcastically, as he dumped all my underwear back into a holdall.

It had come out without thinking, but luckily he

laughed. I was sure the other one would have gone ballistic.

But again I felt degraded; my privacy was being invaded. It was like being stopped at Customs and having all my personal items exposed for all to see.

'You seem to have brought enough clothes for a year. Are you sure you're not intending to live here?'

I declined to answer because he had just picked up my last bag and was about to tip it out on to the table.

'Please don't,' I cried out. 'You'll break something. Could you empty it carefully?'

He looked at me suspiciously as he pulled out two cameras, various lens, films and a collapsible tripod.

'What's all this for?'

'That's none of your business,' I retorted, staring at him challengingly.

I didn't know why I had answered him like that. Maybe I felt that it was safe to provoke him. Perhaps I sensed that his intentions towards me were not 'dishonourable' although the circumstances were, most definitely, questionable.

'If you knew me, you would know that it would not be particularly clever to make me angry. So I'm going to ask you again. Why have you got all this stuff?'

Having seen his eyes and heard his voice, I had to quickly reassess my situation. I wasn't going to get away with another flippant remark, so I answered, somewhat meekly, 'I'm a photographer. It's what I do for a living.'

'And what do you photograph?'

'Promotional pack shots. Are you any the wiser?' I asked, facetiously.

I just couldn't help it. He was making me feel nervous, vulnerable, and I had a tendency to cover it up with sarcasm whenever I felt like this; not that I'd ever had much cause to feel like this. It wasn't often that I was trapped in a house with two fugitives brandishing a gun.

'I work in advertising. I take stills – for brochures, that

kind of stuff,' I continued, not liking the way he had just sat down at the table and put his hand over his mouth. His body language suggested that he was now considering something else – probably what to do with an awkward cow like me.

After the longest pause, he took his hand away from his mouth. 'I'm disappointed,' he answered. 'I would have expected you to be more – creative.'

I bristled with indignation: of course I was creative, but I had to earn a fucking living.

Although, it had to be said, I had been getting less and less work of late. Clients were finding it cheaper to phone up a photography bank than to bring in a photographer. I was doing more promotional pack shots than anything else – work that I found uninspiring and paid me peanuts; but the fact remained that in my field, where computer imaging had just come into its own, commercial photographers like me were in grave danger of becoming redundant.

But how could he have made such a provocative comment? He didn't even know me. He was just a worthless criminal and his opinions were just as worthless. But for some reason, I felt compelled to answer him.

'I don't enjoy what I do for a living, but it pays the bills. In my spare time, I do fine-art photography. I love it and . . . Actually, I'd like to take some pictures of you!'

I didn't know why I had blurted that out. Perhaps I wanted to test the limit; maybe I wanted to make him feel vulnerable for a change. No: I just wanted to capture his ruggedly beautiful image on film, to fantasise about him afterwards.

But he was now looking at me with the strangest expression on his face. I bit my lip, wondering if I had gone over the limit.

'We'll see,' he replied, after a pause, and walked out of the room.

His answer surprised me.

I quickly put on a T-shirt and a pair of old cut-off jeans, then brushed my hair and tied it up. I decided that I might as well leave all my bags in the dining room, since there was no room upstairs for them.

I started in the kitchen. I found all my grandfather's cleaning things under the sink and set about boiling water on the hob to wash the pans and plates that had accumulated. It looked to me as if they had gone two weeks without washing a single utensil.

From the kitchen I could hear Miguel say to his partner, 'Lighten up, Eric. By the time she gets to tell anyone about us, everything will be sorted out or we'll be long gone. Anyway, it could be useful having her around. You can live in all this shit, but it makes me sick. I know you don't like the situation, but you're just going to have to live with it if . . .'

I couldn't hear any more because the voices went quiet, as if they had just realised that I was listening to them. But I now knew which one of them was the dirty bastard.

One hour later and the kitchen was immaculate. There wasn't a fridge, but I was relieved to find plenty of food in the cupboards, including bread. It had probably been bought the day before: it wasn't that stale.

When I came out of the kitchen, Eric (I now knew his name) was sitting in the salon smoking a cigarette. His eyes narrowed when he looked at me but he said nothing.

For some reason he disliked me intensely and I felt that it had nothing to do with me finding them and the possibility of my shopping them. There was something else eating him up.

Carrying my cleaning stuff, I went upstairs to the bathroom.

Miguel was already there, attempting to clean up the sink with his bare hands. He had obviously had a go at the bath, but hadn't made much impact.

'Leave it. I'll do it,' I snapped ungraciously.

Then, totally ignoring him, I leant over the bath and began to scrub at the grime which had built up.

A couple of minutes later, I looked up to find him staring at my arse. Bent over as I was, a good deal of it was probably on display. I straightened automatically, forgetting that he was gay, and he strolled out of the bathroom with a supercilious smile on his face.

I decided that he was looking at me abstractly – pretty much as I might look at another woman who I thought was attractive. It didn't mean that I wanted to sleep with her.

Within half an hour, the bathroom was about the best I could get it. Clean enough for me to have a bath in, anyway.

'I'm going to get washed now,' I called down.

'Leave the door open,' was the reply.

I stripped off and sat in the bath while it was filling up with cold water. God, it was awful. But I was hot and sweaty and I needed to wash desperately. I was just glad I'd brought some nice soaps, fresh towels and shampoo with me.

After I had bathed – obviously I didn't linger – I got out and wrapped a towel round me. Then I leant over the bath to wash my hair under the taps.

When my body was dry and my hair had been combed out, I dressed in a cotton sundress.

I felt drained, physically and mentally, having been driving since the crack of dawn, when I came off the ferry at St Malo. All I wanted to do now was crash out.

When I came downstairs, I couldn't find them in the house, but I heard their voices. After a moment, I realised that they were out on the terrace at the back of the kitchen.

I went outside and found that the table had been laid for lunch – three places – and they were both sitting down smoking but hadn't yet started to eat. They had waited for me. This common courtesy surprised me;

I had thought them incapable of anything but uncouthness.

As I took my seat on one side of Miguel, who was now wearing a T-shirt, they started to eat. I took what I wanted and ate too.

Halfway through the meal, Miguel turned to Eric.

'Have you noticed that you two could pass for brother and sister?'

'Give me a fucking break,' Eric groaned quietly.

'No, I mean it. You're very alike. And even you would have to admit – she's pretty.'

'She's not my type,' Eric retorted.

I couldn't stand any more of this. The boy was regarding me as if I were a pile of dog shit; Miguel was studying me as if I were a new breed of dog at Crufts.

'Do you mind? Having to put up with you being here is one thing, but if you're going to start talking about me, like I'm not even here, then I'll . . . It's fucking rude!' I snapped, changing tack in mid-sentence.

I had suddenly remembered that I was hardly in a position to make threats.

Eric looked up at Miguel almost expectantly, but Miguel just laughed at my last-minute reticence, then continued to eat.

Secretly, I had to agree with Miguel's observation. Eric and I did look related. We were both very blond, with long straight hair. Except that, wet, my hair was down to my waist; and Eric's was just down to his shoulders. We both had blue eyes but, whereas I thought mine were large and open, his were smaller and piercing in their intensity. And of course, we were both tall and slim.

Yes, we could have passed for brother and sister. Me being the older sibling.

'Miguel, I'm really tired. I want to catch up on some sleep this afternoon. Is that OK?' I added sarcastically.

It stuck in my throat to have to be grovelling like this.

He found my compliance amusing, if the smirk on his

face was anything to go by. In any other circumstances, my hand would have been itching to slap it off.

'Yes. You can sleep outside on a sun lounger, where we can keep an eye on you,' he answered.

'How lovely and cosy: just the three of us!' I quipped, giving him a bitter-sweet smile.

At that, Eric abruptly stood up, knocking his chair backwards in the process. 'If you don't tell this bitch to watch her fucking mouth, I swear, Miguel, that I'll . . .' He raised his hand, as if he were going to swipe me from across the table.

I immediately leapt up out of my seat and, without even thinking, ran behind Miguel's back. Now feeling that I was in a much safer position, I retaliated: 'Oh yes? And what are you going to do about it, you –'

'Enough!' Miguel growled, standing up. 'You watch your mouth and you,' he continued, turning to Eric, 'get inside now.'

I could tell that Eric was weighing up whether to slap me one, just for good measure. Then, having cast a quick glance at Miguel, who was striding round the table towards him, he must have thought better of it. Swearing under his breath, he stormed into the house.

Miguel followed him and, a few seconds later, I could hear them talking in low, angry voices.

Feeling extremely uncomfortable, I got up and wandered around the house until I came to my grandfather's sun loungers. They were on another terrace, overlooking the woods and meadows. I sat down on one of them and spread my hair out to dry.

I lay back and shut my eyes, basking in the sunshine, and tried to switch off from this surreal situation. It was difficult. In fact, it was hard to believe that I could actually sunbathe while I was caught up in all this intrigue.

And as if to reinforce the severity of my situation, I heard footsteps running along the terrace. I sat bolt upright and was relieved to find Miguel heading towards me. Seeing that I was sitting down, he slowed down to a walk.

Smiling, half-amused and half-irritated, he sat down beside me.

He combed his hair back off his face, then looked across at me. A combination of the sweltering heat and the warmth of his gorgeous brown eyes made me feel as if I were melting under his gaze.

'I thought you'd made a run for it. I didn't relish the idea of chasing after you in this heat,' he said quietly.

'But you told me I could sit out here.'

'I know. I guess I'm just not used to people being so straightforward. I'm sorry for doubting you.'

The sincerity in his voice astounded me. Almost as if he were talking to a friend he had discredited, rather than the woman he was holding against her will.

But was it against my will? Maybe not. At this moment, I had no wish to be away from here. I liked being near him. I found him incredibly attractive, overwhelmingly so; and he fascinated me. I would have loved to know more about him. The only downside was his lover.

Miguel stood up again and took off his T-shirt. As he raised his arms to pull it over his head, I was treated with a perfect view of his chest and stomach: well muscled and covered in soft dark hair.

I had the urge to reach out and touch him; to feel his hard, hairy body underneath my fingertips. Then I noticed the thick black hair in his armpits, which reminded me of the sight I was greeted with earlier in the day. Uncomfortable with my lustful thoughts, I looked away.

I had never felt like this about anyone before. He had to be the most overtly sexual man I had ever seen. It was such a waste.

When I turned back, he was still standing, going through his pockets looking for something. After a moment, he pulled out a cigarette lighter. He lit a cigarette then sat down next to me. As an afterthought he offered me one, which I refused. I very occasionally smoked, but certainly not the stronger French brands.

He looked at me briefly, then took a drag on his cigarette. 'I'm sorry about Eric's behaviour. He would prefer us to be alone. He'll just have to accept the situation or . . . He'll be sorry if he doesn't,' Miguel added irritably, flicking the end of his cigarette.

I didn't understand what he meant, although there was definitely a threat in there, so I just nodded, sat back and closed my eyes.

Three hours ago and this gorgeous-looking man took me hostage, I mused. So what the fuck are you doing, sunbathing with him? someone screamed inside my head.

I sat bolt upright again.

'Miguel, I want to know why you're staying in my house. Even if I'm your hostage, I think I have a right to know what's going on,' I asked calmly, reasonably.

'So correct, so cool, so fucking English!' he retorted scornfully. 'I think I liked you better when you were frightened. But in answer to your question – you have no right. You have to earn the fucking right. OK?' he demanded angrily.

I nodded, trying not to gulp. Jesus, he was so unpredictable. One minute, offering me a cigarette; the next minute, scaring the shit out of me.

I gave him a quick, sidelong glance and was surprised to find him rubbing his forehead. He seemed pissed off, rather than angry.

Well, I knew exactly how that felt but, since there was nothing I could do about it, I just shut my eyes again.

The smell of him wafted over me. Not just the cigarette smoke, but his hot body smell. Not unpleasant: manly I suppose, maybe with a bit of aftershave or soap thrown in. I felt vaguely aroused and wondered what I would do if he were to touch me.

Probably dangerous thoughts for someone in my situation.

I was woken up by a hand being placed on my shoulder. It took me a moment to remember where I was.

Miguel had disturbed me. He was standing beside my sun lounger, gazing down at me with a faraway look in his eyes. But his expression changed completely when he saw that I was wide awake.

'I want you to come inside. I'm bored sitting out here and you've had enough sun,' he said gruffly.

I looked at my watch and was surprised to find that it was nearly six o'clock. I had been asleep for about two hours.

And he was right, of course. My skin was as white as a lily and I had stupidly been lying out without wearing any sunscreen.

I got up and followed him back into the house. Eric was lying on a settee in the salon, smoking. I supposed that he had been there all afternoon.

I couldn't help thinking that they were both wasting their lives. These two healthy young men were just lounging around, day in and day out. Life was too short to spend it doing so little.

'Where am I sleeping tonight?' I asked Miguel, thinking that I could sort out my bed before it got dark.

'You're sleeping with me,' he replied. 'But don't worry: you'll be quite safe. I think I will be able to restrain myself,' he added sarcastically, seeing my jaw drop to my chest.

'No, it's not that,' I answered, blushing furiously. 'It just doesn't seem right. I mean, you – with Eric and now me here too. I can sleep in the barn. There's a bed there. Then I won't be in your way,' I suggested tactfully.

'I'm afraid that's out of the question. If you sleep outside, then we can't keep an eye on you. You have got to sleep with one of us or both of us. I'm not leaving you alone with Eric. He's not on board with you being here and I don't trust him. Therefore you have to stay with me. If anyone should sleep in the barn it should be him,' Miguel answered, turning to Eric for his response.

'If you think I'm leaving you alone with her, you've got another think coming.'

Miguel shrugged his shoulders. 'Suit yourself.'

I went upstairs to the bedroom. The place was filthy and the sheets were grubby. There was no way I was going to do any more cleaning today, but I couldn't put my head down on one of these pillows. I would have to change the linen.

What a weird night I was going to have. Sleeping with two strange men who just happened to be lovers. It seemed immoral, perverted even. But it was probably better for me that they were gay. If I'd been in this situation with two straight men, I would have been worried.

Thankfully the bed was a large one. It was about 200 years old, made of heavily carved oak. I found some clean sheets and pillow cases in my grandfather's old linen chest then proceeded to change the bed.

Afterwards I opened all the windows to get some fresh air into the room. The lace nets billowed in the welcome breeze. I kicked all their clothes into one big pile in the corner of the room; I certainly wasn't going to touch them. Then I went back downstairs.

Miguel was reading a book, probably one of my grandfather's. Eric was dozing.

I remembered that I had brought loads of books with me from England, ones that I hadn't yet had a chance to read. And since reading was going to be a better way of passing the time than just twiddling my thumbs, I went to fetch a book from one of my bags.

I stacked the books on the dining-room table as I unpacked them. There were a couple of tomes on the history of photography as art. I thought they might give me inspiration, but I couldn't face reading anything too academic.

Nancy Friday's *Women on Top* – 'How real life has

changed women's sexual fantasies'? Probably not a good idea, this evening.

I suddenly spotted a Joanna Trollope, and pounced on it with something like relief. *A Passionate Man*? Well, the content was probably safe enough, but the title? Definitely not the title.

In the end, having found one too many reasons not to read Jilly Cooper and the like, I opted for *Pride and Prejudice*. It didn't matter that I had read it about four times since school. It was infinitely more sensible on my part to be on safer ground.

As it began to get dark outside, Miguel lit some candles. I watched him as he moved silently around the ground floor, placing them here and there.

Looking about me, at the flickering candles in every room, the house seemed to be enchanted, almost magical. These strange men had created a mood, an aura, where time and convention had no place.

It occurred to me that my grandfather would have approved of this. This was how he had lived his life. What a strange coincidence that these men had stumbled upon the home of a like-minded drop-out.

And I realised that, to an outsider, it would have seemed as if all three of us shared a contented silence; as if we were totally relaxed in each other's company or had known each other for years.

But this wasn't the case at all. My stomach was churning with tension and I was dripping with perspiration. Every time I looked up from my book, I found them staring at me: Eric, as if I were a large cockroach that he ought to step on, and Miguel, loath as I was to admit it, like he hadn't eaten for days and I was a bag of chips.

As the hours ticked by, I became more and more wound up.

I was having to share my home with two fugitives, albeit drop-dead-gorgeous fugitives, and I needed to know how this would all end.

I wasn't going to see anyone else, unless I made a trip into town, so why was I allowing this thing to go on? I had nothing to fear but Eric's gun and I felt sure that, if it came to it, Miguel would protect me or at least keep him in check. I should be demanding an explanation . . . Even a hostage was entitled to some sort of explanation.

'Katie,' Miguel called across the room, making me jump. 'Come into the kitchen with me. You can make us something to eat.'

What was I . . . his servant?

By the time I reached the kitchen, my temper was at boiling point and I decided that now was the time to tackle him again.

'Miguel, I need to talk to you. Now I'm not interested in what you and Eric have done,' I said, willing myself to stay calm, 'but I am concerned about –'

Taking me completely by surprise, he grabbed me by the shoulders and pushed me against the kitchen wall.

'I'm concerned too,' he whispered in my ear. 'I'm very concerned that you have been lying to me.'

As his eyes bored into mine, my heart started to pound. I then realised, with something like horror, that the adrenalin rush was more to do with excitement than anxiety.

'I don't know what you're talking about,' I retorted indignantly.

But my mind was racing. Which lie was he referring to?

'I'm talking about – this,' he went on, producing my mobile from his back pocket.

I was temporarily at a loss for words. I wondered if I should feign surprise, even incredulity, but then I thought better of it.

Miguel had just found one of the cards I had been keeping up my sleeve. He knew and I knew it. I decided to come clean and just admit it.

'What the fuck did you expect? I find two men in my house. You have a gun. You ask me all these questions, yet I don't know anything about you and . . . What are you doing?' I snapped, seeing that he was switching on the phone.

He handed it to me. 'Keep it, Katie,' he said flippantly. 'I couldn't give a damn. There's no mobile reception here. But don't lie to me ever again, because . . .' He suddenly broke off, closed his eyes and ran his fingers through his hair. He seemed – frustrated.

I suddenly realised that I was as much taken with his mannerisms as I was with his looks. Perhaps, in the absence of the words, they told me more about him.

He looked at me so seriously, while he continued to comb his fingers through his hair, that I got the feeling he was weighing me up.

And then, suddenly, it was as if he had come to a monumental decision.

'Come with me,' he said gruffly, gripping me by the wrist. He evidently wasn't going to give me any choice in the matter.

Until he'd given me this last order, my sense of self-preservation had been sadly failing me. It finally kicked in as he dragged me out on to the terrace.

'Leave me alone!' I shouted, struggling to free myself of his grip.

'I'm not going to hurt you,' he said, laughing at my futile efforts. 'Look!'

He unclenched his hand and – suddenly – I was free.

Not wanting to waste a moment, I jumped off the terrace and ran. I didn't know where I was running: it was pitch black and I couldn't see a thing. All I knew was that I had to get away from him.

I'd probably got only twenty feet when I felt his hand on my shoulder.

'Where do you think you're going?' he demanded, pulling me up to a stop.

He spun me round violently and I fell against his chest.

The air was hot and humid. I was panting and dripping with sweat. But above the heavy atmosphere, above my anxiety as to Miguel's next move, I felt an exhilaration as we made physical contact.

I was scared of him, but more angry with myself for finding him so attractive.

'Get away from me,' I yelled, punching him in the chest as hard as I could.

It was like punching a brick wall.

'If you touch me,' I continued, with a kick that was meant for his shins, but didn't even connect, 'I'll –'

'You'll what? What will you do?' he demanded angrily, seizing me by the forearms and lifting me up. 'Tell me, because I'd really like to know.'

I didn't answer him, because I didn't have an answer. It was too dark for me to see him, but I didn't need eyes to feel how strong he was; how easily he could overpower me.

Then, just for a second – no, not even a second – I felt his tongue lick my throat. I gasped with shock as his unshaven jaw grazed my chest and his tongue flicked up my neck.

His action had been incredibly carnal – and yet totally primitive. It was as if he had wanted to taste me; to savour the sweat that was running down my neck.

Of course, it was impossible for this to be sexual, so what else could he have meant by such bizarre behaviour?

Suddenly it came to me; after all, it was an age-old ritual. He was making his mark on me. He was telling me that he was the predator and I was his prey.

And yet he must have tasted my fear, for he suddenly dropped me as suddenly as he had picked me up. But his hands stayed on my arms.

'OK. Let's calm down,' he whispered brusquely. 'This is getting out of hand. And you're making this more difficult than it needs to be. I'll let you go if you promise not to run away. OK?'

'OK,' I agreed breathlessly.

If he did but know, his sexy voice had been enough to take the wind right out of my sails. And I had indeed calmed down, sufficiently to notice that I was still close enough to hear him breathing; still close enough to feel the heat coming off his body; still close enough to smell him.

I was still panting, but it was no longer with fear.

He continued to hold me. I had no idea what he was thinking; I still couldn't see his face. Then, abruptly, he let me go.

'Come on. Let's go inside and make something to eat. Eric will be wondering where we've got to.'

One minute so intense; the next minute so flippant. Bewildered by his mood swings and completely stumped as to why he'd wanted to take me outside in the first place, I followed him back in.

I took a clean pair of knickers and a T-shirt up to the bathroom with me, since I didn't have nightclothes as such and I couldn't very well sleep naked. And when I finally climbed into bed, I left a candle burning on a nearby table.

I felt uncomfortable – uptight about sharing a bed with these two people that I didn't know – but I didn't feel scared. However unpredictable Miguel was, whatever crimes he'd committed, for some reason I thought I could trust him. I still felt relatively safe.

I must have fallen asleep because I woke up later, feeling very thirsty; I needed some water desperately.

I looked at my watch. It had gone midnight but they still hadn't come up to bed. The candle had nearly burnt out so I decided to go downstairs before it went out and get myself a drink.

As I went down the stairs, the house seemed unnaturally quiet. I wondered if they had fallen asleep, since several of the candles had already extinguished themselves.

I saw them as I got to the bottom. They were in the

salon. They were doing something that I had never seen before. At least, I had never seen other people doing it.

Miguel was sitting in a chair; lying back in a chair, rather. He was still dressed in his jeans but his flies were undone. Eric was crouching on the floor between Miguel's legs, evidently giving him a blow job. Eric was naked.

There was enough light in the room for me to see that Miguel was quite detached – switched off from what was happening to him. His eyes were shut, his arms folded behind his head. Eric was putting in so much effort, obviously relishing what he was doing, but Miguel seemed both unappreciative and unresponsive, not once putting a hand to Eric's bent golden head.

Miguel was definitely the dominant one, Eric the submissive one. I knew that now for sure.

I would have loved to take pictures; they looked so beautiful together. Eric's blond locks against Miguel's dark pelvis. Eric's beautiful buttocks gleaming white against the background of Miguel's tanned skin.

For one fleeting moment, Eric reminded me of a ministering angel, although that image was in complete contrast to the act he was performing. Perhaps it was his hair, shining like a golden halo in the candlelight. Maybe it was because, in the shadows, Miguel looked even darker, even more mysterious; like a dark angel.

They were perfect male specimens and yet exact opposites.

I felt a wave of jealousy. I wished that I could push Eric aside and take over. I wanted to worship Miguel as Eric was doing, to show him that I thought he was beautiful too. But Miguel wouldn't have wanted me; that was not what he was about.

I stood there for maybe five, ten minutes, before I realised that Miguel was watching me. I had no idea how long he had been aware of me, but it was probably long enough for him to realise that, far from being shocked or repelled by seeing them together, I was fascinated, even aroused, by watching them.

His dark brooding eyes were boring into mine and I suddenly felt ashamed of myself, even perverted. But I still couldn't bring myself to turn away.

And he had not stopped Eric. Incredibly, he was letting his lover continue, oblivious to the spectator behind him.

Miguel's body started to shudder. He grabbed Eric's head and thrust his cock hard into him. I saw his stomach muscles contracting; he was coming. Poor Eric has to be gagging on him, I thought; he is so big.

And the whole time Miguel never took his eyes off me.

I now felt uncomfortable for another reason. I knew that, somehow, I had been part of it. I had made him come by watching.

With my heart beating way too fast, I walked into the kitchen and got myself a glass of water. Without looking in their direction, I ran upstairs and climbed into bed.

The linen sheets cooled my legs. I was hot and sticky but it had nothing to do with the temperature.

Chapter Two

When I woke up in the morning they were both still asleep. I rolled over carefully and found that I was on one side of Miguel and Eric was on the other. Eric was naked; Miguel was wearing a pair of boxer shorts.

I was surprised, knowing that I had seen him naked yesterday morning. Perhaps they were for my benefit: trying to bring a shred of decency into this bizarre situation.

I got out of bed as quietly as I could and walked to the bathroom. I wanted a bath but, not wishing to disturb them with the sound of running water, I closed the door. Bracing myself against the cold, I stepped into the bath.

Actually it was quite invigorating. In a few minutes I got used to it and, after washing myself, I was able to lie back and rinse off.

Suddenly the door was thrown open and Miguel stormed in. I looked for some way of covering myself up but there wasn't one. I had to lie there, pretending it didn't matter.

He looked at me, his eyes sweeping over my body before returning to my face. 'I told you never to shut the door,' he said gruffly.

'I didn't want to disturb you. I thought you were asleep.'

'Well, don't do it again. I thought you'd gone – I couldn't hear you.'

I sat up and pulled out the plug. I started to stand up, wondering why I felt so self-conscious in front of him. I should treat him as if he's a woman, I told myself. He won't fancy me, so modesty on my part is completely unnecessary.

He handed me my towel and, having wrapped it round my body, I got out.

'Would you like a coffee?' he asked, watching me as I attempted to dry myself without revealing any more flesh than was absolutely necessary.

Still feeling uncomfortable under his intense gaze, I accepted.

I breathed a huge sigh of relief when he walked out of the bathroom, leaving me alone to get dressed.

When I went down, he was sitting on the terrace in jeans and a shirt. There were just two mugs of coffee on the table. Obviously he was not expecting Eric to be up so early.

'Why did you come downstairs last night?' he asked, watching my face intently.

I blushed guiltily. 'Not to spy on you two, if that's what you think. I was thirsty and I wanted a drink.'

'It took you a long time to get the drink!' he said facetiously. Then he added, 'But don't get me wrong: I like it that you wanted to watch. It tells me something about you. And once Eric gets over the shock of you being here, he'll see it in you too.'

I didn't know what he was implying, but I was cringing nonetheless.

'So how long do you intend to stay?' I asked, sounding light and conversational, so as not to convey the fact that I needed to know – really badly.

'I can't answer that.'

His abrupt answer quashed any ideas I might have

had about him opening up to me and we drank our coffees in silence.

After a while Miguel spoke again. 'We need to get some food. And you had better phone your family, in case they suspect anything untoward has happened to you. I think we should go into town this morning. You can drive. Wait here while I tell Eric we're going.'

I waited all right, but I was bristling with indignation by the time he got back. The way he spoke to me, so offhandedly; I just couldn't stomach it.

'Right, now you wait here,' I said pointedly, 'while I get my mobile and my handbag. I might want to buy something.'

I marched inside, not waiting for an answer.

When I came out on to the terrace again, I immediately caught sight of the gun, now lying on the table. I stopped dead in my tracks, suddenly very frightened. It reminded me how vulnerable I was. And that Miguel was not a casual acquaintance – he was a desperate fugitive.

'Katie, I'm taking this with me,' he said, shoving it into the belt of his jeans and pulling his shirt out to hide it. 'If you make any stupid moves, you know what will happen. I don't have to spell it out for you, do I?'

I shook my head, feeling sick with nerves. Not that I had intended to do anything anyway. I didn't need a gun to feel overpowered by Miguel. Just standing near him was enough.

He gave me my car keys and we walked round to the front of the house. I got in the driver's side and he sat next to me.

'Where shall I drive to?' I asked.

'Do you know the area?'

I nodded.

'Head for Eauze. We can get everything we need from there and I'm sure there'll be mobile reception.'

Eauze was about fifteen miles to the east of us. I'd

been there many times with my grandfather so I remembered the way.

As I drove along the country lanes I was aware of Miguel staring at me.

'Have you got a boyfriend, Katie?' he asked, after a while.

'No,' I snapped.

I could have expanded, but I didn't. I felt that my situation would be even more precarious if they knew too much about me. It was better that I was an unknown entity.

'How old are you?'

'Why the inquisition?' I was irritated by his interest, not being able to account for it. After all, he wasn't being friendly: he had a gun in his pocket.

'I'm just wondering why a girl like you should be keen to stay alone, in the middle of nowhere.'

'I'm twenty-seven,' I answered, ignoring his last comment. The fact that I used to spend every summer here, on my own, while my grandfather worked in his studio, wasn't any of Miguel's business.

'Have you ever been involved with anyone?'

'Yes,' I snapped. There was no way I was going to expand on this one.

'This is a nice car. Is it new?'

I didn't want to discuss anything that might make my situation more untenable, but I decided that my MG was fairly safe ground. 'You ask a lot of questions. Yes, I got it a few weeks ago.'

'You must be a good photographer, then.'

I shrugged my shoulders. 'I get by.'

My fear had vanished within minutes of us getting into the car, and Miguel's questions, while being direct to the point of rudeness, showed me that he was interested in me, or at least a little curious. I wished it was because he liked me.

I then asked myself why it should be so important for someone like him, a man on the run, to actually like me.

Any normal person would be praying for the day that the pair of them would leave.

If I only knew what he was hiding from, if I only knew his crime, then I would be able to determine whether I was making a huge mistake by letting him get inside my head like this. If I knew the worst, I would be able to pull myself together. I would stop harbouring lustful thoughts about someone who was, at best, a loser, and, at worst, a psychopath.

Since he had asked me so many questions this morning, I felt perfectly justified in asking him one too. 'Miguel, why are you staying in my house? Are you in hiding?' I asked, having eventually summoned up the courage.

I felt him turn to look at me. I felt his big brown eyes on my face, almost burning me in their intensity, although mine were still fixed on the road.

I couldn't bear it: I didn't know whether he was angry or uneasy. After a minute I began to chew my lip, thinking I had gone too far.

'Katie, you know I can't answer that – right now,' he answered eventually.

I swallowed nervously, then tried again. 'So have you or Eric done something really terrible? Because I – I think it would really help me if I could . . .'

I wasn't quite sure how to finish the sentence.

I gasped when he dropped his hand on to my thigh and gripped it. I didn't know whether he had done it to reassure me or to warn me. 'Everything will be fine, as long as you don't ask me any more questions like this,' he replied in a brusque voice. 'I'll tell you when I'm ready and not before.'

He slid his hand slowly down my thigh before removing it and returning it to his own. I found the gesture very disconcerting. Surprisingly intimate, strangely sensual, and very reminiscent of last night, when he had licked my neck.

I swallowed, nodded to show my understanding, but

kept my eyes glued to the road. I didn't want him to see how much he frightened me . . . how much he excited me.

We spent the rest of the journey in silence, but now I found it totally distracting, sitting so close to him in my little sports car. He was unpredictable, scary, yet so incredibly sexy. His thigh was inches from my own and I would have loved to be able to put my hand on him too, just to feel him; to feel his hardness inside his jeans. I reminded myself that he wouldn't get an erection on my account.

And as I was thinking this, we arrived in Eauze.

'Why don't you phone your family now and get it over with? And I speak English, so be careful. Act perfectly naturally. If you make them suspicious, you will suffer the consequences. OK?'

I nodded my head and, with butterflies in my stomach, phoned my mother.

'Hi, Mum. It's me.'

'Hello, Katie. Are you at the house?'

'Yes, I got here yesterday morning.'

'Is everything all right?'

Now I looked at Miguel; he was watching me carefully.

'Yes, fine, except that there's no hot water and electricity, of course. I shall get on to the companies about it.'

'And have you seen anyone?'

Now I was nervous; I thought that perhaps Miguel could hear her and the question was a little odd – I hadn't expected it.

'Well, nobody is likely to come visiting, are they? And I've only just come out now, to phone you. So no, I haven't seen anyone.'

'Robert's been phoning me two or three times a day. He's very upset, Katie. What do you want me to say to him?'

Sighing, I threw my head back and shut my eyes,

forgetting for a moment that I was not alone. 'Tell him to fuck off and leave you alone.'

'I can't do that. He wants me to tell him where you are.'

'Don't you dare tell him.That's the last thing I need at the moment –' I nearly added, 'him coming down here,' but, remembering that Miguel was beside me, I stopped myself just in time. 'Just tell him that I want nothing more to do with him. He'll get the message eventually.'

'All right, Katie. When will you phone me again?'

Looking at Miguel, I said, 'I don't know. Maybe in a couple of days?'

He nodded his head and made a sign for me to finish the call.

'Mum, I've got to go now. I'll speak to you soon. Bye.'

When I had disconnected the call, Miguel smiled wryly.

'You can learn far more about a person by listening to their phone calls. Do you know that?'

'Really? Well, perhaps you'd like to make a phone call?' I replied sarcastically, handing him the phone.

'No. I don't have anybody that I would want to speak to,' he answered quite seriously.

'Poor you! Well, at least you've got Eric,' I retorted.

'OK, get out of the car. We've got shopping to do,' he said, ignoring my last comment. 'And remember what I said – don't get careless. I don't want to hurt you, but I will if I have to.'

Nodding in agreement, I got out.

Our first stop was a baker's shop. Unfortunately for me, the lady behind the counter recognised me, having seen me in there years ago with my grandfather.

I sensed, rather than saw, Miguel's hand go to his waist, and I acted as naturally as I could in such a tense situation.

I introduced Miguel as my boyfriend – it was the only thing I could think of, probably wishful thinking – and they shook hands.

She enquired after my mother and we chatted for a couple of minutes, but meanwhile another customer had walked into the shop and was waiting to be served. Thankfully our conversation was cut short and I was able to buy some bread quickly, then leave.

Once outside, I gave a huge sigh of relief, my churning stomach beginning to calm down.

We hadn't got very far down the road before Miguel turned on me.

'What are you playing at? Do that again and I'll hurt them before I hurt you. Is that clear?'

Starting to cry with real anxiety, I answered, 'I'm sorry, Miguel. I haven't been here for at least four or five years; I didn't know she would still be there. This could happen in any of these shops. I used to spend every summer here.'

I began to get the impression that my crying was unsettling him; even making him feel guilty. He must have realised that it had been a genuine mistake.

He just stood there, watching me, running his fingers through his hair, as if he didn't know quite what to do; then he said, 'OK. Stop crying. I'm sorry. Perhaps if it happens again you should tell them I'm your boyfriend. It's a good idea. It's quite feasible that you would come down here with someone. Just don't invite any long-lost friends round for dinner. OK?' He smiled at me almost affectionately and, despite everything, my heart missed a beat.

I decided there and then that he was a bit too soft-hearted to be a hardened criminal. He was probably an amateur if my tears could affect him.

I wiped my eyes and nodded. 'Don't worry, no one would expect me to. My grandfather never invited anyone to the house; he was a recluse. They probably think we're all a bit odd anyway.'

'Good. So let's finish the shopping and get back. I don't like being around all these people either.'

* * *

When we got back to the house, Eric was sitting on the terrace.

'You took your fucking time!'

'Well, we had to buy a lot of shopping,' Miguel answered coldly.

I threw Eric a look of contempt then quickly walked into the kitchen and started to unpack. I knew that I shouldn't provoke him; the tension was almost intolerable when the three of us were together anyway, without me aggravating the situation. But for some reason, I just couldn't help myself. Eric was bringing out the worst in me.

'Miguel, I'm just going down to the barn,' I announced after lunch.

I hadn't been inside my grandfather's studio for years and it held fond memories for me.

'Yes, I'll allow you to go to the barn,' he answered, his tone heavy with innuendo. 'But I'll come with you.'

I shrugged my shoulders and bit back the childish retort that would have been forthcoming under normal circumstances.

We strolled over the lawns until we came to a cluster of outbuildings. It then dawned on me that one of them, probably Miguel, had been cutting the grass. Certainly, having been left empty for three years, the garden should have looked like a jungle.

'Someone's been keeping the garden tidy. Is it you?'

He seemed almost embarrassed by the question. 'Yes. I couldn't bear to see everything going to rack and ruin. I found an old lawn mower in one of the sheds and managed to get it going. I'm no gardener, but it looks a lot better than it did.'

Passing one of the outbuildings, I noticed a couple of motorbikes parked up, half-covered by an old tarpaulin.

'Are they yours?'

Again, he looked uncomfortable that I had seen them, but he acknowledged that they were.

I had been wondering how they had got here. It was too far from anywhere for them to have walked; and without a fridge in the house, they had to have been going shopping fairly regularly.

But I was surprised: the bikes looked to be fairly new. One was Japanese and the other was Italian, probably quite expensive. I wondered how they could have afforded to buy them. And how they managed to buy their food. It didn't go unnoticed that Miguel had paid cash for the shopping today, including mine. I had offered to pay my share but he'd refused. It now occurred to me that they might be bank robbers in hiding.

As I opened the door to the barn, I gasped in amazement.

It was as if my grandfather were still alive. Everything looked so clean and tidy. Much of his work still hung on the walls and there were one or two partially finished pieces still pinned to boards. Yet I had been informed by his solicitors that all his remaining work had been sold after he passed away.

On closer inspection, I realised that the paint had been freshly mixed. The oils hadn't dried up, which they most certainly would have done after any length of time, and the art wasn't exactly in his style.

For a moment it crossed my mind that perhaps he hadn't died. Maybe it was a final stunt to get total solitude: that's what he had always wished for. Then it dawned on me. Someone else had been using his studio.

I walked up to the first piece, still in a state of shock. Whoever it was, they were extremely good, incredibly talented; I knew enough about art to see that.

I turned to Miguel. He was looking at me carefully, as if he wanted to gauge my reaction. At long last, the penny dropped.

'This is your stuff, isn't it? I had no idea you could paint.'

'It's what I do for a living,' he answered, not meeting my eyes, as if he were embarrassed.

'Really? You sell them? I don't mean to be rude; they're certainly good enough. But you just didn't seem the type to actually work for a living. The way you're shacked up in my house . . . Do you make a lot of money painting?' I asked, changing tack quickly.

He shrugged his shoulders and answered me in exactly the same way as I had answered him earlier. 'I get by.'

He had thrown me completely. I had been trying to build up a character in my head, piecing together all the bits that I had picked up in the last 28 hours. Now that I had discovered he was a budding artist, I was back to square one.

His paintings were of people. Men with men; men with women; women with women. But I didn't think he would have had anyone pose for him. It was pure fantasy; escapism.

They were very erotic, some depicting bondage, domination and submission. Others were just of beautiful people making love, but often more than two people.

I tried to look at them abstractly, without thinking about the man who had created them. I had to admit that they were beautiful, every one of them. And if a painting could be explicit, without a trace of obscenity, then his were. He obviously had a wonderful imagination, and being able to transfer it to canvas was a rare talent.

I looked at each picture for several minutes, and sometimes I went back again for a second look. I loved them. He had expressed what I sometimes felt inside; some of my most deep and private fantasies.

How I wished I could take a photograph in the way he could paint a picture; not that I, personally, could ever be as liberated with my camera. I was actually aroused by just looking at his work.

Now I understood why he had let me watch him last

night. He knew that I had found the scene erotic and for him that was OK. He empathised with that.

I wondered what he would do if I turned round now and told him how I felt about him. That just being in the same room as him made me hot and sticky between my legs; and if he wanted me to, I would lie down on the floor right now and let him fuck me.

I reminded myself that he was gay and would probably find the very idea of touching me abhorrent. Also, it was becoming increasingly obvious to me that he liked me; and probably the worst thing I could do at this moment, when things were progressing so nicely in that department, would be to announce my burning desire for him.

I turned round and looked at him. He was staring at me with a mixture of amusement and uncertainty on his face. He was pleased that I liked his paintings, but felt that his privacy was being invaded. I could understand that.

I wanted to ask him if they reflected his fantasies; whether he had ever actually indulged in any of these scenes and where he got his inspiration from. 'How often do you come out here and work?' was all I dared to ask.

He smiled, maybe a little cynically, as if he knew what I was thinking and found my lack of courage amusing, but he answered me nonetheless. 'All the time – until you arrived. I can't very well disappear down here, leaving you in the house. You might run away.'

'I won't, you know. It's my house and I'm going to stay here.'

As soon as I had said, I realised that I meant it. Escape was the last thing on my mind now.

'Besides, I can't go back to England at the moment,' I added, as an afterthought.

'Reading between the lines, I take it that you're trying to avoid someone at the moment? And they don't know where you are?'

I nodded.

'Then I guess we're both trying to keep a low profile,' he added with a wry smile.

It was strange: having seen his paintings, it made me feel even more for him than I already did. I felt that they had given me an insight to his personality. As I had seen his naked body when I arrived yesterday, now I had seen his mind. For some reason I felt closer to him. I understood him without knowing anything about him.

We were interrupted by Eric barging into the studio. 'What the fuck is going on? You've spent no time with me since she's been here and why are you two in here with the door shut?'

'If you'll excuse me, I'll just leave you two love birds alone,' I quipped, making a quick exit. I didn't want to aggravate Eric any more than I already had, by being closeted in the barn with his lover.

But I must have aggravated him a little bit more, because I heard him say to Miguel, just before I got out of earshot, 'What is the matter with you? Why are you letting her talk to you like this? The bitch is just asking for a slap and . . .'

I realised that I was jealous of Eric. I found his possessiveness oppressive and I hoped that Miguel did too. But I knew that I was being unfair. I wouldn't have liked anyone barging in on my relationship. Two was company, three a crowd.

Again I went to bed before them. At some point in the night I woke up. I felt hot and sticky; the room was like an oven and there were three bodies burning off heat.

It was pitch black. I couldn't see them but I felt their nearness. I was on one side, turned towards the window. I was sure that Miguel was in the middle and Eric on the far side of him.

With each moment that passed, I became more and more alert. I turned on to my back.

I thought Miguel was lying on my hair so I carefully

pulled it out from under him. My hand accidentally touched his arm and I caught my breath, not wanting to disturb him, but wondering what he would do if I had. I was both excited and apprehensive. I imagined that he was lying on his back too. I could hear him breathing.

The heat, and my proximity to him, turned me on. I kept thinking about his paintings, and the thoughts that must have floated around in his head to have produced such work.

As I became more aroused, I couldn't resist putting my hand inside my knickers. I was wet. I wanted to masturbate. Knowing that I had two gorgeous men in the bed, completely out of bounds to me, was frustrating. I needed some sort of release.

I parted my legs a little and started to rub my clitoris. Just delicate little movements; I didn't want to disturb them. But I became more and more aroused.

I put one hand under my T-shirt and felt my breast. My nipple became erect under my touch. I continued to stroke myself, but my movements were becoming a little more vigorous.

The risk of being discovered only added to my fervour, as if I were a little schoolgirl, getting a kick out of doing something naughty.

I felt my clitoris becoming numb, my pussy beginning to throb with the oncoming orgasm. I was like a coil, slowly winding myself up.

Suddenly I sprang open, the vibrations reverberating throughout my body, every muscle in my pelvis and thighs spasming with the force. I bit my lips to stop myself crying out as I came and kept my fingers working for several more minutes, dragging it out. Apart from my sporadic intakes of breath I had been completely silent.

Relieved but not fulfilled, I turned on to one side.

I felt someone climb over me and stand up. Absolutely mortified, I realised that Miguel had been awake the whole time and would have known exactly what I was doing. And, unless I was mistaken, I had felt an erection as he had got off the bed.

I heard him as he had a piss, then wash himself in cold water. He stayed in the bathroom several minutes, then came back into the room.

Silently he climbed over me and lay down. His skin was wet where he had accidentally touched me. He hadn't bothered to dry himself. How I would have loved to dry him with my hair, my tongue, but I decided to banish him from my thoughts altogether. I had shamed myself enough for one night.

I tried to sleep. Eventually I did doze off.

They had obviously left me to sleep in, because I was alone in the bedroom and I could smell Eric's cigarette smoke wafting in through the open window. They were probably out on the terrace.

I sat up in bed to find the sheets on the floor. We had all been hot and one of them must have thrown them off. But I had been left wearing nothing but a pair of skimpy knickers and a T-shirt which had rolled halfway up my back.

I consoled myself with the thought that they wouldn't have even noticed. Like sleeping with my brothers, they were completely indifferent to me sexually.

I thought about Miguel's erection. It was probably for Eric rather than for me. He was more than likely frustrated that he couldn't very well do anything with me in the bed too.

The sky looked overcast so I ran downstairs and dressed in a pair of jeans and a T-shirt. I made some breakfast, then carried it out to the terrace. Miguel said good morning to me; Eric ignored me.

As I ate, I was conscious of Miguel looking at me from time to time. I prayed that he wasn't thinking about my activities during the night.

I decided to speak about the sleeping arrangements. If I could sleep on the floor, we would all get a better night's sleep and I would be able to keep a check on my desire for Miguel.

'It's so hot at night that I can't sleep!' I suddenly blurted out. 'I think I might be able to, if I was somewhere – on the floor.'

Miguel looked up from his book slowly. If anything, he seemed irritated, but Eric jumped in first. 'That's a good idea. If she sleeps under the window, she can't leave the room without us noticing; any less than if she were in the bed with us.'

'No, I don't like it. Not only because she might leave, but because she's a girl and it's her house. It's not right that she sleeps on the floor. It's got to be one of us, Eric, so who's it to be: you or me?'

'Well, I don't want to sleep with her –'

'Look, there's really no need for all this,' I cut in. 'There's a mattress down at the studio. If you carry it up for me, I shall be just as comfortable on that, if not more so, and I'm not splitting you two up.'

'Yes, we can do that. But you're staying on the bed. I don't know you well enough to trust you. I've made up my mind. Eric, you're on the floor.'

Eric was about to protest; he looked genuinely hurt. But Miguel wouldn't have any of it. 'I was stupid to even consider you sharing the bed with her. I know what you're like. I wouldn't put it past you to watch her leave, then tell me about it afterwards.'

I went into the house, not being able to handle Eric's look of hatred. I was sure he was capable of killing me and Miguel knew it. That was probably why he was keeping him away from me.

I couldn't understand where all this vehemence was coming from. I was no threat to Eric's relationship. I had feelings for Miguel but they were obviously one way. And I hadn't done anything to threaten their safety. I was toeing the line.

Still, in Eric's eyes, I had won a minor battle. I was now to be sleeping alone with Miguel.

But I hadn't wanted this. The whole reason I had brought up the sleeping arrangements was so that I could get away from Miguel. Thoughts of him and what I would like to do with him were keeping me awake at night.

I decided to clean up the rest of the house. The salon was still in a pretty bad way and so was the bedroom.

As I dusted the salon, I found Miguel's book, left open, on a table. Wanting to discover as much as I could, about him as a person, I peeped at the cover. *Che Guevara – A Revolutionary Life*; definitely not one of my grandfather's!

I worked until about three o'clock, only stopping for lunch. Just as I finished, the storm broke.

The rain was torrential. Miguel and Eric moved inside, off the terrace where they had been sitting for most of the day. To me, it was too inviting to resist.

'I'm going for a walk!'

'Then I'm going to watch you,' Miguel retorted. 'But do you think it's wise to walk under trees in a thunderstorm?'

I didn't answer him. I loved the rain and we seldom got it like this in England. I ran across the grass and sat on a garden seat. I was drenched within about ten seconds but I didn't care. The weather had been oppressively warm all day and I had worked hard. This was so refreshing.

I pulled out my ponytail and the rain quickly saturated my hair. I got up and continued to walk down towards the woods, past the barn and the outbuildings. The rain had started to ease off now and was becoming more of a shower than a downpour. The thunder and lightning had blown on to another hill.

'Katie!'

I spun around; Miguel was about ten feet away from me.

'I've been calling you. Where are you going?'

'Nowhere in particular. I just wanted to get some fresh air.'

Then, seeing that he was also drenched, I added, 'I'm sorry; you're wet too! What did you want?'

'What I wanted was for you not to go wandering off. I want to know where you are all the time. Do you understand?'

He had started off angry, but by the end he was almost smiling. He must have realised that I was being thoughtless rather than unco-operative.

'Well, why don't you come for a walk with me? It's got to be more interesting than sitting in the salon or on the terrace all day,' I said.

I hoped that he wouldn't be angry with my familiarity. I knew that he wasn't far off being a kidnapper, but I felt totally safe with him around the house. I thought that, if he was going to do something to me, he would have done it already.

He looked towards the house, frowning. I knew he was thinking about Eric, and what he would make of us going on a little jaunt. Then he obviously dismissed Eric from his mind, because he shrugged his shoulders and walked towards me.

He looked beautiful. My eyes took in everything: his hair hanging wet and long; his face streaming with rain; his long eyelashes wet and weighed down with the rain drops.

Smiling at him, I held out my hand for him to take it.

He frowned again as he took my offered hand, as if he thought there was an ulterior motive behind my invitation. He ran his other hand through his hair, uncertainly. He looked – irresistible.

Taking his hand had been an unconscious act on my part; I had meant nothing by it. I often went for walks back in England with my ex-boyfriend or another friend, and we always held hands. It was habit as much as anything else, but it had obviously made Miguel feel uncomfortable.

We walked into the woods, just as the rain became heavier again. We were walking into the storm. It got so heavy at one point that Miguel stopped me.

'This is silly. Let's just wait here for a while. It will pass shortly.'

'OK. Shall we sit under that big tree?'

I pointed to a nearby pine tree, which was as wide as it was tall, and would offer us some shelter under its umbrella branches.

He agreed and we sat underneath on a damp grassy mound.

'"Miguel". That's a Spanish name, not French.'

'Yes. My parents were Spanish.'

That would account for all the expressive mannerisms, I told myself. They definitely weren't French.

'So where are they now?'

'They're dead.'

'I'm sorry. I wouldn't have . . .'

'How could you have known? But it was a long time ago. I've got over it.'

I wondered how he could have got over something like that – he must have been quite young – but I didn't like to ask him any more about it so I changed the subject.

'How old are you, Miguel?'

'I'm thirty-one. Now, no more questions. You know I don't like it.'

Why was he being so defensive? My questions had been fairly innocuous. Certainly I knew better than to ask him anything too contentious, after the warning he had given me in the car yesterday.

So what was he trying to hide? I now knew that he was an artist and made money from his work, so I could assume that he wasn't a criminal. But he was running away from something. Perhaps it was to do with Eric.

I started to pick up handfuls of my hair and wring it. The water poured out. He smiled, in spite of the uncomfortable silence.

'Do you have any idea what you look like?' he asked brusquely.

'A drowned rat?'

'Yes, but I didn't mean that. You're really beautiful. The prettiest girl I have ever seen.'

I looked up sharply, hardly believing my ears.

'I mean it. You've got everything. A beautiful face and a stunning body.'

His hand reached out and he put a finger on my cheek. I held my breath while he absentmindedly followed a raindrop that was running down it. It splashed off my chin, but his finger traced an imaginary line down my neck, down my chest to my breast.

My heart was pounding as he gently ran his finger across my wet T-shirt to my nipple.

At which point he dropped his hand and abruptly stood up.

'Come on. Let's go,' he snapped, clearly irritated.

I stood up and followed him, totally baffled by his erratic behaviour.

What had all that been about? Why had he touched me in that way? It had been very sensual. He had made me breathless with anticipation, then he had deliberately spoilt the moment.

As I fell in step beside him, I looked down at myself. I blushed with embarrassment. My T-shirt was completely transparent, being white. He had seen, and still could see, everything.

Self-consciously, I pulled my hair forward. It covered me like a cape and I felt a little bit more respectable.

We were still walking away from the house. I told him about a path on the far side of the woods that led eventually up to the road. We could take it and follow the road back to the front of the house. He agreed and we continued to stroll through the woods.

Once we picked up the path, it started to climb quite drastically. I had forgotten this, being years since I had been here, and I slipped a couple of times on the mud.

He took my hand this time, to help me, and he half pulled me up on to the road.

Once on the road, it stopped raining altogether and the sun came out for the first time that day. Everything looked fresh and green. The heat from the sun made the puddles evaporate and the steam rise on the tarmac.

Miguel and I started to dry out too. It felt good to be out with him, surrounded by all this natural beauty. I could have walked miles. He was still holding my hand. Perhaps he had forgotten to let go. But we didn't talk.

If nothing else, we could be friends, I consoled myself. Despite the fact that I was nearly overcome with lust every time I clapped eyes on him, there was definitely an unspoken communication between us. Perhaps it was because we were both artistic, insular people. We felt comfortable with each other even if we weren't talking.

Again, I had to remind myself that I was daydreaming about a drifter, a squatter, and possibly a criminal. Hardly the basis for any sort of relationship – friendship or love.

After about half an hour, the house came into view. We had been gone nearly two hours; Eric would not be happy.

Reading my thoughts, Miguel let go of my hand.

As we entered the door, Eric started. 'Where the hell have you been? I thought you'd gone away with her –'

'Shut the fuck up, Eric. She went for a walk. I couldn't see her from the house and I ended up going with her. Don't read any more into it than that.'

Eric had obviously seen a side to Miguel that I hadn't, because, yet again, his deep voice, laced with suppressed anger, was enough to silence Eric – completely.

I was dreading going to bed. It was going to be even more awkward now that I was alone with Miguel. But by ten o'clock, I was ready to sleep and I left them downstairs, as on the two previous occasions.

I had a quick cold bath, then got into bed. The fresh

air had made me sleepy and, although there were butterflies in my stomach as part of me waited for Miguel to come up, I fell asleep quickly.

I was awakened by strange noises. Panting and groaning from within the room, yet I was alone in the bed. I recognised the noises – rather I knew what they meant – but I couldn't understand where they were coming from.

Suddenly the moon came out from behind a cloud and I caught sight of two silhouettes moving on the far side of the room. As my eyes adjusted to the darkness, I saw quite clearly what was happening. Very quietly, I lifted my head up and rested it on my elbow.

Miguel was leaning over Eric. Eric was leaning over a chair. They were both naked. Miguel had hold of Eric's hair and was pulling him backwards and forwards while he fucked him.

There was no affection, no touching. Eric was being sodomised, but he was enjoying every second of it. And Miguel looked detached, like he was just using him, as if he felt nothing.

My heart beat faster and faster as I continued to watch them. Like before, I was becoming aroused by their abandoned display. And like before, I wished that Miguel would cast Eric aside and use me instead.

They were beautiful. Even in the dark I could see Miguel's biceps and the muscles in his buttocks and thighs flexing. I had never seen this act before and I was fascinated. The ecstasy on Eric's face, as he was penetrated, was incredible.

I wished that I could somehow become more involved; join them in some way. But, of course, I was redundant. They didn't need me or want me.

My hand slipped inside my knickers. Almost unconsciously, I started to stroke myself as I watched Miguel thrust into Eric. God, how I wanted him to come over to the bed and fuck me.

At that moment, something made Miguel look towards the bed. The blood rushed to my head when I realised that he could clearly see me, watching them. There was no way I could drop down and pretend to be asleep; it was too late. And I had done just about everything, bar puffing up the pillows, to make myself comfortable for the show.

Feeling both guilty and perverted, I slid my hand out of my knickers.

His eyes were fixed on my face. Even in the dark I could see them smouldering. I held my breath as he pulled Eric's head back even harder. Eric let out a groan, but I didn't think it was with pain. Miguel clenched his buttocks and rammed him hard several times. He groaned as he came, then suddenly released his hold on Eric. He hadn't taken his eyes off me for a moment.

He walked out of the room and went to the bathroom. He was in there some time, obviously having a cold bath. After about twenty minutes he came out, walked across the room and climbed into bed beside me.

Eric, who had been lying on his mattress, now went to the bathroom.

It was strange that there was so little communication between these two. It was hard to imagine that there was any love at all between them; yet there must have been.

I turned away from Miguel and looked towards the window. Suddenly he leant over me and whispered in my ear, 'Did you enjoy it?'

Then he nipped my earlobe spitefully.

I held my breath, hoping for more, but he just moved away from me.

He was playing a game with me, I realised. Maybe he was pushing me to see how far I would go; how low I would stoop. But I didn't understand why. He could tease me sexually; I would be a willing playmate. But what was the point when he couldn't deliver – wouldn't want to deliver?

* * *

I opened my eyes and saw the brilliant blue sky through the window. The storm yesterday had done its job: we would now be in for some really scorching weather.

I rolled on to my back and my heart leapt when I found Miguel, lying just a couple of inches away, wide awake and watching me, with his arms folded behind his head.

I would have loved to have been able to roll into him, nuzzle into his armpit, run my fingers over his chest, even kiss him. But I couldn't, so I quietly slipped out of the bed and went to the bathroom.

As I sat in the bath washing, he walked in. Without even glancing in my direction, he nonchalantly took a piss. Although I found it hard not to look at him, wearing nothing but a pair of boxer shorts, his familiarity made me cross.

'I thought you said that you would respect my privacy?' I demanded.

Now he looked at me long enough to make me feel uncomfortable again. And if I hadn't known he was gay, if I hadn't seen the evidence, I would have said that he was looking me over, the way most men would have looked over a naked woman – speculatively.

'Well, I would do, only you don't seem too bothered about other people's privacy. I didn't think it was that important to you. I mean, it's got to work both ways, don't you think?'

I knew he was talking about me watching them again and I blushed.

'I suppose so,' I answered rather lamely, sinking down into the cold water to cool my burning cheeks.

When he had finished cleaning his teeth, he picked up my towel. He held it out for me, although I hadn't thought to get out of the bath at that particular moment.

I stood up rather awkwardly and went to take the offered towel.

With a rakish smile, he put it behind his back.

Feeling embarrassed, I asked him to give it to me.

He continued to hold it behind him, while he leant back against the wall. 'If you want it, take it!'

I was shocked. Not by his words, but that they had come from him. I felt very unsure of myself. He was giving me conflicting messages and I didn't know how to take him. I had accepted that Eric and he had a relationship – I could still worship him from afar. But now he was pushing me to take part in a game where I just didn't know the rules.

'Miguel, don't play games; just give me the towel. What would Eric think if he saw you in here?'

'I'm not playing games. This is serious. If you want the towel, take it from me. If not – leave the room,' he added dismissively.

With a heart beating way too fast, I moved towards him. Standing next to him stark naked was making my legs turn to jelly. Strange that I was overwhelmed by him now, but I had managed to sleep with him three times without being this close to making a fool of myself. The difference was, of course, Eric wasn't with us.

Taking a deep breath, I put my hands round his waist and snatched the towel out of his hands. As I did so, he laughed and his arms went about me. He pulled me in to him and I felt a kind of shock run through me as our skin made contact, my breasts grazing his hard chest. As I looked up at his face to try to understand, he bent his head down and kissed me.

It was a long, demanding kiss. His tongue pushed through my teeth and found my tongue. His stubble scraped against my chin. As he withdrew from me, his teeth caught my lip and nipped it. I opened my eyes to find his, burning into mine, watching me – watching my reaction to him.

As quickly as he had grabbed me, he let me go again. I took a step back, absolutely stunned. Laughing at my expression, he left the bathroom.

This time there was no mistake; he had an erection in

his shorts. It had pushed against my stomach while he'd been holding me.

He was probably bisexual. It was all I could think of to account for it. He had definitely been aroused by being near me.

The realisation of this gave me some hope. If he found me attractive, then I could probably have some sort of relationship with him. I didn't care how much or how little he gave me. Just to be able to share something with him would be wonderful; more than I had ever dreamt would be possible.

But I would let things take their course. I had to be careful: not read too much into his actions. He could still just be teasing me. And of course, there was Eric. What I had seen last night was no dream. It had happened. He had used Eric like he was no more animated than a piece of meat; and while it had turned me on, I wouldn't have liked him to treat me the same way.

In an ideal world, I would have wanted love and passion from Miguel. His beautiful face promised these things; so did his paintings. But I had seen nothing of it in his actions.

I went down to the dining room and dressed slowly, totally preoccupied with the thoughts buzzing around in my brain. From now on, whatever we did or said to each other would have other implications. His kiss had changed everything.

I put on a T-shirt and short denim skirt. I slipped on a pair of leather mules and plaited my hair back to keep me cool.

I had quite a pile of dirty washing now and that irritated me. I would have to do something about it. If I had been alone here, I would have gone to the launderette by now; or, even more likely, had the electricity connected.

'Katie, are you supposed to phone your mother today?' Miguel asked, as I walked outside.

'Yes, she'll be expecting me to call.'

'Then we'll have to go into town early, before it gets too hot.'

'OK. And I want to get my clothes washed. There are all the dirty towels and sheets you've used – I'd like to get them all done.'

'We can go to the launderette. There's one in Barbotan. I've used it before – believe it or not!'

'Well, I guess there must come a point when your clothes get too dirty for even you to wear. You couldn't have brought that many things with you on a bike.'

He seemed uncomfortable with what I'd just said. I was sure it wasn't the comment about his dirty clothes; he wasn't that sensitive. It was to do with the bikes.

'Miguel, if you bring down your washing and strip off the bed, then we can get everything done in one go. Give me the keys and I'll start loading up the car.'

'Don't push your luck. I'll open the car but you're not having the keys until I'm sitting beside you. I don't want to lose you.'

I looked at him sharply. His choice of words had been odd, but he didn't seem to have noticed.

He should have said 'I don't want you to run away' or 'escape'. To 'lose' me suggested that he put some sort of value on me. Neither I nor my family were exactly wealthy: it wouldn't have been a particularly fruitful exercise to hold me to ransom.

I put the roof up on my car, then tucked what I could behind the seats.There was a mountain of washing behind me; I couldn't see out of my rear-view mirror, but it probably didn't matter; the roads were virtually deserted in this part of the world.

'All right, so I'll drive to Barbotan?' I asked, as I pulled off.

Miguel nodded but he didn't say anything. He had pulled the gun out from under his shirt.

'For fuck's sake, Miguel. Do you have to do that while I'm driving? It's dangerous.'

'Something tells me that you like danger. Am I right?'

I slowed down to look at him. His face was deadly serious, but there was a challenge in his eyes.

'I don't know what you mean. If you think I like you waving that around in my face, you're mistaken.'

'Katie, pull over. I want to talk to you.'

I did as he asked, feeling a little nervous. I found him totally unpredictable and I certainly didn't like the gun being out.

I looked up and down the road. Of course we were totally isolated; nothing but forests on either side. He must have seen my consternation because he gave me a wry smile. Then, completely unexpectedly, he opened the glove compartment and chucked the gun inside it.

He turned to look at me. His expression was unreadable, but he was shaking his head as if he were disappointed with himself or irritated with me.

Perhaps he took it as a sign of weakness on his part, that he didn't have the heart to frighten me. Maybe he was angry with himself, for feeling obliged to put the gun away.

But then he reached out his hand and stroked a strand of hair lying on my shoulder. And a second later, his hand slid to my neck.

I felt his fingers stroking my throat. They were making tiny, circular motions and his touch was very gentle; yet I was acutely aware of the strength in those fingers as they skimmed over my quickened pulse.

I wasn't sure if I was scared or excited, or a mixture of both. He must have seen my heart thumping in my chest fit to burst.

'I couldn't hurt anything as lovely as you,' he said quietly.

I steeled myself not to look at him. I kept my eyes fixed on the empty road. If he had seen my expression, he would have known that I was his for the taking.

He ran his hand down my neck to my chest, following the line his finger had taken yesterday, then across to my breast. I knew then that he was playing with me. He couldn't hurt me.

My apprehension had evaporated; now I was just incredibly aroused. It was all I could do to stop myself squirming in my seat.

'I think you would like to live dangerously – live on the edge,' he said, looking at the gun lying in the open glove compartment. 'And I think my gun is just the excuse you need, right now, to let me do anything I want with you.

I didn't answer him because at that moment, I would have had to agree with him.

'Shall I prove it to you?' he whispered in my ear.

I blinked, but again, I didn't answer him. I was now playing a game of my own.

His hand left my breast. Moving down my stomach, it continued to trace an imaginary line down one of my legs. I caught my breath as he suddenly pushed his hand up, under my skirt, between my thighs.

He leant over me and, placing one hand across my chest, he held me back in my seat by my shoulder. 'Open your legs,' he commanded.

I saw the glitter in his eyes. I had to do what he asked. But, of course, I wanted to. Gun or no gun, I would have done anything he wanted – at that moment in time.

He lifted up my skirt. His fingers hooked into the top of my knickers and literally ripped them off me. I bit my lip to stop any sound escaping.

He then pushed two fingers inside me. I was wet; it was easy.

He let go of my shoulder and ran his hand down to my breast. He played with my nipple incredibly gently while his fingers entered me, just a little way, down below.

'Recline your seat,' he ordered rather than asked.

I did as I was told; I was now lying back. He was still leaning over me and his hand left my breast and travelled down to my pussy. He parted my labia and began to rhythmically stroke my clitoris as his other fingers penetrated me more and more deeply.

The whole time Miguel watched me. Sometimes he looked at my pussy, sometimes my face. I couldn't take my eyes off him either. I wanted to know what he was thinking and feeling. And I wanted *him* to fuck me, not his fingers.

I knew I was going to come. The sordidness of it all, the fact that he was only doing this to prove a point, just added to the intensity of what I was already feeling, having his hands all over me.

I came in great long shudders. My whole body arched and shook. As I cried out, Miguel leant over and put his mouth on mine to stop the noise.

He broke away from me when I had at last become still. Then, giving me a wicked smile, he pulled down my skirt.

I didn't return the smile. I had been finger fucked just to demonstrate my wantoness. And whilst I had found it erotic, there had been a total lack of sensuality . . . Apart from that kiss at the end. And that was the confusing part.

I struggled to regain my composure, but it was difficult after what had just taken place.

'Did you like it?' he asked, still smiling.

'No I didn't,' I lied.

He laughed, then almost as an afterthought, he took the gun out of the glove compartment. He opened up the barrel and showed me that it was, in fact, empty.

'If I had told you beforehand, that the gun wasn't loaded, I don't think I would have got quite the same result from you. The danger turned you on. And it gave you the excuse you needed, to let yourself go with me. I think you and I are the same. We are attracted to, and drawn by, the same things. You wouldn't have come all this way, on your own, unless you were looking for something. If you were content with your life, you would never have come here.'

'That's crap, Miguel. I only came here to get away from an unpleasant situation at home. I like this place because it is so remote; where no one would bother me –'

'Where you can escape from all the shit in the real world . . . into a fantasy.'

He was right, of course. This was the only place I had ever known where I could totally relax, forget about all the mundane things in my life and daydream to my heart's content. I was very like my grandfather in that.

But I didn't think I would ever meet a man who felt as we did. Who was happy to cut himself off from everything, just to live in his own private fantasy.

It was such a pity that our fantasies weren't compatible. He was the epitome of mine.

'You don't like women much, do you, judging by what you've just done to me?'

I couldn't resist it; I had to find out where I stood with him.

'On the contrary, I love women. I love everything about them. And I find you particularly fascinating . . . Come on; let's get going. I don't want to be in town all day – it's too hot.'

I was more confused by his reply than ever. He certainly hadn't enlightened me over his sexuality. He had merely acknowledged an interest in women.

I turned on the engine and we sped off down the road.

After we had gone a couple of miles, he said, 'I'm telling you this for your own peace of mind. The gun hasn't been loaded since you've been here. Eric just kept it in the bedside cabinet in case we ever had unexpected visitors and we needed to make a quick exit. We knew that someone was going to show up sooner or later and it might not have been you. Eric may resent you, but he's not capable of shooting anybody. I took it off him when you arrived because you weren't a threat to us, on your own, and I didn't see the point of scaring you needlessly.

'But don't make any mistake about it. If you try to leave before I give you permission to, or if you draw attention to us in any way, I could just as easily put my hands round your neck and throttle you as I could pull a trigger. So the same rules apply – with or without the gun.'

I nodded very gravely, to show him that I understood – absolutely.

When we arrived in Barbotan, I parked two doors down from the launderette. I switched on my mobile. There was reception, but it wasn't brilliant.

As before, Miguel warned me to be careful.

'Mum, it's me. I'll have to be quick because my battery is running low. Is everything all right?'

'Yes, fine. Have you got the electricity on at the house yet?'

'No, but I will. I've cleaned the house and I've tidied up outside. Everything's fine. Is he still bothering you?'

'Yes. He came round yesterday. He wanted your address. It's very awkward, Katie.'

'No, it isn't. Just don't let him in. Have some sort of loyalty to me, for God's sake. And if you tell him where I am, I'll never forgive you.'

'All right, Katie, take care. Phone me in a couple of days.'

I said goodbye and disconnected the call.

I looked towards Miguel, wondering if he really understood that much English. His next words confirmed that he did.

'When men fall in love, they fall much more deeply than women. Do you know that more men die of broken hearts than women?'

'No, I didn't. But that has nothing to do with what's going on in my life. He would be more likely to die of hurt pride than a broken heart!'

Miguel laughed and I said nothing more on the subject. Robert was history as far as I was concerned. I had a new object of passion.

We had three loads of washing to do; it was going to take a couple of hours. So while the machines were running, we walked around the town and did some shopping to see us through the next couple of days.

Since we still had another half-hour to kill before the final load was finished, Miguel asked me if I fancied a coffee. Pleasantly surprised, I agreed.

We strolled to a nearby café and took a table on the pavement, under an umbrella. Miguel ordered two coffees, then began to chat to me.

I found myself feeling totally at ease with him, as if he really were a boyfriend rather than someone holding me hostage. And it was at that moment I realised. If he were to suddenly announce that he was leaving my house, I would be very upset . . . devastated.

While we sat chatting, I noticed that we drew people's attention. Looking at Miguel, I could understand it. Relaxed, smoking a cigarette, he seemed totally oblivious to his own good-looks and the effect he had on other people. But I saw what they saw – a tall, extremely handsome man wearing sunglasses. He could have been a model.

After a while, he noticed too. 'People are looking at us. They must think we make a strange couple. You are so blonde and beautiful; I am so dark. I have a big build and you are slender. We're complete opposites.'

I shrugged my shoulders, not wishing to say what I thought: that he was beautiful too. 'We have a saying in England – "opposites attract". And it works in your case. Look at you and Eric: you're exact opposites. As it happens, I think you're more attractive than Eric, and that's probably because he is too much like me. Different is more interesting. But I can still appreciate that he's handsome.'

'Surely you wouldn't be interested in Eric, because he makes it fairly obvious that he doesn't like women?'

'So what? Eric's not in the least camp; he's just very standoffish. Some women find that very attractive – it's more of a challenge. And as for myself, a person's sexuality doesn't come into it. It just makes some men out of bounds to me. Besides, you said the other day that I looked like Eric. If you think Eric's attractive then you would have to acknowledge that I am too – even if you're gay. It doesn't mean you want to fuck me,' I added, deliberately trying to draw him out.

The waiter came over and Miguel paid for the coffees. As we got up from the table, he said in a low voice, 'But you know I find you attractive. I've already told you that I think you're beautiful. And I do want to fuck you.'

He walked away from the table, and I stood there for a moment, wondering if I had misheard him. He turned round and waited for me to catch up, laughing at my bemused expression.

No, I definitely hadn't misheard him.

Back in the launderette, it was as if we had never had the conversation. But the whole time I was folding up the washing, I kept wondering about him: what I meant to him, what Eric meant to him, and what kind of path he was leading me down.

I couldn't wait to find out.

Chapter Three

The three of us sat on the terrace and ate lunch. I found it hard to believe that, less than three hours earlier, I had allowed Miguel to put his hands between my legs. Just thinking about it made me feel hot and sticky all over again.

The usual silence had resumed. I realised that it was because of Eric. His face was permanently that of a petulant child, and Miguel seemed to be easily irritated by him. I just kept quiet in Eric's company, not wishing him to pick up on the attraction I felt towards his lover.

Halfway through the meal, Miguel turned to me.

'Why don't you tell us about your French family?'

I was startled, wondering what he meant. Then I realised that he was referring to my grandfather.

'Why?' I asked, torn between a desire to withhold as much information as possible and an even greater one – to become better acquainted with him.

'I'm just curious,' he replied offhandedly, pushing his plate away and lighting a cigarette.

I shrugged my shoulders. 'There's nothing much to tell. My grandfather lived here; he died three years ago. As far as I know, he had no other relatives. But he was a recluse, so he probably wouldn't have kept in touch with his family, even if he had any.'

'So your mother lives in England?'

'Yes. When she was eighteen, she went to university in England. She met my father and never came back – except to visit occasionally. To be honest, I saw more of my grandfather towards the end than she did.'

'And what about your grandmother?'

'I never knew her. I don't think my mother remembers her either. She died when my mother was about two. My grandfather was only about twenty-three at the time; they hadn't been married long. He had to bring my mother up on his own, but he was a successful artist and was able to send my mother to boarding school.'

As I talked, I noticed for the first time in three days that I had Eric's undivided attention. He was virtually hanging on my every word. I thought it quite out of character, seeing that he spent most of his time in a vegetative state, and I just couldn't account for his fascination with my family history.

'So you have no other French relations?'

'No. My mother was an only child and my grandfather never married again. Why?'

Miguel ignored my question and asked me another: 'Did you see much of your grandfather?'

'Yes. I was close to him. Closer than my mother was, I think. She spent most of her life away at school so she didn't get to spend as much time with him as I did. And I am more like he was in nature. After he died, I was too upset to come down here. And this is the first chance I've had to get away since.'

The inquisition was over and I continued to eat my lunch. But I couldn't help wondering where this sudden inquisitiveness had sprung from. Perhaps they were curious to know more about the man who had owned this house. Miguel might have even felt a certain empathy with him, being an artist, too. In fact, Miguel reminded me of my grandfather; not in looks, of course, but in his intensity and insularity.

After lunch I went into the dining room and put all my clean clothes away. The temperature outside felt like the mid-90s so I pulled a bikini out of my bag. I applied some suntan lotion, picked up my book and went into the kitchen to get a Coke.

I walked past Miguel and Eric, who were still sitting on the terrace, intending to find somewhere in the garden that was a little bit cooler. I thought the heat on the terrace was unbearable, but their skins were so tanned already it probably didn't bother them.

'Where do you think you're going?' Miguel called out.

'I can't sit up here. I want to find somewhere with a bit of shade. I'm hardly likely to be going anywhere dressed like this, am I? I won't get very far with just a book.'

I couldn't help the sarcasm: I felt he was too paranoid about me escaping. Surely he would realise that it was the last thing I intended to do?

'Watch your tone, Katie. I told you that I want to know where you are all the time. And, on the contrary, you could go a long way dressed like that. Couldn't she, Eric?'

Eric gave me the once-over, then returned his gaze to Miguel and nodded.

I saw his uneasiness and for the first time felt a little sorry for him. He saw me as a threat, which simply acknowledged to me that Miguel liked women as well as men. If Miguel had hated women, Eric wouldn't have been in the slightest bit bothered about me.

But I was still standing there like an idiot and started to feel cross. 'Can I go then, or what?'

'Yes, but don't wander off like you did yesterday.'

I dragged one of my grandfather's sun loungers across the lawn to the edge of the woods. I positioned it so that I was half in and half out of the trees.

Lying there was very pleasant. The slightest of breezes

kept me cool and I became engrossed in my book. I had moved on to *Sense and Sensibility*. It had been a bit like rubbing salt into my wounds, reading about Darcy's underlying passion for Elizabeth.

About an hour later Miguel strolled across the lawn towards me. I was lying on my stomach so I lifted my head up to watch him. 'Now what?' I snapped, as he squatted down beside me.

'I'm going into the barn and I shall be there for some time. I will be watching you so I'm trusting you not to do anything stupid. And I don't want you going back to the house without me. OK?'

I nodded, realising that he was concerned about Eric; or rather, Eric and I being alone together.

Miguel strolled down to the barn and I turned on to my back to watch him. I saw him open the doors wide and open up the windows. I thought he was moving things around, but I could just see his head and shoulders through the window. After a few minutes I realised that he had positioned himself so that he could paint but still keep his eye on me.

I closed my book and made myself comfortable. I put my hands behind my head to cushion it, and took more pleasure from watching his beautiful face than from reading my book.

I could clearly see his mannerisms: the way he frowned at something he'd done, knitting his black eyebrows together; or combing his hair off his face in frustration. He was totally absorbed in what he was doing. Now and again he looked up at me, to check on me, I supposed, but he didn't acknowledge me with a smile; his face was serious.

As the afternoon wore on, the sun moved round. It was now shining directly on me. I closed my eyes, feeling languid – enveloped in the scent of the pine and the humidity in the air.

I dozed off.

When I awoke, my first thought was to look at Miguel. He wasn't in sight.

I sat up, wondering why he hadn't told me he was finished – that he was going back to the house.

I was thirsty so I reached under the sunbed for my can of Coke. As I tipped back my head to drink from the can, a movement in the woods caught my attention. Miguel was about twenty yards away, leaning against a tree trunk. He had lit a cigarette - that was what had caught my eye – and he was staring at me intently, his face devoid of all expression.

I smiled at him, but he didn't return it. Then I raised my Coke as if to offer him some.

He now nodded and gave a half-smile, accepting my offer of the drink. After a moment I realised that he wanted me to bring it to him.

I walked up to him and, saying nothing, handed him the can. I watched him while he tipped his head back and finished it off.

'It's not very nice warm, is it?' I said, to break the silence.

'Yes, a fridge would be good. If you arrange for the electricity to be put on, I'll buy one.'

'No, I can buy one. It's my house.'

'But I think that, as we're uninvited guests, the least we can do is buy you a fridge. I'll sort it out next time we go to town.'

As a breeze stirred the leaves above us, I suddenly shivered.

'Are you cold? How could you be – in this weather?' he asked, looking at my breasts rather than my face.

'My back's wet with perspiration where I've been lying asleep in the sun. Now I'm standing in the shade, I feel cold,' I replied, flicking my damp plait off my neck irritably, like a horse swishing its tail.

'Let me feel,' he whispered.

'Excuse me?' I asked, wondering whether I had misheard him.

'I want to feel your skin.'

'You're not going to strangle me or anything, are you?' I asked, as I tentatively stepped towards him and lifted my face to meet his eyes.

I felt that I was offering myself to him. I wanted him to touch me. Whatever he asked me to do, I would do, no matter how strange or perverse. He had his reasons for this unusual request, even if they were unfathomable.

I felt that he was in another world. And although the things he did would seem unnatural to most people, even to me, to those drawn into his sphere anything he did was acceptable.

Perhaps Miguel was as nature intended us to be. Following basic instincts with no care for convention and conformity. What was important to the rest of us meant nothing to him.

I hoped that he might kiss me again, but he didn't. He put his hands round my neck as if he really were going to strangle me. I continued to look him in the eyes, but began to feel apprehensive: he was so unpredictable. But he smiled at me almost affectionately.

'You don't know whether to trust me or not, do you?'

'Well, you haven't given me a reason not to trust you, but I still don't know anything about you.'

'Just follow your instincts,' he replied, in little more than a whisper.

He kept one hand on my throat; I'm sure he could have crushed it with just one hand if he had wanted to; and the other slid round my back.

His big brown shoulders were so powerful; so too were his arms, with his well-defined muscles flexing as he reached out to touch me.

But it was his eyes which mesmerised me; their intensity. They seemed to smoulder all the time, whatever he was thinking or feeling.

He ran his hand from the nape of my neck down my hot sticky back to my bikini strap.

Suddenly, and taking me by complete surprise, he unclipped it. It fell to the ground and I was standing there naked, bar my bikini bottoms. I caught my breath.

Hearing it, he looked up from my breasts to my face. His eyes were laden with sexual intent. There was no mistake.

'Turn around.'

I did as he asked, then he placed his hands on my shoulders and pushed me down. He got down with me. I was now sitting on the ground, between his legs. He was leaning back against the tree. My back grazed his chest. I could feel his body hair sticking to me.

'I just want to be close to you for a while.'

I felt his hands on my hair. He was pulling out my plait. Within a few seconds it was loose and falling about me. He put his arm across my chest and drew me into him. I could feel his erection in the small of my back.

Still holding me, his other hand came up to my breast and stroked it. Of course, my nipple was erect with desire for him.

I was panting with anticipation. He would unexpectedly tweak or pull my nipple, then run his hand all over me, avoiding the one place I wanted him to touch.

At long last, the hand that was holding me to him slid down my stomach and went inside my bikini bottoms. His fingers parted my labia, while his other hand left my breast and slid down to my pussy, which was already wet with wanting him. He immediately located my clitoris and began to finger it roughly.

I wanted to sit on his lap, squirm on his crotch, even capture his cock; but he hadn't given me permission and I wouldn't have dared to take the liberty.

His fingers were driving me mad; he was driving me mad. I had to be still; I had to let him do what he wanted. He wanted to tease me, but he obviously didn't want to fuck me.

I felt my stomach starting to tighten as his fingers did

their job. He must have seen my chest heaving with the build-up to orgasm.

Keeping one finger on my clitoris, he slid another finger inside me. It began pushing in and out gently like a little cock, skilfully pressing some secret, internal button, which just intensified my reaction to his other busy finger.

I dropped my head back on his shoulder and closed my eyes. He brought his head down next to mine, and gently licked my neck, my ear. His tongue pushed inside my ear as his hands continued to work on my pussy.

I groaned as I came, the force of it reverberating through every fibre of my body. I pushed myself back into him, feeling his hard body against me, supporting me. Regardless, he continued to stroke me and fuck me with his finger. It went on and on; he wouldn't let up, dragging out the aftershocks of my ecstasy.

Then it happened again; another explosion from deep inside me. Incredibly, it was stronger, more overwhelming than the last one. And I thought he had already exhausted me.

As soon as I had recovered, I opened my eyes and begged him to stop. He was torturing me needlessly. My body was a numb and trembling wreck.

He slid his hands out of my bikini but his arm remained across my chest, holding me tight to him, almost crushing me. He must have felt every spasm that I had felt as they slowly subsided.

After a couple of minutes, I spoke. 'Miguel, why did you do that? It can't be very satisfying for you.'

'That's where you're wrong. It gives me a great deal of pleasure to watch you come. I love the expression on your face; feeling the way your body responds. I've thought of nothing else since I felt you masturbating in bed the other night.'

He hadn't really answered my question. It may have turned him on, but ultimately he was unfulfilled.

I began to think that he might be homosexual after all,

and while he could touch me because he liked me as a person and wanted to please me, he found the idea of putting his cock anywhere near me . . . abhorrent.

But he still had hold of me; it was like I was stuck to him. My hair was the only thing that came between his skin and mine. I felt hot and bothered, and strangely frustrated. I pushed his arm off me irritably and moved away from his body.

I turned round so that I could see him. His eyes were still smouldering; I didn't know why.

I picked up my bikini top and started to put it back on. I lifted up my hair, which was stuck to my back, and shook it out.

'You are really lovely, Katie. I could just sit and watch you twenty-four hours a day.'

And I feel the same about you, I thought to myself. And watching you is about the nearest I'm ever going to get to fucking you, the way things are.

'And do you feel like that about Eric?' I asked, my voice laced with bitterness.

He looked surprised. 'No, I don't. Why do you ask?'

'Well, I just thought that because you two had a sexual relationship, you would find him more attractive than you do me.'

'Well, Eric would disagree with me, I'm sure, but I think women are far more beautiful than men. I would rather look at you any day than Eric. And as regards a relationship, don't you think we've had one going from the moment we met?'

I didn't say anything. I looked down at the ground to hide my feelings. He continued, nonetheless. 'Katie, any two people can fuck; it doesn't mean anything. I want much more than that and I think you do too.'

So he had acknowledged that there was something between us – a mutual attraction, something special and different – from the very beginning. But I wondered whether it was to culminate in sexual intercourse, or just this continual foreplay.

He was driving me crazy but, if that was all he could offer me, then I would take it and welcome.

I was sitting alone at the table while Miguel cooked our evening meal on the barbecue. It had been my grandfather's idea to convert it from the original bread oven which had been built into a wall on the other side of the property.

Eric came outside and sat down opposite me. He stared at me sullenly for a couple of minutes, until I finally decided to build some bridges.

'Eric, why don't you like me? I've tried to give you and Miguel some space, as much as he allows me to, anyway. And I don't want to come between you. So – what's the problem?'

He looked at me for a few moments, irritated that I had forced him into a corner; that he would have to answer me. 'I don't dislike you. I hate you. And it has nothing to do with Miguel, if that's what you think. Miguel is a free spirit; he can do what he wants, when he wants. I can't change that. But you are a total hypocrite, just like the rest of your family.'

I opened my mouth to speak, but no words were forthcoming. I was gobsmacked by the sheer venom in his tone.

'You come down here after all these years,' he continued, now in full swing, 'walking around like you fucking own the place –'

'I do fucking own the place,' I managed to slip in quickly.

'It makes me sick. You make out you were fond of the old man; you didn't give a shit. You think you're like him; that's a joke. And now Miguel thinks he's found a kindred spirit. I wish we had left the day you arrived. I wish you were dead. So – now you know!'

He was obviously crazy. I had thought him neurotic, jealous even; but now I knew it went beyond Miguel. He was confused – talking rubbish. Everything I had told them about myself had become jumbled up in his head.

Miguel came round the corner with a plate of meat from the barbecue. I was obviously pale and shaken; Eric angry. 'What's been going on?' he demanded, addressing Eric.

'She wanted to know why I didn't like her. The bitch can't take criticism. That's not my problem.'

Miguel slammed the plate down on the table, which startled me. He looked absolutely furious – menacing. He walked round the table and hit Eric across the face with the back of his hand. Eric just sat there in a daze. Miguel had knocked the anger right out of him. Eric wiped the side of his mouth with his hand, and I saw smeared blood as he brought his hand down again.

'Go inside,' Miguel shouted at me, his eyes blazing. He didn't have to ask me twice. I immediately got up and scuttled away.

Miguel had frightened me, too: that he could become so angry, so quickly. I climbed the stairs to take refuge in the bedroom, but not quick enough to avoid hearing the angry words Miguel gave to Eric.

'What's the matter with you? Can't I trust you to be alone with her for five fucking minutes before going off the deep end? And I told you before she came that you were to keep your big mouth shut. If you're not careful, you'll spoil everything and then I'll wash my hands of you. It will all be over between us.'

Then he added in a quieter, more controlled voice, 'I know it wasn't supposed to be like this, but it's not her fault – it's theirs. You're blaming everything on her, but it has nothing to do with her.'

I wondered what on earth was going on. What Miguel had said made no more sense to me than what Eric had said. And how did he know that I was coming here? I didn't know myself until about three days beforehand.

Now I had something else to worry about. There was

more to their being here than simply squatting or hiding out; and I was somehow involved.

I had to get to the bottom of it, but knew that I would get no joy from Eric. I would have to ask Miguel. Though I would have to pick my moment carefully: he was obviously more volatile than I had thought.

They talked quietly downstairs for some time. It was maybe half an hour before Miguel came up to me.

'You know Eric resents you. Why did you have to provoke him like that?' he demanded.

'I didn't provoke him at all. I asked him nicely why he didn't like me, and if I had done something to upset him,' I answered, a bitter-sweet smile on my face.

'But I told you what his problem is. He doesn't want you here. Now I suggest you keep your nose out of other people's business, before things get out of hand.'

'But he said lots of things that didn't make any sense. He was talking rubbish. What's wrong with Eric? Is he crazy? If he is, you should tell me. You're making me sleep in the same room as him!'

'No, he's not crazy, and as long as you give him plenty of space and stay around me, he'll never do anything to upset or hurt you. He knows I'd kill him. Now just forget all about it and come and have your dinner.'

I stood up and followed him out of the room. I went back out on the terrace to find Eric as quiet and withdrawn as ever. I sat as far away from him as possible and we started to eat.

All evening we sat outside reading by candlelight. I was feeling apprehensive; my stomach was churning without knowing the reason why.

I kept going over Miguel and Eric's words, trying to make some sense of them; but of course, I couldn't.

Everything wasn't as straightforward as it had at first seemed. I wasn't just shacked up with two fugitives.There was definitely a mystery to be solved. And

Miguel, the most beautiful man I'd ever laid eyes on, was harbouring something unsavoury; dangerous even.

If my grandfather hadn't died of a heart attack, I could have sworn that these two had murdered him.

About ten o'clock I announced that I was going up to bed. Miguel hadn't spoken to me since he'd had words with me upstairs, and he just murmured a good-night without looking up.

How different he was from this afternoon, when he had held me and said those things to me.

I extinguished the candle and tried to sleep, but I was too nervous. I really didn't like the idea of sleeping with them now. At first it had appealed to me, sharing a room with two gorgeous men, but now I knew them better. One was erratic and the other volatile. I felt extremely vulnerable.

After about twenty minutes of tossing and turning, I heard the strangest noise, which seemed to get louder and louder with every passing moment. At first it was a rumbling sound but as it got louder I realised that it was the sound of engines; perhaps motorbikes or cars.

I jumped out of bed, thinking for one awful moment that Miguel and Eric were leaving; they'd had enough of me. I looked out of the window, hardly believing the sight before me. Coming up the road towards the house was a procession of various vehicles.

This in itself was incredible. The road was virtually unused and to have suddenly become the equivalent of the M25 was bizarre, especially so late at night.

I hadn't heard Miguel come into the room behind me. I was unaware of his presence until I inadvertently touched him with my arm.

'Miguel, what is it? What's going on?' I asked in a shaky voice.

'It's nothing to be worried about. They're just passing through.'

As he spoke, I realised that he was amused.

I turned back to the strange procession, and realised with increasing horror that they were pulling off the road. They were starting to park up all around the house, on the drive, on the lawns and even in a nearby meadow that belonged to the property.

Seeing all the cars, bikes and caravans, it occurred to me that they were Gypsies. And realising what they were, I was even more frightened.

'Miguel, they're Gypsies. What shall we do? They can't stay here. I'll have to call the police.'

'Don't be silly, Katie. They won't do any harm. They'll stay a day or two, then move on.'

'No, Miguel, you're wrong. They'll nick everything I've got, and you won't be able to do a thing about it. They're awful people.'

'I'm sorry you feel like that. Perhaps you should stay up here then, until they've gone. Good night.'

He spun around and stormed out of the room, slamming the door behind him. He had spoken with such a tone of bitterness, almost hatred, that I was hurt, shocked and frightened.

He was obviously very naive. Back in England I had often seen the debris and mayhem, not to mention the petty crimes, resulting from a Gypsy encampment. And how could he expect me to condone them parking up on my land?

Even so, his reaction made me feel as if I were the one in the wrong.

I watched Miguel as he left the house and walked towards a group of people who had already parked up and were wandering around. I was staggered when I saw them throw their arms round him, hugging and kissing him like he was a long-lost friend. And I was equally amazed to spot Eric, a couple of moments later, getting a similar response from another group.

Children started to run about the place. Dogs were barking. People were unloading tables and chairs, lighting lanterns and siting them in various locations, on tables and in trees.

I watched, totally mesmerised, as my grandfather's house turned into a campsite in less than half an hour.

I lost count after about fifty people because everyone was milling around, talking and laughing. I imagined there were at least sixty of them, though. And Miguel and Eric seemed to know every single one of them, from the youngest child to the oldest woman.

After a while, people started to sit down. They were opening bottles of wine by the dozen, eating, drinking and smoking to their hearts' content. I had never seen anything like it – and I had a bird's eye view.

A man walked into my line of vision carrying a guitar. He started to play and others started to sing. The sounds wafted up to my window; it was unmistakably Spanish music.

I remembered that we were not too far from the Spanish border; it was feasible that these people had come from Spain. And as I was thinking this, a beautiful young woman walked into the midst of the largest group. As everyone cleared a space for her, she began to dance flamenco.

Knowing that these people were Spanish Gypsies, it was only natural for me to connect them, then, to Miguel. He had admitted that he was Spanish; both he and Eric had been given the most incredible greeting; and even now, they were sitting at tables drinking with them.

Miguel and Eric were Gypsies. That was why he had seemed so offended – no, angry – when I had cast aspersions on them. I was absolutely sure of it, but I now wondered, more than ever, why they were shacking up in my house.

They had obviously not fallen out with their people, so why had they chosen not to move around with them? If they were hiding from the police, then they would be more secure buried in the midst of their friends. There was safety in numbers.

The beautiful Spanish woman had finished her dance. Everyone was whistling and clapping. I was overcome with jealousy when I saw her run up to Miguel, throw her arms about him and give him a big kiss on the mouth. He laughed, absolutely delighted, and pulled her on to his knee.

I turned my head to see what Eric had made of this little scenario but, incredibly, he was laughing at Miguel good-naturedly, completely at ease with the situation.

Alone in the bedroom, I felt suddenly lonely, hurt and rejected. If I hadn't said those things to Miguel, he would have brought me down to sit with him. And perhaps he wouldn't have turned to the Spanish woman.

I couldn't bear to watch any more. I'd seen enough. Whether Miguel was or wasn't gay, he was enjoying her attention, and I was the last thing on his mind at the moment.

I contemplated getting my car keys and leaving. Driving through the night if I had to and arriving back in England tomorrow evening. If I could have done it, then I would have done.

But, of course, I realised that even if I did get as far as the car and was able to start the engine, there would have been at least fifty Gypsies within twenty feet of me, to stop me from going any further. And having already seen Miguel's temper unleashed once today, I didn't relish getting the full brunt of it.

I climbed into bed and shut my eyes. I lay awake for what seemed like hours, listening to their music and laughter. In the end I buried my head under the pillows to shut out the sounds.

It took me a moment or two to remember the events of last evening. I still had a pillow over my head and I felt hot and sweaty. I lifted myself up and looked about.

Judging by the tidiness of Eric's makeshift bed on the

floor and the sheets still tucked into the other side of my bed, Miguel and Eric hadn't come up last night. So who had Miguel slept with? I could accept him screwing Eric, but another woman?

I had never been so jealous in all my life as I was at that moment. Not even when I had discovered my boyfriend's infidelity. And yet I was aware of how unhealthy my feelings were. Miguel was, as Eric had said, a free spirit. He could do whatever he wanted; he was not committed to me in any way, shape or form. For Christ's sake, he hadn't even fucked me. But unfortunately for me, I had feelings for him that went way beyond the physical.

I realised that I didn't know him at all and it was probably safer for me that I didn't; yet it didn't stop me from feeling more and more for him with each passing day.

I got up and looked out of the window. All the vehicles were still there, but it was deadly quiet. No sign of anyone except for a couple of children playing, and a few dogs lying outside their respective caravans.

I quietly went into the bathroom and washed. I imagined that there would be loads of people downstairs, kipping on the floor. I began to feel quite indignant about it. Miguel and Eric staying here uninvited was one thing, but to expect me to just accept their whole clan without batting an eyelid was pushing it too far.

I crept down the stairs, aware that I was only wearing my T-shirt and knickers, but was amazed to find the salon deserted and as tidy as it had been yesterday morning. Obviously nobody had been inside.

I quickly donned a pair of jeans and a shirt, then went to open the kitchen door that led out to the terrace. I was surprised to find it locked. For some reason, Miguel had locked it last night.

I went back into the salon and tried to open the front door. That too was locked and the key that was normally on the inside had been removed.

I decided that Miguel was stupid if he thought that locking me in would stop me escaping. I could have opened any of the windows on the ground floor and jumped out. Then it occurred to me that he hadn't done it to keep me in, but to keep people out. I wondered whether he had done it to protect me or the house.

But I wasn't about to open a window and get out now. I felt ashamed of myself for the things that I had said last night; especially now that I knew he was a Gypsy too.

And I would have felt uncomfortable seeing Miguel with that woman. I didn't know how I would react so it was better that I stayed away from them. Hopefully they would leave in a day or two, as Miguel had said they would.

I prayed that he didn't go with them. He and Eric might have been in hiding, waiting to be picked up by their people on the way through. The idea that Miguel would be out of my life as quickly as he had come into it made me feel sick with dread.

And yet, when Miguel came in through the kitchen door just before lunch, to check on me I supposed, I felt the dread quickly reverting back to jealousy. I couldn't even bring myself to answer his greeting.

He stood in the doorway of the salon watching me, but I didn't look up from the book I was pretending to read. All I could think about was who he had been with and what he had done with them.

After a while he spoke to me in a gruff voice, obviously irritated by my behaviour. 'You're obviously fine in here, enjoying your book, so I won't disturb you. You may have noticed that I've locked the doors for you, so you don't have to worry about these awful people coming in and robbing you blind. I'll see you later.'

He spun on his heel and left the room. I heard him slam the kitchen door and lock it behind him.

I mentally kicked myself for my behaviour. If anything, I would have driven him further away by sulking.

He found it hard to tolerate Eric's petulance, so how could he tolerate mine, a relative stranger? He had only come in to make sure that I was all right.

What I should have done was apologise for my thoughtless comments. He would have forgiven me and probably would have made an effort to include me. The way things were now, I might never see him again. He could ride off on his motorbike into the sunset with that Spanish tart on the back.

I spent the day feeling lonely and miserable. I didn't eat any lunch and I only ate lightly in the evening. As it got dark I watched them outside by the light from their lamps, drinking, eating and singing. The guitar player strummed and the Spanish bitch danced.

From the salon window I could see her more clearly than from the bedroom. She was very beautiful: dark-skinned, flashing eyes, long black hair . . . She made me sick. And even more so when I saw Miguel watching her with a relaxed, contented expression on his face. He was drinking heavily too, I noticed.

About ten o'clock, I saw that they were starting to clear the tables and pack things up. They were obviously getting ready to move on. I imagined that I would discover within the next few hours whether Miguel would be leaving with them.

Perhaps, then, I would beg him to stay.

As I lay in the bath, in total darkness apart from one flickering candle, I heard voices downstairs: a man and a woman whispering together, but I couldn't make out what they were saying. When they climbed the stairs, I realised that they weren't speaking French: they were speaking Spanish, which I couldn't understand.

They had reached the top of the stairs and were walking into the bedroom. I realised that the next stop would be the bathroom, so as quietly as I could, but with nerves making my heart pound, I stepped out of the bath.

I grabbed a towel and was just about to wrap it round myself when the door swung open.

Miguel stood in the doorway, holding a candle.

'God, I was so frightened. Why didn't you call out to me?'

In a deep quiet voice he answered, 'What did you think, Katie, that some Gypsy was stalking around the house, looking to rape and pillage?'

With a cynical smile on his face, his eyes ran over me. If I hadn't known better, I would have assumed that he was looking to do the very same thing.

I shivered with the cold water on my skin, and because the way he was still looking at me made me feel very vulnerable. I wrapped myself in my towel and just shrugged my shoulders in answer.

He reached out and took my hand. 'Katie, there's someone I'd like you to meet.'

He pulled me out of the bathroom and into the bedroom. Standing by the window was the Spanish woman. In the candlelight I could see that she was several years older than me, but still very striking.

I swallowed nervously, wondering if this was the point when Miguel was going to announce his departure or his new-found love.

She turned to look at me and, as Miguel had done a few minutes before, she gave me the once-over. When her eyes returned to my face, she was smiling. She said something in Spanish to Miguel and he answered her quickly. It was then that I realised – Miguel's first language had to be Spanish. Being English myself, I hadn't detected that his French had an accent.

The woman came towards me and startled me by taking my face in her hand and tilting it up for her to inspect more closely. I was annoyed and went to pull away from her, but Miguel still had hold of my hand firmly. Laughing at my discomfort, he said quietly, 'Katie, this is my sister.'

I looked at him incredulously, then turned my eyes

back to her. Of course, their likeness was all too apparent. How could I have thought that they were anything other than related? My heart lifted somewhat as his words sank in, but at the same time hoped that she wouldn't be taking him away from me.

He let go of my hand and walked towards the window. He sat on the window sill and watched, almost expectantly, while his sister pushed me gently backwards, until my legs touched the bed.

She motioned for me to sit down and I had no choice but to do so, without appearing churlish. But my heart was starting to pound with a mixture of nerves and anticipation.

The way Miguel was watching us so intently, it was as if he were waiting for his sister to perform more flamenco. But I had a vague idea that this wasn't on the cards. Whatever he was waiting for, it somehow involved me.

She sat down beside me and I was almost overwhelmed by her heavy perfume: exotically spicy, actually very musky, conjuring up images of Arab women and harems.

Her hand reached up to my head and her fingers pulled out the knot that I had made to stop my hair getting wet in the bath. Running her fingers through my hair as if she had never felt silky, straight hair before, she spoke in Spanish to Miguel.

'My sister thinks you are beautiful. She wants to know if you have ever been with a woman before?'

I looked beyond her to Miguel, hardly believing my ears. His laughing face confirmed that I had heard him correctly and, full of outrageous indignation, I went to stand up.

She laughed and, putting her hands on my shoulders, held me down. As I opened my mouth to protest, her mouth covered mine, and her tongue stopped the words.

I was shocked and mortified that this could be happening to me; that Miguel wanted to watch this happen.

But just thinking about Miguel watching, and the sexual pleasure it would undoubtedly give him, sent a bolt of exhilaration rushing through me which blasted away the shock.

My towel had fallen away so that she caught a glimpse of my naked breasts. Her hand left my shoulder and travelled down to my nipple. She teased it while she kissed me again more forcefully, using her weight to hold me down.

I began to feel aroused in spite of myself. Not because she was a woman, but because of what she was doing to me. My nipple was sending the usual messages down to my pussy, and I felt strangely excited, struggling naked underneath her.

She was rough, but her mouth was soft, much softer than a man's; and I began to find the sensation pleasurable.

Like in a dream, I was losing control. Everything was just happening and I was reacting instinctively to every moment. There was nothing else I could do. I was smothered by her musky scent, smothered by her erotic kisses; I was almost overcome.

After a few minutes, her mouth left my lips and her tongue gently descended to my other nipple. I gave a little gasp as she took it in her mouth and gently bit it with her teeth. Then she began to suck it demandingly.

I was vaguely aware that Miguel was still in the background, studying the picture, relishing the image, but I no longer cared. I was now really aroused.

I reached up and, putting my hands on her head, buried my fingers in her lustrous hair. I tried to push her down; I wanted her down – between my legs.

Suddenly she stopped everything, moved back and looked at me. She could see that I was panting with desire for her. She said something to Miguel and he moved towards us. He sat on the bed, just a few feet away from us, and his eyes studied my face. I had no idea what he was thinking.

She stood up and quickly peeled off her dress. She was naked in seconds. She had a good body, strong and firm; the female equivalent of Miguel's, I supposed.

When I looked up at him again, to see what sort of impact his sister's nakedness had made on him, I found that he was not even looking at her; he was still gazing at me intently. I knew then that he was not interested in her at all.

She climbed on to the bed and lay down beside me, but the opposite way round this time. Her face was near my pussy and my face was near hers. I knew what she wanted to do.

I gasped again, as she ran her hands over my arse and drew me towards her mouth. Holding me firmly, she ran her tongue up and down the inside of my thighs. I was aching for her to go to my pussy.

I knew that she was teasing me. I wondered what I could do to make her go down on me. Almost instinctively, my hand reached down and found her breast.

It was a shock when I touched it: so soft and yielding; not like a man's chest, firm and hard.

Her breasts were bigger than mine; she was altogether more voluptuous. I had a sudden desire to hurt her for being so feminine; I wanted her to be her brother. My fingers found her nipple and I pinched it spitefully. She responded by nipping my thigh with her teeth.

She positioned herself so that her pussy was just inches from my face and then, at last, her tongue moved to my cunt.

Her fingers parted my labia, and her tongue immediately focused on my already throbbing clitoris. She began to stroke it rhythmically. I knew that it wouldn't take long for me to come; I was halfway there already.

As my stomach muscles started to tighten involuntarily, she seemed to sense this. She quickly wrapped her legs round my head, drawing me into her pussy. I knew what she wanted and, as I desperately wanted her to take me all the way, I had no choice but to do it.

Holding her arse in my hands, I buried my face in her pussy and breathed in her overwhelming femininity. My tongue tentatively found her clitoris.

This was uncharted territory for me; it seemed utterly bizarre that I was even in this situation. For a moment, I was distracted from my own selfish desire for fulfilment, to thoughts about what this could mean. I had never ever fantasised about being with a woman, and yet, amazingly, I felt no distaste.

I wanted to do it – now. It seemed erotic, decadent; I was responding so positively to this woman who was dominating me. But why? Where was this coming from? I had no idea that I had such desires within me.

It was the strangest sensation, going down on her; so different from doing it with a man. And yet I knew what to do. It was easy – like masturbating. And she obviously liked what I was doing.

I felt her squirming under my mouth – as I must have been doing under hers. I tasted her flowing juices and I felt her body shuddering. She was coming; her whole body jerking with spasms. She cried out in Spanish and I let go of her buttocks, which I had been gripping, almost desperately, to my face.

But she was still between my legs, wanting me to come. I closed my eyes, forgetting everything but what she was doing to me. I relished every little sensation her wonderful tongue was bestowing on me.

As I felt my body building up for orgasm, I wrapped my thighs tight round her head. I pulled her hard into me, so that she had no choice but to breathe me and drink me.

For a while I had forgotten that we were being watched. I opened my eyes and looked up, to meet Miguel's, looking deep into mine, seeing everything, probably feeling everything, through my eyes. And in the end, he brought me to the point of climax. Or rather, his eyes, smouldering as he watched my face and body. And his hand, rubbing the hardness inside his jeans.

He was aroused by what we were doing. In the same way that I was aroused by watching him with Eric. With that one thought, I came. Violently, in great long shudders.

She immediately got off me, speaking to Miguel in a low voice. He just nodded, still watching me with his beautiful dark eyes.

I now felt dirty and sordid, having performed like that in front of Miguel. To have done it with a woman was one thing, but to have done it in front of her brother was something else.

I reconciled myself with the thought that neither of them cared in the slightest. And I had seen Miguel do as much, if not worse.

I decided that they were strange, perverted people, who had no moral code and no inhibitions.

And I was little better. I would and could do anything, with just a little encouragement.

It could have even been that Miguel had seen something in me that told him I would respond in this way; that I was open to sexual experiment and would go with the flow.

But despite what I thought about him and his principles, or lack of them, I hoped that he would stay with me.

I climbed under the sheet to cover my nakedness, although it was a little late in the day for modesty; and Miguel got off the bed and walked towards the door. His sister, now dressed, followed him. Just as she reached the door, she turned and blew me a kiss.

I lay back in the pillows and thought about what we had done. I had to be honest with myself: I had enjoyed it. I had found it erotic in the extreme. I just felt ashamed now that it was over and done with. And I dreaded having to face Miguel.

I dozed on and off to the sounds of people shouting, dogs barking, cars and vans hooting. The vehicles were on the move. I wondered if Miguel and Eric were going with them.

About an hour later, I felt someone climb into the bed beside me. It was Miguel, of course. He had brought a candle in with him and had placed it on the bedside cabinet.

I had my back to him and was looking towards the window. I could see his reflection in the glass, as he could see mine, but I didn't speak to him.

He reached out his hand and put it on my shoulder. 'You're incredibly beautiful, incredibly sensual, and I got as much pleasure from watching you tonight as you did from doing it. Do you know that?' he asked, whispering in my ear.

I chose to ignore him, because I was still feeling disconcerted, actually very confused, by what was happening here. But my heart was pounding with excitement, in spite of the way I felt. Just his proximity to me, him leaning over me and touching me, was enough to send it racing.

'Are you OK, Katie?' he asked, a moment later.

I shrugged his hand off. 'I'm fine.'

He tugged me hard, rolling me on to my back. 'Don't play games with me. We have one sulky brat in the house. We don't need another one.'

'If anyone's playing games – it's not me. Good night!'

I rolled back towards the window and shut my eyes, making out that I wanted to sleep. He dropped back into the pillows and swore under his breath.

He was irritated with me but I didn't care now. Whatever his reasons were, he was staying with me.

Safe in the knowledge that he was beside me, I soon fell asleep.

When I awoke in the morning, it was as if the Gypsies had never been there. Miguel was fast asleep in the bed beside me and Eric was on the floor.

I quietly slipped out of the bed and made my way to the door.

I stood there for a few moments just watching Miguel sleeping. He was frowning, obviously having a dream, and I watched as his brows kept furrowing then clearing, his long eyelashes flickering on his cheeks. He looked like a little boy and I would have loved to be able to kiss him on the mouth or stroke away his frown with my hand.

I went downstairs to look at the devastation. Actually, there wasn't any. A few empty bottles and bags of rubbish; nothing that Miguel couldn't have sorted out within about half an hour. I was going to have to swallow my pride and apologise to him.

But now the Gypsies had left the property, my earlier problem came to mind. What had Miguel and Eric meant when they had said that they knew I was coming; and what were they doing here in the first place? I needed these questions answered and soon, because, the way I was starting to feel about Miguel, it wouldn't be too long before I would accept anything he'd done without question.

After about an hour, Miguel came outside and sat down without speaking. Our eyes met briefly and I could see that he was still annoyed with me.

I decided to apologise, thereby smoothing the path for further conversation. 'Miguel, I'm sorry for the things I said about your friends the other night. We have a lot of trouble with Gypsies where I live in England, and I thought they would be the same. I was wrong.'

He looked at me for a moment before he answered me. 'I imagine that the people you are talking about aren't genuine Gypsies. As you have probably guessed, Eric and I are from Gypsy stock. Our families have lived this way for generations; they are essentially people that like to travel. They don't put down roots in any particular place, but they work for their living, passing down their trades from generation to generation.

'The people you describe probably don't do it for their love of the open roads. They just want to live life the easy way, copping out and avoiding the rules that most people have to live by.'

'What about you then, Miguel? Don't you love travelling around, not putting down roots?'

'No. I'm a painter and the life I was born into doesn't lend itself to what I do best. I like peace and solitude. Living with one big extended family offers me neither of these things.'

'Well, why doesn't Eric stay with them? He doesn't share your interest.'

Miguel hesitated before he answered my question; I sensed that he was selecting his words carefully. It made me all the more suspicious.

'Eric has spent all his life with me. I'm seven years older and I've always looked after him. And for some years we have not moved around with the rest of them. Like me, he prefers staying in one place.

'Then there's his sexuality. Gypsies are very family-orientated, and while they accept the way he is, he is unlikely to have a fulfilling relationship in their environment.'

'And I suppose that applies to you too,' I slipped in quickly.

He just shrugged his shoulders, not bothering to reply.

As I walked inside to fetch my book, Eric pushed past me.

'Do you mind?' I snapped indignantly.

But he ignored me, as always, and spoke to Miguel. 'I'm going into town to get my clothes washed. Do you want anything?'

'Get us some bread and some meat, and that will see us through today. I'll go tomorrow with Katie and do a big shop.'

A few minutes later, Eric came back out with a backpack bursting with clothes, and walked down to the outhouse where they kept their bikes. He wheeled out the Japanese bike and started the engine.

Seconds later he was off, up on to the road, and disappearing from view. With his blond hair flying behind him and his unshaven good looks, I imagined that he would get plenty of attention from girls along the way; not that he would have been interested.

My book was open on my lap, but I wasn't taking anything in. I just couldn't relate to my heroine's cool restraint when I was sweltering in the heat and burning up under Miguel's smouldering glances.

Suddenly he stubbed out his cigarette and stood up.

'I want you to come down to the barn with me. You can read in there while I paint.'

Miguel threw open all the doors and windows while I dragged a chair over to one of the windows and settled down in it. It was very warm inside the barn, although it was still fairly early in the day.

Miguel positioned his easel on the other side of the studio and started to mix up colours. As on the other occasion when he painted, I preferred to watch him than read, and it was difficult for me not to just shut my book, sit back and openly stare at him. But after a while he became so absorbed in what he was doing that I thought he had all but forgotten me.

I was startled when he spoke to me. 'Katie, why don't you talk to me? I can listen as well as paint.'

I answered without thinking, 'I don't think you'd like what I'd say!'

He put his brush down and looked up at me. 'What is it you want to say to me?'

'Well, it's more of a question really, although you told me that I mustn't ask you anything like this. I want to know what you and Eric were talking about the day before yesterday, after he had a go at me. It made no sense to me but I know something's going on.

'You're staying in a house that doesn't belong to you

and I'm accepting that, aren't I? Because I could have told someone by now, you know, when we've been out. I'm not stupid. But I haven't, because I don't want to get you into trouble.

'I wish you would just tell me what you're about. Then I can put my mind at rest, or not, as the case may be. You make me feel as if I'm in some sort of danger and I can't relax.'

He walked towards me, looking so grave that I was nervous. I should have kept my big mouth shut. He now felt threatened by my inquisitiveness and was going to explode. But instead, he squatted down on the floor in front of me and took my hand.

'I promise you that I wouldn't do anything to hurt you, unless you do something to hurt me. At this moment, the worst thing you could do is run away. You have nothing to worry about. I'll take care of Eric. And believe me when I say that the most illegal thing I've ever done is stay in this house which isn't mine.'

I didn't know whether I should, but I believed him. He seemed so sincere. His big brown eyes boring into mine cast away all my doubts. If his worst crime was staying here uninvited, then he wasn't a criminal in my eyes. I wanted him to be here.

I inwardly gave a huge sigh of relief. Eric was still an unknown entity; I wouldn't have trusted him as far as I could throw him. But perhaps I could trust Miguel enough to protect me.

Still holding my hand, he spoke again. 'I've answered you as best I can. When we know each other better, I will explain everything. So now I have a question for you. Who do you find more attractive – my sister or me?'

I felt the colour flooding to my cheeks. I was mortified.

I looked at him but there was no laughter in his eyes and I felt compelled to answer. Looking down at my lap, I replied, 'I find you both very beautiful; you as a man, she as a woman.'

He tipped my face up with his hand, forcing me to look at him. 'That's not what I asked you. Who do you find more attractive?'

'Well, I'm not a lesbian, if that's what you think,' I retorted, irritated by his persistence and my own discomfort. 'Anyone could do those things and make me come. It wasn't because of the person, but for the act itself.'

Miguel stood up with a supercilious smile on his face. 'That's exactly how I feel. We're very alike.'

He walked across the studio, picked up his brush and started painting again. Well, he still hadn't enlightened me as to his own sexuality, but he had implied that for him, too, anyone could make it happen just by performing the act.

And yet I had always been led to believe that a gay man would find the prospect of sleeping with a woman abhorrent; and that a straight man would find the idea of fucking another man the worst thing imaginable. I was more baffled than ever.

Miguel painted for about an hour without even looking at me. Until the silence was broken by the sound of Eric's bike.

He threw down his brush, shut all the windows, which told me that he wouldn't be painting any more today, then together we strolled up to the house.

Chapter Four

'Do you fancy going swimming this afternoon? It's going to be really hot and I'm bored just sitting around,' Miguel asked Eric after lunch.

'OK, but what about her?' Eric asked, nodding his head at me as if I were a piece of dog shit that he had just spotted on the terrace.

'Well, Katie will have to come too, of course. We'll keep a close eye on her,' he added, giving me a wry smile.

'I won't be able to fit you both in my car. It's only a two-seater.'

'We'll go by bike. Get your things together and we'll leave in ten minutes.'

I knew where he would go. There was a large swimming lake just outside the town and I often went there as a child.

I went into the dining room and got undressed. I put on my bikini then slipped my jeans and a sweatshirt over the top. I was nervous about going on a bike; I hadn't been on one in years. I threw a towel, some suntan lotion and my book into a bag then went outside.

'I want you to put this on, Katie. I know it's hot but you'll be safer,' Miguel said, handing me a padded leather jacket which was way too big for me.

I could smell him on it. I liked that he had given me his jacket. And it told me something. Regardless of all else, he was a caring person.

He also gave me a crash helmet and seeing me struggle with the clasp, he came over to help me. I watched his face as he did up the strap, intent on what he was doing. When he'd finished, he smiled almost affectionately and his hand stroked my cheek.

I nearly swooned.

'If we're going to do this again, I'd feel happier buying you a helmet that fitted you properly. Wait there while we bring the bikes up.'

Miguel and Eric wheeled their bikes out and started the engines. The noise was deafening. Miguel climbed on his and rode it up to the house. He put his legs down to support it and told me to climb on the back. Tentatively I did as he asked.

'Don't be nervous; I'll ride sensibly. Just remember to lean with me on bends. Don't try to lean the other way or the bike will be unbalanced.'

I nodded and, putting my hands round his waist, we pulled off.

Once on the road, Eric took the lead. They both drove so quickly that at first I was petrified, hanging on to Miguel for dear life. But after a while I started to relax and, actually, enjoy it.

It felt good being so close to him, my arms wrapped round him, my thighs rubbing against his, his natural body smell wafting over me as he slowed down sometimes . . . I could have suffered this for hours!

We reached Barbotan in under ten minutes and I was surprised when they didn't stop. They just drove straight through it. I couldn't think where we were going.

We followed the main road westwards and pretty soon I realised they were heading for the coast. This was turning out to be a major excursion, but I thought it would be nice to spend an afternoon on the beach. As a child we had only gone to the coast once or twice when I was here, simply because it took at least two hours by car.

I had to admit, both Eric and Miguel looked very sexy on motorbikes. I often caught Miguel's reflection in shop windows as we drove through the villages – he could have been a model for a poster.

I wondered if he would let me take some pictures of him. Having to live with such perfect male specimens, day in and day out, was very frustrating for me as a would-be fine-art photographer. Generally I worked in black and white and I had loved playing around with exposure times in my darkroom back in England, watching the effect it'd had on skin tones and so on, almost as much as I had loved taking the actual photographs. I had only used a photo lab for processing my commissioned work.

But I would use colour, I decided, with Miguel and Eric. The contrast between them – Eric, blue-eyed, blond-haired; Miguel, dark-haired, moody; the richness of their colouring – the mahogany tints in Miguel's black hair, the corn-coloured streaks in Eric's fair hair; their different shades of skin . . .

My dream, probably along with every other photographer, was to have some of my work shown at an exhibition, or even featured in a book. And now that I was no longer working, it was the perfect time for me to focus on my art. Art for art's sake, rather than for the clients who paid me. And now that I had found Miguel and Eric literally on my doorstep . . . I had to look no further for my inspiration.

Of course, Miguel and Eric still had no idea that I had taken that one shot, the day I arrived. I had hidden my camera under the bed that night and it was still there; not that I would have used it as evidence now.

I discreetly studied Eric's silhouette, now that he was riding just in front of us or alongside us. Just for once, I got a certain amount of pleasure from watching him.

Torn, faded jeans; rugged, tanned faces; long, clean, hair. We were certainly pulling looks as we drove along and the girls weren't looking at the bikes.

After about an hour, we arrived in a town called Hossegor. We followed the signs for the beach and parked in a nearby street. I got off the bike and Miguel put it on its side stand.

Eric started to head for the beach with Miguel and I following him.

Walking behind Eric, I saw again the reaction he was getting from women as he passed them by. They were openly staring at him before their eyes turned to Miguel. It was rare to see two such good-looking men together. Even I had appreciated that, when I first laid eyes on them. And now I just felt proud that I was with them, despite the fact that Eric hated my guts.

The beach was packed mainly with young people surfing and sunbathing. The place had a fantastic atmosphere; everyone bent on having a good time. Eric chose a spot to sit down and we dumped all our stuff.

I was the only one with a towel, but it didn't seem to bother them.They immediately stripped off their shirts and jeans and lay them out to sit on. Miguel and Eric were both wearing swimming trunks under their jeans. They had obviously donned these while I had been in the dining room getting changed.

I sat down on my towel beside Miguel and slapped on some suntan lotion, then, as an afterthought, I offered him some. He refused, laughing at me like I was mad.

Thinking about it, I could see his point. His skin was already the colour of mahogany. It was a little late in the day for him to start worrying about protection factors.

After about half an hour, Eric stood up. 'I'll be back in ten minutes. Do you want anything from the shops?' he asked Miguel.

'Yes. Get some cigarettes and a couple of cold cokes for Katie and me. Do you want anything else?' Miguel asked, turning to me.

I appreciated this little acknowledgement of my existence; after all, I was invisible as far as Eric was concerned; but I just shook my head in response.

Eric nodded and walked off up the beach.

'Do you often come here?' I asked Miguel.

'Quite a lot. There's another nice beach a couple of miles away, Capbreton, but Eric prefers the waves here. Would you like to go swimming?'

'Yes I would. But is the water cold? It's the Atlantic.'

Miguel stood up. 'Try it and find out.'

I got up and walked with him to the edge of the water. He waded straight out and started to swim, avoiding all the surf boards. I dipped my toes in and, finding it cold, braced myself before I moved into deeper water. I held my breath as it reached my stomach, gasped as it reached my chest.

The waves were really strong. I found that they were practically picking me up and carrying me further out. I swam towards Miguel. 'It's fucking freezing,' I said, somewhat breathlessly, when I reached him.

'No, it's great when you get used to it. Just watch out for the surfers. Half of them don't look where they're going.'

I swam around for about five minutes then told Miguel that I was getting out. He said that he would come with me. As we swam into the shallow water and stood up, the waves nearly knocked me over. Miguel had to put his arm around me, just to steady me until we reached the shore.

'Do you want to share my towel? Otherwise you'll get covered in sand,' I pointed out, as we sat down.

'Yes, please – if you don't mind?'

I shrugged my indifference, then moved over for him to lie beside me. I leant to one side and wrung the sea water out of my hair as best I could, then stayed sitting up, waiting for it to dry off a little. I glanced down at Miguel. He was watching me with a hand over his eyes to shield them from the sun.

His hair was drying already and going really curly. He never looked more like a Gypsy. All he needed was an earring to complete the picture. As I thought about this, my eyes strayed to his ears. One of them had been pierced. I wondered why he didn't wear an earring any more.

'With your long golden hair, you look just like a mermaid. Do you know the superstition about them? Sailors used to believe that if they ever saw a mermaid, they were doomed.'

'Yes I know. I think it's an English superstition, in fact. But don't worry, I don't swim well enough to be a mermaid!' I quipped, to cover up the emotions that were bubbling away inside me. When he was being so nice to me, it was easy to forget what he was, who he was, what he did with Eric . . .

I lay down on the towel, my head just an inch from his. He rolled on to one side and looked down at me. 'But you're beautiful enough to be one. And sometimes I do feel doomed because, having seen you, no one else will ever compare.'

I swallowed the lump which had suddenly sprung to my throat. It was the most romantic thing anyone had ever said to me, even if he didn't mean it!

He was so expressive at times; perhaps it was the artist in him. His words, even his deep, sexy voice, stirred me emotionally – almost as much as his looks did. I would never again be able to look at any other man without comparing him to Miguel. And of course, whoever he was, would fall well short. Miguel was perfect in my eyes.

I closed my eyes, embarrassed by his intense stare. A second later, I felt his mouth on mine, his tongue entering my mouth and searching for mine.

I opened my eyes in surprise. His eyes were shut; I didn't know what he was thinking.

I felt his naked chest touching mine, his hair caressing my shoulders. I forgot where we were, the people all around us, and just relished this open display of 'affection'; I didn't know what else it could be. But how I wanted him to do more. His kisses were sending tiny, but effective, electrical impulses all over my body. My pussy was responding without any stimulation. I wanted him desperately.

As suddenly as he had started kissing me, he stopped. He lifted up his head and rolled on to his stomach. 'I'm sorry. With your eyes shut and your mouth slightly open – I couldn't resist it. And here comes Eric, just in time!'

'Time for what?' Eric asked irritably, dropping down on the sand next to him. He must have seen Miguel kissing me.

'Just in time to distract me from Katie. Give me a cigarette then we'll take turns to surf.'

He took the packet of cigarettes Eric was offering him, then I noticed that Eric had two surf boards beside him.

'How are you going to get those back on a bike?' I asked, forgetting for a moment that he didn't actually talk to me.

I was stunned when he answered me good-naturedly enough. 'I've just borrowed them from one of the surf schools. We often do it. This bit of coast has some of the best waves in the world.'

Possibly the prospect of surfing made him feel better disposed towards me, so I pretended to be impressed. In fact, I knew next to nothing about surfing, but Eric fitted the picture perfectly. He looked like a Californian beach bum. I wondered if he had stolen the boards. A moment later, I had to dismiss this line of thought.

'I should mention at this point that Eric knows what he's talking about. He's won a major surfing competition that's held here, several times. And he's worked at one of the surf schools for years.'

Well, I had certainly underestimated Eric. Not that surfing as a career greatly impressed me, but I had to acknowledge that he was not the lazy bastard I had thought he was.

And for all I knew, winning competitions and working in a surf school paid well; at least he was doing something which he thoroughly enjoyed. Not many people could say that about their jobs.

What they were doing in my house was still a mystery, but, as the days went by, I was learning more and more about them. And Eric certainly seemed a lot happier with himself, and me, here on the beach.

I enjoyed watching them surf. Miguel was good but Eric was excellent. People actually stood and watched him and, as more and more surfers arrived during the course of the afternoon, they came over to greet him. Incredibly, he seemed to be well known and really well liked!

About six o'clock Miguel asked me if I would like to eat before we went home. I agreed and we packed up our things. The three of us walked up the beach on to the busy street and made our way to a little Italian restaurant. Eric did a detour to return the surf boards.

We sat outside the restaurant for several hours, eating pizza, drinking beers and watching the world go by. It was wonderful being out with them both, while Eric was actually behaving like a human being. I felt like I was with two good friends – the three of us on holiday together. The only time I was reminded of my somewhat bizarre circumstances was when I got up to go to the toilet.

'Where do you think you're going?' Miguel asked me as I started to walk away from our table.

'I'm just going to ask the waiter where the loos are. Is that all right? You can come with me if you want to,' I added sarcastically.

'Yes, I think I will. I'm sure there're plenty of men here who would be only too willing to help a beautiful blonde in distress.'

I gave him a withering look and walked up to the waiter. As he pointed out to me where the toilets were, I noticed Miguel standing behind me.

I rolled my eyes to the ceiling, feigning irritation. He was taking this a bit too far. I hadn't the slightest intention of 'escaping' and he should have realised this by now.

We got back on the bikes at sunset. The air was a little cooler and I was glad for the leather jacket. I wondered if Miguel was cold wearing just a shirt and jeans; Eric had pulled a leather jacket out of his back pack and put it on.

It was nearly dark when we got home. I told them that I was going straight upstairs to have a bath and wash my hair. Miguel nodded; Eric said nothing. Back in the house, his sullenness had returned.

I dried my hair with a towel as best I could, then, having put on a clean T-shirt and knickers, called down the stairs that I was going to bed.

A little while later, Miguel walked into the bedroom. Watching him through half-closed eyes, I saw by the light of the candle he was carrying that he was naked.

My heart began to beat faster with excitement. It was going to be the first time that we were in bed together, awake, without Eric being in the room. Except for last night, of course, but I was cross with him then.

He placed the candle on the bedside cabinet, then drew back the sheet to get in beside me.

'Katie, would you do something for me? It's not a very big thing.'

My heart was now pounding with anticipation.

'What?' I asked him dubiously.

'I'd like you to take your clothes off. Eric's not interested; seeing you naked would do nothing for him, but it would do a lot for me. I like looking at you.'

Without waiting for an answer, he leant across and pulled my knickers off. He threw them on the floor and then, sitting up, he pulled my T-shirt up over my head. As he did so, I saw his erection.

His next move took me totally by surprise. He rolled on top of me, forcing my legs apart with his. He took my hands and, raising them above my head, he held them down . . . just like my fantasies.

He looked down at me for a couple of seconds, his eyes seemingly searching mine, and then I knew. He was going to fuck me. This was what I had wanted from the first moment I saw him.

'Miguel, what would Eric think if he saw us like this? I don't think it's a good idea –'

'Forget Eric. He understands. And besides, you owe me.'

'What do you mean? I don't owe you anything –'

He stopped me from saying any more. He dropped his mouth down on mine and kissed me passionately. His tongue took mine and he held me like this for several minutes. When he stopped, I was gasping for air – and more.

'You are so fucking beautiful. If I died right now, I'd die happy.'

He kissed me again, his mouth becoming rougher, more demanding. He bit my lips and when I squeaked with the pain, he licked them better. A few minutes later he would do it again.

I felt his cock pushing into my groin, wanting the way in, but he didn't enter me. Still holding my hands above my head, he moved his mouth down my neck to my breasts. He sucked and licked each nipple alternately; occasionally nipping them with his teeth . . . so like my fantasies.

As he sucked my nipples, they were sending messages down to my pussy. It was wet and waiting for him. And after a couple of minutes of him teasing me, I couldn't stand it any longer.

'Fuck me!' I whispered in his ear.

'What did you say?'

I knew he'd heard me but I said it again anyway. This time I made it a command.

Transferring my wrists to one hand, but still holding

them high above my head, he used his other hand to push himself inside me.

As his cock entered me, I felt overwhelmed with relief. This was what my body had been craving for – the whole of my adult life.

Whatever his sexual inclinations were, whatever he had indulged in up until now; I knew, the moment my pussy encapsulated his shaft, that he was everything that I had ever wanted in a man. And even if he were to withdraw from me, never to go near me again, no other man would ever make me feel so complete, so fulfilled, as I was, at this moment, with him.

He was like the missing piece in my puzzle. He had instantaneously put himself in the right place; for me, the perfect place; and I just prayed that he could feel the same way as I did, and learn to accept the inevitable.

He closed his eyes as he started to move slowly in and out of me. I kept mine wide open.

In the flickering candlelight his long black eyelashes cast shadows on his cheeks. His hair, falling forward, stroked my face. His eyebrows were furrowed into a frown and he groaned very quietly with every thrust. He, too, seemed relieved to be inside me.

He started to move faster. His mouth came down on to mine and stayed there, entering me with his tongue as he entered me down below.

Now he released my wrists and put his hands on my buttocks. He held me tight as he thrust into me, harder, deeper.

I had to touch him; I couldn't resist it. I had to make sure that he was real, not another fantasy. I put my hands on his head, burying my fingers in his thick hair as he kissed me.

I ran my hands down his shoulders, feeling every muscle flexing as he lifted himself up and down. My hands continued their exploration, down to his waist then around to his back. At last they came to rest on his arse. I dug my nails into his flesh; it was so hard and firm that I couldn't resist it. I must have hurt him for he did the same to me.

As he started to breathe more rapidly, he lifted his mouth off mine and dropped his head to my shoulder. He squeezed my buttocks even tighter as his body began to shudder. His thrusts became even harder as he slowed right down towards the end. He groaned as he came.

He stayed on top of me for several minutes, his head still buried in my shoulder. As I felt his heart rate return to normal, I suddenly realised that I hadn't come. Incredibly, it had made no difference. The man I physically worshipped had fucked me – had actually wanted to fuck me. It had been passionate, sensuous – just how I had always fantasised it to be. And the fact that he had come meant everything.

When he at last rolled off me, I found that I was bathed in sweat. I sat up, intending to go to the bathroom.

I was stunned to find Eric, sitting on a chair, just three feet away from us. He was naked; he had a huge erection and he had probably watched – everything.

I walked past him, yet again wondering about their relationship and ours; and how it all fitted together.

I sat on the toilet thinking about Miguel. He had kissed me and touched me the whole time. So different from the way he acted with Eric. Even Eric must have noticed this.

Perhaps it was because I was new; it was the first time with me and I was something different from his usual sexual experiences. Maybe over time, he would become as detached in his love-making with me as he was with Eric. If that were so, he would break my heart.

Miguel was lying next to me, fast asleep, with one arm draped across me almost possessively. Ever so gently, I moved it off me and got up.

It was ironic that I had left my boyfriend because he had been unfaithful to me; and within a matter of days I had fallen in love with somebody who seemed to treat sex so lightly; something I could have never understood or condoned back home.

Perhaps it was the house that was having this effect on me. My mother had always hated the place. She said that she had dreaded coming to stay here when she was young; she said it had an atmosphere.

I felt an atmosphere, but not a menacing one. I felt languid, sensual and aroused in this hot sultry climate. It filled my head with erotic desires that I would never have entertained back in England.

Miguel felt it too, I was sure. I had seen his paintings; and I remembered my grandfather's. Both their work was very sensual, very provoking.

When I caught Miguel's silhouette out of the corner of my eye, I was startled; I hadn't expected him to be up so early.

I smiled at him in greeting, then noticed that he was wet; he'd just taken a bath.

Imagining that my eyes were my camera, I captured the moment as this Greek god stood before me, the sun caressing his mahogany-coloured skin, emphasising the contours of his well-defined muscles; his wet body hair sleek and glistening against his dark torso, his hair dripping water, turning to rivulets as they landed on his bronzed shoulders; even the black shadow he cast on the white wall behind him . . . everything about him was so fucking beautiful.

But he seemed perturbed; he wasn't smiling.

'What's the matter?'

'I wish you would tell me when you're going downstairs. I woke up; you weren't there. I thought you'd gone.'

'I didn't like to wake you up; you were fast asleep. But you know, Miguel; I'm not going anywhere. I wish you'd just accept that.'

'Well, if that's true then I'm happy. Stay there while I get some coffee.'

He came out after about five minutes, dressed in jeans and a T-shirt. I watched him as he sat down, combed his hair back with his fingers then tied it in a ponytail.

Looking at him now, so quiet, so seemingly unobtainable, it was hard to believe that he had made love to me last night.

He looked at me too with a puzzled expression on his face. Perhaps he was feeling a little confused, wondering about this development in our relationship. It must have felt strange for him, to have made love to a woman. But I was sure he had feelings for me.

'Do you think you could live here, Katie?' he asked me after a while.

'What do you mean – in France or here, in this house?'

'In this house.'

'Yes I could, very easily. I feel very at home here.'

In fact, I had informed everybody, including my mother, that I was never going back home. And that was why my ex-boyfriend was now freaking out. Initially Robert had assumed that I would get over his little indiscretion and within a few weeks we would be back together again. Now that I had left England, with no intention of returning, it had knocked him for six.

But I didn't say all this to Miguel.

'Are you going to do anything about getting the gas and electricity connected then? It would make it a bit more comfortable for you, wouldn't it?'

'Yes, it would be nice to have hot water, although to be honest I quite like the place lit with candles rather than light bulbs. It creates a lovely atmosphere.'

'Well, there's nothing to stop you using candles if you prefer them. But you need a fridge. I'll buy you one today. We'll go into town in a little while and sort it out.'

I went inside and changed out of my cut-off jeans and a T-shirt into a long summer dress. I plaited my hair, put on my mules, then I was ready.

As we drove towards Eauze, I was aware of Miguel's

eyes on me the whole time. His face was turned towards me and, whenever I glanced at him, he was frowning.

'What is it, Miguel? I can't concentrate on driving if you keep looking at me like that.'

'I'm thinking that you're the most beautiful thing I've ever seen. I can hardly believe last night. I want to thank you. You made me very happy.'

'Are you saying that you're not happy now? What's changed since last night?'

'Well, I suppose, being realistic, it can't last. You've got a life, a family, back in England. And that's why I can't stop looking at you. I'm drinking in as much as I can, committing you to memory, before you leave me.'

'But, Miguel, you said that I wasn't allowed to leave?'

'When you arrived the other day, I didn't want you storming off and causing trouble. I wanted to get to know you. There was only one way of doing it under the circumstances. I forbade you to leave and watched you like a hawk. Now that I know you better, of course I would let you go – if you were unhappy with us.

'And I'm glad that you've found us. It means that Eric and I have to make some decisions about our future. Otherwise we would have just drifted along, staying in your place . . . I'll explain everything to you, one of these days.'

'So when do you think you'll leave?' I asked, trying to keep my voice on an even keel.

'Eric and I are kind of playing it by ear, but if you asked me to stay on with you, then of course, I would.'

'Miguel, I'm totally confused. Are you saying that you would live with me – long term? What about Eric? Don't you love him?'

'Eric has nothing to do with this. This is me; what I want. Of course I love Eric, but not in the way that you think. I love him like a brother and he loves me in the same way.'

'Well, you have a funny way of showing your affection. It verges on incest,' I quipped bitterly.

Miguel shrugged his shoulders but didn't respond.

'Miguel, am I the first woman you've ever been with?'

'Don't be stupid. I'm thirty-one years old. Of course I've slept with other women; too many to remember off hand. I haven't been serious about any one of them – because I've never wanted to be.'

'But I thought you were gay. I've seen you with Eric, don't forget. I thought that maybe I'm just something new and different you want to experience. You can be honest with me; it won't upset me. If you want to see how far you can go in a heterosexual relationship, it's OK. I can accept that.'

'I'm afraid you've got me completely wrong. For a start, I don't like being categorised, but if you feel the need to do it, then call me straight. I rarely find other men attractive and even when I do, I have no wish to fuck them unless there's a –'

'Miguel! How can you say that when you've –?'

He raised a hand to stop me, then he continued. 'If I could choose between a man or a woman, then I would choose a woman every time. But I won't deny that I find certain situations very erotic. You've seen my pictures, so you know what I'm talking about. And in the past I have responded to certain situations, regardless of whether it's a man, a woman, both, because at the time it's turned me on. To put it another way, I am as likely to be aroused by an erotic atmosphere, as I am by gender.'

I was just opening my mouth to speak, when he raised his hand again.

'I haven't finished yet,' he said, giving me a wry smile. 'So far, I've been talking about strangers. Now I'll talk about Eric and you.

'I have spent weeks at a time seeing no one but Eric – by choice I might add. And to be perfectly honest, getting a blow-job off Eric is better than having a wank.

It doesn't mean that I'm gay. I just have a good imagination and he does things which turn me on. He's good-looking, we protect ourselves . . . And be honest, Katie, you had sex with my sister for the same reasons. It doesn't mean that you're a lesbian.

'But Eric, on the other hand, is actively gay. He gets the opportunity but hasn't yet met anyone he feels able to have a long-term relationship with. That's why he chooses to stay with me.

'But I would rather have one night with you than the rest of my life with him. That's the difference.'

'So why were you doing things with him, even after I arrived?'

'Because I felt so frustrated – watching you, sleeping with you, and not being able to do anything about it. Eric was there. He understood; I hoped that you would understand. I even hoped that you might have wanted to join us!'

'Why didn't you just do it with me instead?'

'Come on, Katie – just think about it. You freaked out, the night you arrived, just because I grabbed your arm. If I had jumped on you, you would have died of fright. Especially having told you that you weren't allowed to leave.

'And under the circumstances, it was better that you did think we were both gay, initially. It made you feel less threatened by me and allowed you to drop your guard a little. I wanted to wait, to see if you liked me. The last thing I wanted to do was force myself on you.'

'But, Miguel, I wanted you from the moment I first saw you. I just didn't think you'd be interested in me.'

'Give me your hand. I want to show you something.'

I gave him my hand and he placed it between his legs and held it there. I felt his rigid cock encased in his jeans. 'That's how interested I am in you – all the time.'

When we arrived in Eauze, I parked in a car park. Reaching for my mobile, I told Miguel that I ought to phone my mother. He nodded.

'Hi, Mum; it's me.'

'Oh, Katie, I'm so glad you phoned. I've tried to reach you on the mobile several times, but it's always switched off.'

'Well, there's no point in keeping it on when there's no reception. And I don't go into town very often. I've phoned you each time I have. What's the problem?'

'I don't know how to tell you this, Katie, but it's Robert. He's been nagging me day and night to tell him where you've gone. I feel so sorry for him; he's devastated that you left him –'

'Well, he should have thought about that before he had his little fling then, shouldn't he?' I cut in.

'But he's so sorry. He wants to make it up to you. He's coming down to you; he's leaving today. I couldn't stop him, but it's for the best. You should sort it out between you, once and for all, then we'll all have a bit of peace.'

My blood ran cold as the realisation of what she had said dawned on me. I didn't know what to say to her with Miguel just inches away. I had no choice but to disconnect the call.

'Is everything all right?' Miguel asked, studying my face intently.

'Yes, fine; the battery's dead. My ex has been giving my mother grief, that's all.'

I tried to keep my voice on an even keel. I prayed that Miguel didn't notice my shaking hands. There was no way I could tell Miguel; not now; not after he had been so open with me. It would spoil everything. He would probably pack up and leave.

The whole time we walked around the shops I was thinking about what to do. If I didn't tell Miguel and Robert just turned up on the doorstep, he would know that I knew he was coming. He would go ballistic of course but, even worse, he would hate me.

This was so typical of my mother. She hadn't done this for my benefit, but for hers. She wanted Robert out of her hair and she hadn't even considered what he had done to me. But how could I have hoped, expected, her to act any differently? She had always been self-centred. Family loyalty was not one of her strong points; not something she had ever subscribed to – I only had to look at the way she had treated her father, to see that.

We went into a shop selling electrical appliances and ordered a fridge. We organised the reconnection of the electricity supply and I also arranged for the gas tanks to be regularly filled with gas.

At least I was going to be able to do the washing at home now. And hot water to bathe and wash my hair in would be a luxury.

'I would have liked to take you out for lunch, but we'd better get back because there's no food in the house for Eric. Perhaps we could do it next time,' Miguel said, as we walked back to the car.

I smiled in reply.

If there is a next time, I added in my head.

'Eric, we're just going down to the barn for a couple of hours,' Miguel announced.

Eric just nodded, not even bothering to look up from the bike magazine he was reading.

Once inside the studio, Miguel threw open all the windows to change the air, but made a point of shutting the doors again. I watched him with a questioning frown and he laughed when he saw it.

Walking towards me, he said, 'I want you to humour me for a little while. Just let me do what I want, OK?'

I nodded, my heart beating fast with anticipation. I still found him unpredictable.

He put his arms around me and bent his head down to kiss me. My mouth opened under his automatically and I shut my eyes, relishing our closeness.

Suddenly he let go of me and I gasped, not a little disappointed. I had hoped that this was just the beginning of what he had in store for me. Obviously not.

'Just stay exactly where you are. Don't move. And please keep your eyes closed. I want you to feel the element of surprise.'

I did as he asked, wondering what he was up to. I could hear him rummaging around in a drawer. I was tempted to peek, but I didn't want him to be irritated with me, so I kept my eyes tight shut.

After about a minute, he was back beside me. 'Keep your eyes shut, OK?'

I nodded.

He undid my plait and combed out my hair. Then I felt his mouth on mine again, this time a little more demanding, almost spiteful. He took my hand and placed it on his crotch. I felt his cock, big and hard, restricted in his jeans. I rubbed it while he continued to kiss me.

Suddenly I felt him putting something soft on my face. It felt like material – silk. I felt him pulling it around my head; he was tying it at the back, over my hair. 'OK, you can open your eyes now.'

I opened my eyes but, of course, I couldn't see anything. He had blindfolded me.

'Now I want to undress you.'

I felt his hands stroke my breasts through the material before his fingers went to the buttons. By the time my dress had slipped off my shoulders and I was standing there naked, my nipples were erect with desire for him.

I trembled as he put his hands all over me, feeling me, examining me. I was really aroused; all I wished was for him just to lay me down on the floor and fuck me. But he obviously had something else in mind.

He ran his hands down my arms to my wrists and drew them behind my back. A second later, I felt him attaching something cold, probably steel, to my wrists and snapping them shut. I tried to move my arms, but, of course, I couldn't. He had handcuffed my hands behind my back.

'Do you trust me, Katie?'

'I think so – I mean, I want to. What are you going to do with me now?'

'Nothing at all. I just want to look at you. I could come right now, just looking at you. You look beautiful – so vulnerable. I could do anything I liked with you and there's not a thing you could do to stop me.'

He must have seen my chest heaving up and down with excitement. His words were turning me on, just as much as his touch had done.

'I can't stand here like this, Miguel. I feel totally disorientated. I feel that I might fall over or something.'

He didn't answer me because he had begun to kiss me again. His mouth left my face and moved down to my neck. He placed his hands on my buttocks and held me while his tongue ran down a breast and sucked a nipple. My legs began to feel wobbly. I couldn't bear the suspense and the frustration. He must have heard my erratic intakes of breath because he started to laugh quietly.

His tongue left my nipple and trailed down my stomach to the tops of my thighs, unfortunately bypassing my pussy. I could feel myself getting so wet: it was actually seeping out of me.

His tongue ran up and down my thighs several times, before he stopped for a moment at the very top. Now he's going to lick me, I thought to myself.

But instead, he must have stood up because I felt his hand on my face, pushing my head to one side. A moment later I felt his teeth on my earlobe, gently nibbling it, before his tongue began to circle my ear, then enter it, slowly, sensually, thrusting it in and out.

I felt my juices actually running down my legs. God, how I wished he would just finish what he had started.

'Would you like me to do this somewhere else, Katie?' he whispered in my ear, before picking up my earlobe with his teeth and gently sucking on it.

I nodded vigorously.

'Here?' he asked, moving to my other ear.

I shook my head vigorously.

I was going to have to tell him. He knew damn well what I wanted him to do, but this little game of his would go on all afternoon if I didn't say the actual words. It suddenly occurred to me that this was what he was waiting for – he wanted me to express myself. Perhaps he was teaching me a lesson. After all, the attraction which we had held for each other, the lust we had felt since the moment we met, had not been expressed until today, due to a lack of communication.

Drawing a deep breath, I said, 'I want you to go down on me. I want you to bury your face in my pussy and eat me. Is that what you wanted me to say?'

'Yes, that's what I wanted you to say. And from now on, you have to tell me everything that you want. Anything you desire, all you have to do is ask. I could, and would, do absolutely anything for you, so we can't have any more misunderstandings.'

He had been thinking the same as I. And whilst his words had promised limitless possibilities, giving me mental pictures which were hardly wholesome, I realised that he had only expressed how I felt about him. Not only were we on the same wavelength, but we were of the same mind.

I felt his fingers parting my labia and then I felt his tongue on my clitoris, gently at first, then becoming more determined and rhythmic in its movements. Several times it moved off my clitoris altogether and slipped inside me; after a few moments it would be back again.

Now my whole body was shaking with the wonderful sensations emanating from my pussy.

Miguel placed his hands on my arse and held me firmly while he took my clitoris between his teeth and alternately nipped and sucked. At first he was gentle, then he became more and more demanding. My clitoris had never been worked over so thoroughly; it was becoming numb, almost losing its sensitivity, to all this exquisite abuse.

My orgasm was upon me suddenly, taking me by surprise. I came in great long shudders. I would have toppled backwards if Miguel hadn't still been holding me tight.

He continued to suck my clitoris. I begged him to stop but he ignored me. I couldn't stand it. It was like being electrocuted, receiving intense shocks over and over again, making my body jerk uncontrollably. With my hands cuffed behind my back, I couldn't break away.

At last he stopped. He stood up, and taking my arms, gently manoeuvred me back towards a chair. When I felt it against the back of my legs, I sat down. I felt as if his mouth had sucked me dry. He had drained me of all energy.

'Are you going to let me go now?'

'Not yet. I want you to sit there for a while.'

He put his hand on the back of my head, tipping my face up. He kissed me on the mouth again, then I heard him walk across the wooden floor.

By the noises he was making, dragging things around, I realised that he was going to paint.

Sighing with resignation, I settled back into the cushions on the old wicker chair, making myself as comfortable as possible, restrained as I was.

It was strange that the blindfold had taken away my inhibitions. Lying naked in front of him, on a chair in broad daylight, would have made me feel terribly self conscious at any other time. But the blindfold had given me exemption. I couldn't see him looking so it didn't really matter.

And having taken away my sight, my sense of touch had become more finely tuned than it had ever been before. My skin had become my eyes. The material covering the cushions stuck to my back; I felt the sun's hot rays pouring in through the barn window on to my breasts and thighs; I felt the lightest of breezes playing on my hair.

And earlier, when Miguel had touched me, it had felt

incredible. I had been so aroused that I was sure I could have come just from having him kiss and stroke me.

He had taught me something today. There was more to sex than fucking. It was about stimulating all the senses, tantalising each and every one them, bringing the body to a level of sensual awareness never reached before. Miguel was obviously very good at this.

'Stand up!' he ordered.

I stood up just as a gust of wind blew in through the open window. I felt my hair floating around my breasts, seemingly caressing my nipples. A combination of that, the erotic atmosphere within the barn and my own vulnerability, caused them to pulse with desire.

'Would you like me to own you?'

I nodded, my chest heaving with excitement.

'But do you understand the implications, Katie? It means that I would be your master. I would expect you to do anything I asked.'

I nodded in total agreement. I had read *The Story of O*, after all. And at this moment, I would have done anything – anything at all.

Suddenly, the barn door slammed.

'Miguel?' I called out tentatively.

'I'm here,' he answered.

'What was that?'

'Eric's just left,' he answered nonchalantly.

I gasped in alarm.

'Did he – see me?' I asked, dreading the answer.

'He saw you. Actually, he stood beside you for several minutes. He thought you looked – stunning.'

I didn't ask Miguel why he'd compromised me in such a way. I already knew the answer. He had admitted earlier that the eroticism of a situation would appeal to him as much as the actual act, possibly even more so. And because he was an artist, and incredibly hedonistic, he would have found the image of a handsome man standing over a naked woman, bound and blindfolded, extremely erotic.

By the same token, he would also have understood that the very idea of Eric surveying me in this context aroused me – beyond belief.

As I was thinking this, he said, 'Sit down and part your thighs. I want to look at you – all of you.'

His words alone gave me another rush. Not an hour had passed since my orgasm and I was panting with sexual anticipation.

Without even thinking about it, I parted my thighs.

Again, the blindfold allowed me to overcome my modesty and enact a fantasy. I had certainly fantasised before today, about being in bondage, at the mercy of a man like Miguel.

I could imagine spending the rest of my life with him – growing old together. He would paint; I would watch him. And we would live here, away from the real world, escaping into our own private fantasies – our utopia.

And as I sat in the chair, totally restrained yet liberated, Robert rudely interrupted my daydreams. If I didn't sort it out, Miguel and I wouldn't have a future. We wouldn't last for another day, never mind the rest of our lives.

But I was frightened; frightened that he would leave and frightened that he would be angry.

Even so, his temper would be nothing compared to what it would be tomorrow morning, when Robert knocked on the door. And if Miguel didn't kill me then, Eric certainly would.

I decided that I would tell him at some point today – when the moment felt right.

At last Miguel came over to me. He kissed me, then his hands went to the blindfold and started to undo it.

When he had removed it, I was at first dazzled by the brightness of the sunlight shining in through the windows. It took a second or two for my eyes to adjust. When they did, Miguel was squatting down in front of me, smiling. Now I felt embarrassed under his intense gaze.

He put his arms under mine and pulled me up. He fished in his pocket for the keys to the handcuffs and spun me around.

'I was going to let you go, but I've changed my mind. Turn around and kneel on the floor.'

Once again his words aroused me. He steadied me with his hand as I knelt on the floor.

I heard him as he unzipped his jeans. I felt his hard prick, pushing between my buttocks, and I was suddenly reminded of Eric. I clenched my muscles, expecting him to take me the same way.

Seeing my reaction, he laughed. He leant against me, pushing me forward on to the chair until my face was buried in the cushions.

He ran his hands under my arms and grasped my breasts. He kneaded my nipples roughly between his fingers; they were erect, actually throbbing, sending messages down to my pussy to be ready for him. But his cock was still nestled between my buttocks.

Now he started to rub it rhythmically against me. Every now and then he would stop and push it a little way into my most private place. I held my breath, scared that he would hurt me, but incredibly aroused at the same time. Part of me, a large part of me, wanted him to use me as he saw fit.

After a few minutes of this teasing, he stopped touching my breasts and moved a hand to my hips. He lifted my bottom up even higher, which automatically tipped my head even more into the cushions. I was virtually suffocating in them now, which only intensified my urge to be taken and subjugated.

Keeping one hand on my hip bone, the other hand went to the back of my head. He took a handful of my hair and pulled it cruelly. I cried out, but I didn't know whether it was with pain or frustration.

Finally he pushed his cock down, away from my anus, and entered my pussy from behind.

He started to move me backwards and forwards on

his shaft. Plundering me deeper and deeper, filling me with his cock. I groaned softly every time he thrust into me.

He was controlling me, controlling my movements with his hands. He was my master; I felt like a dog on a leash. He was pulling me on to him by my hair and my hips. He moved me faster and faster, penetrating me deeper and deeper, until in the end he let go of my hair, put his hand on my other hip, and slowed me right down. The last three or four thrusts were deliberately deep, deliberately long, while he came inside me. I felt his whole body shudder as he released himself.

He continued to hold me for a few minutes, then he picked up the keys, withdrew from me and released my hands.

My arms were stiff and my muscles sore from having been restrained for so long. I brought them round to the front of me slowly. My wrists were marked from where the cuffs had bitten into the skin. I rubbed them to try and lose the marks.

Miguel, seeing my wrists, took them in his hands and kissed them all over.

'I'm sorry. I didn't think I'd done them that tight. Do they hurt?'

'Not that much,' I said, smiling. 'Actually I liked them. They made me feel helpless, but at the same time more abandoned – less inhibited. I suppose it sounds stupid, but restraining me kind of released me. Do you know what I mean?'

He nodded, but he didn't answer.

Later, as we were walking up to the house, he turned to me. 'When Eric gets around to making a decision about his future, then I'll come clean and tell you everything. I want us to have an open relationship, without secrets. I want you to know everything about me and then you can tell me if we have a future together. I know that as far as I'm concerned, I want to spend the rest of my life with you.'

My heart should have soared at his words. I was crazy about him after all. But instead my heart felt heavy with fear. I was being deceitful – now was the time to tell him about Robert – but I chickened out. I just couldn't do it after he had given me such hope for the future. I knew I was playing with an unexploded bomb. Whenever he found out, he was going to go ballistic. And not just because of my dishonesty, but because of the potential danger I was putting Eric and him in. Robert would, of course, question why these men had taken refuge in my house and he would, without a doubt, report them.

I supposed that I wanted another couple of hours imagining what it would be like to have a full-blown relationship with Miguel before the shit hit the fan. In years to come, I would look back on these last few days, and think about what could have been if . . .

Chapter Five

I got the impression that Eric was feeling a little better disposed towards me. As Miguel's and my relationship began to develop into something more tangible, Eric was becoming more relaxed. I had obviously misread him before. He wasn't so much jealous of me with Miguel as concerned about the potential threat I was to them both.

He would now see that, whatever Miguel's feelings were for me, they were reciprocated. Perhaps it made Eric feel more inclined to accept me. After all, if I hurt him then I would be hurting Miguel too.

Well, at some point in the next few hours, I was really going to rock his boat.

The three of us sat out on the terrace after it got dark, reading by candlelight. But I was tired, worn out with nervous tension. I still couldn't bring myself to warn them about their forthcoming visitor. With a churning stomach, I announced that I was going to bed.

I slipped under the sheets, naked, as requested the night before, but I hoped that I would be asleep before Miguel came up. I dreaded him picking up on where he had left off this afternoon. The more he revealed himself to me, the more he was going to hate me for it later. He was obviously a man who took his relationships seriously. Of course he did. He hadn't wanted any up until now.

Miguel walked into the bedroom with a candle, placed it on the bedside cabinet and climbed into bed.

'Is everything all right, Katie? You seemed a little on edge this evening. Eric hasn't upset you, has he?'

Do it now, I told myself. 'No, everything's fine. I'm just tired.'

'How tired?'

He was lying on his side, his head resting on his elbow. His hair hung down, touching the pillow; his eyes searched my face. He knew something was wrong.

I reached out my hand and touched his face, stroking his unshaven cheek. I slipped my hand round the back of his head and drew him towards me. I kissed him on the mouth, the first time I had ever done it to him, then, becoming aroused in spite of the way I was feeling, I pushed my body against his.

I felt his erection pushing against my stomach, my nipples grazing his hard hairy chest. He was so beautiful; I was so lucky. And I was going to blow it.

I wanted to make it special; please him this one time so that afterwards he would always remember something nice about me, even if he hated me.

I pushed him on to his back and climbed on top of him, straddling his hips. His prick was trapped against my pussy, holding it down.

I put my hands on his shoulders and leant down to kiss him again on the mouth. He lay there almost submissively, letting me take control.

As I kissed him, pushing my tongue inside his mouth, I put one hand behind my back and stroked his balls. I felt his stomach muscles flexing; he wanted to be inside me but I didn't free his cock.

Instead I started to squirm on it, moistening it with my own wetness. I sat back and, picking up his hands, placed them on my breasts. He started to stroke my nipples, sometimes pinching and pulling them.

I put my fingers in my mouth and licked them. Then I put my hand between my legs and started to run the tips of my wet fingers around the end of his trapped cock. My other hand was still stroking his balls and I could feel his stomach muscles flexing even more, trying to manoeuvre himself inside me.

I leant down again and kissed him. I kissed his neck, his ears. My tongue went inside his ear and back to his mouth, then entered his ear again.The whole time I was playing with his balls and the tip of his cock, my fingers sticky from the fluid secreted in his arousal. Without thinking, I put them in my mouth and tasted his sweetness.

Abruptly he stopped touching my breasts and put his hands on my bottom. He lifted me up and dropped me down again, entering me at the same time. I had been so wet from sitting on his cock that he had literally slipped inside me.

I started to ride up and down on him. My hands held his shoulders for support. As I moved on his shaft, my hair stroked his chest and face. 'You're so beautiful, Katie, I want –'

My mouth stopped him from saying any more. I didn't want to know what he wanted. He would want me long gone in the morning.

His hands were still on my buttocks, guiding my movements as I rode him; even with me on top he was controlling the speed. How I would love to restrain him, I thought to myself. Unfortunately I would never get the chance.

Suddenly I felt another pair of hands on me, sliding under my arms to my breasts. I gasped, genuinely startled, for I had realised immediately whose hands they were.

Eric had climbed on to the bed, unbeknown to me, and was behind me.

I felt his chest against my back; I felt his erection against the base of my spine. He was starting to stroke my nipples, as Miguel had been doing only minutes before.

Although I felt bewildered, I continued to ride up and down on Miguel. Actually I had no choice; Miguel was still holding me firmly by my arse.

He had known Eric was there, of course; he must have seen him watching us. And like me, on those two occasions when I had watched Eric and Miguel together, Eric had wanted to join in; to be involved in some way.

Eric dropped one hand down between my legs and, parting my labia with his fingers, he started to rub my clitoris. I was shocked; not only because I was in a threesome, but because Eric actually wanted to do this.

I felt sordid, dirty; what we were doing was perverted. But I found it erotic and incredibly exciting. I was being fondled by the two most gorgeous men I'd ever seen. All right, so one of them was gay, but he was still willing to give me pleasure; and I was fucking the one I loved.

Eric pulled me back so that I was sitting up. Miguel was watching my face intently; he could see that I was really turned on. Eric rubbed my clitoris a little harder and his fingers pulled my nipple a little more roughly. I felt his prick rubbing against the base of my spine, almost between my buttocks, as I moved.

I could feel myself building up for orgasm. My pussy was on fire and my stomach muscles were starting to spasm.

Miguel was now gripping my buttocks so tight that they hurt; he groaned each time he penetrated me, filling me with his manhood. He was coming.

The look of ecstasy on his face, his cock inside me and Eric's hands, were just too much for me to bear. I cried out as I came in great long shudders.

Eric removed his hands and dropped down on the bed beside Miguel. I got up, feeling totally disorientated by what we had just done, and went to the bathroom to wash.

Poor Eric; he would be feeling totally frustrated and unfulfilled. But then, what did he normally do? Miguel had told me that their sexual relationship had been very one way – even I had noticed that.

I couldn't help feeling sorry for him. With his looks, people should have been beating down the door for him, male or female. Perhaps his erratic behaviour put people off. I could understand that.

When I walked back into the bedroom, Miguel and Eric were lying side by side on the bed, talking quietly. They stopped when they saw me standing there.

I was startled to find Eric nonchalantly wanking off, even as he was chatting to Miguel.

Completely relaxed, Miguel stood up and walked to the bathroom, giving me an affectionate kiss on the way out.

I had to go to the bed; I couldn't stand in the doorway like an idiot. I went and lay down next to Eric, keeping my eyes fixed to the ceiling. There was nowhere else for me to look at the moment.

After a while, I couldn't help taking a sneaky look, not because he was masturbating – I'd seen my ex doing that before – but because he was a handsome man and whether he was straight or gay, I still found him aesthetically pleasing.

'You can watch me if you want. I don't care,' he said, startling me. He had evidently been watching me and had seen my barely disguised interest.

Knowing that he knew what I was thinking, it would have been silly for me to pretend otherwise. I rolled on to my side and watched him.

'You can help me if you want to,' he said, after a moment.

'How? What could I do for you?'

'Just give me your hand. That's all I want. Just because I'm gay, it doesn't mean I function any differently from other men. Although I liked touching you, I didn't want to fuck you, but it turned me on.'

Eric took my hand and placed it on his cock. I was torn between not wanting to appear churlish – especially after what he'd done for me – and concern as to what Miguel would make of this.

Eric, sensing my reticence, placed his hand over mine, and gently squeezing my fingers around his prick, he forced me to move my hand up and down.

I then reminded myself that Miguel had watched Eric touching me tonight and, if anything, he had found it as erotic to watch as I had found it to be touched. He wouldn't bat an eyelid, I decided.

I began to take over, working my hand independently and, within seconds, Eric had removed his hand and laid it on his pelvis.

'I'd like to bet that if I did want to fuck you, you'd let me,' Eric whispered brusquely. 'I've been watching you. I think you'd let us do anything, as long as you enjoyed it. I might even prove it to you.'

I declined to answer, but wondered why my stomach had given a little flutter at his words. Eric and me together? To be fucked by someone who hated me, just to teach me a lesson? I dismissed the thought from my mind, finding the idea rather unwholesome, yet strangely arousing.

I was becoming more depraved with each passing day, I decided. I wondered if it was Miguel's influence, or the house's languid, sensual atmosphere.

I continued to move my hand up and down, sensing the change as his cock became thicker, more distended, my fingers feeling every ridge, every contour of his throbbing shaft. I watched his muscles flexing; I watched his chest heaving. He was now actually thrusting his pelvis upwards, forcing his cock into my curled fingers and, in that moment, I did indeed imagine being fucked by Eric.

He shuddered as he came. He groaned quietly as the

semen spurted over his stomach. I quickly slipped my hand away.

He got up off the bed and walked towards the door. He stopped in the doorway and turned around, as if he had forgotten something. 'Miguel likes you because he sees something of himself in you. You should just follow your natural inclinations – be yourself. That's all he would ever ask of you.'

It was almost as if he had been reading my mind; and, in actual fact, he had given me sound advice. Miguel was not like any other man I had ever met. He was not bound by morality and convention. He was a law unto himself. For him, sex was something to enjoy with no holds barred.

In this little corner of France, we were far removed from everything I had adhered to back home. I should simply go with the flow. This was what Eric had been telling me – nicely.

I realised, with something like shock, that I was beginning to like Eric.

Miguel walked back into the bedroom and lay down beside me.

'Miguel, can I ask you something?'

'You can but, depending on what it is, I might not answer you.'

'If you like me as you say you do, how could you let Eric touch me? How could you let him be involved in what we do? Surely in a relationship, sex should be just between the two people involved?'

'Because with Eric it's different. I told you he's like my brother – more than my brother. We've slept together most of our lives and always shared everything.

'He was touching you because he felt left out, but I thought you looked beautiful together. And I liked the fact that you were enjoying it. You found it erotic and I found it erotic to watch you. But I could only share you with the people that I love and trust; who understand what I'm about and know the limits. And of course, it would have to be what you wanted too. I think you find Eric sexually attractive.'

'So what would you do if you walked into the bedroom and found me fucking Eric?'

'Well, I'd be very upset if you were doing it behind my back. Eric knows how I feel about you. I would have to assume he was trying to hurt me, or that you had feelings for each other that went way beyond what we have together. But if you and I were making love and Eric joined in, or if he talked to me about what he wanted, whether it was for the experience or to get closer to you, I wouldn't mind as long as you were on board with it. All I want is for you to be happy.

'Is there anything else you want to ask me?'

I shook my head and, a moment later, Eric walked back into the room and dropped down on to his mattress. Miguel blew out the candle and I tried to sleep.

I awoke in the morning with my stomach churning. It took me a moment or two to remember why. When it all came back to me I sat up suddenly, realising that I was alone in the bedroom.

I checked my watch; it had gone nine o'clock. I leapt out of bed, then ran downstairs to get dressed.

I chose clothes that I thought made me look attractive. If push came to shove, I would use anything to stop Miguel leaving.

I put on cut-off jeans, a vest that just about covered my breasts, my platform mules and I wore my hair loose. It looked as if I had just casually thrown them on; they were all old clothes; but everything emphasised my figure. My legs looked long and my breasts looked full. And wearing my hair loose completed the picture. He liked my hair.

I walked into the kitchen and drank some water; my mouth was dry with nerves. Then I took a deep breath and went outside.They were both sitting on the terrace as usual, drinking coffee and smoking.

'Miguel, I've got something to tell you. I should have done it yesterday but I just couldn't bring myself to. I have to tell you now, so you've got time to do something about it.'

'What is it, Katie?' he asked, his eyes narrowing suspiciously. I noticed that I had Eric's full attention too.

'Yesterday, when I was talking to my mother on the phone, she told me that my ex was leaving to come down here. It's not my fault; I repeatedly asked her not to tell him where I was, but she's told him anyway. I'm really sorry; I didn't want this to happen.'

I held my breath, waiting for the eruption. It came ten seconds later.

Miguel stood up and in a flash he was around the table and grabbing me by the shoulders. 'You knew this yesterday and you didn't tell me? Give me one good reason why you didn't tell me before,' he growled, beginning to shake me roughly.

Feeling that my head was being snapped backwards and forwards, as if I were little more than a rag doll, was all that was needed for my fear to revert to rage.

'Get your hands off me,' I screamed, with an anger to match his.

He stopped shaking me but he didn't let go. I could now feel his fingers almost digging into my shoulders as he gripped me even harder.

'You bitch,' he whispered. 'I could hate you so easily.'

In that moment I saw that his eyes were indeed smouldering with hatred rather than rage.

My self-respect would not allow him to treat me this way, or even to talk to me this way, without some kind of retaliation. And in that very same moment, I forgot how much I loved him.

I put my hand down and fumbled around on the table for a knife. My fingers closed over one and, in an instant, I had brought it up to his chest.

'I swear to God, Miguel, if you don't let go of me, I'm going to take this knife and –'

'And . . . nothing,' said a cool, detached voice behind me.

Eric grabbed hold of my wrist and forcibly peeled open my fingers. I watched, with tears of rage burning down my cheeks, as the knife fell to the ground.

Miguel's eyes were still smouldering and he still had his hands on my shoulders. I grabbed at his hands and clawed at them; I even tried biting his wrist. All to no avail.

I looked up at Eric. He was now standing beside me. Hovering beside me, for want of a better word – like he didn't know what to do for the best.

Perhaps he thought I was going to stab his lover the minute his back was turned. Chance would be a fine thing.

Then, suddenly, something came over Eric's face. I didn't know what it was; whether he was responding to the anger and frustration evident on mine, or whether he was worried about Miguel going too far, I wasn't sure. Either way, he put his hand on Miguel's arm and squeezed it hard.

'OK, let go of her. You don't want to hurt her. And I won't let you hurt her. It's not her fault – it's the mother's. Calm down and we can sort it out. If you go off the deep end, we'll all end up in the shit,' he said quietly.

Miguel pulled his eyes away from mine with something like amazement written all over his face. But he had obviously listened because he abruptly released me. Eric removed his hand from Miguel's arm and I stepped back.

I threw Eric a look of gratitude, which Miguel probably noticed, but I didn't care. Despite the fact that Eric despised me, regardless of my personal feelings for him, which hovered between tolerance and hatred, he had protected me.

'I knew you would react like this. That's why I didn't

want to tell you before. I'm only telling you now because you have to know,' I said somewhat breathlessly, gripping the back of a chair for support.

I was actually trembling now, with emotional exhaustion. I hardly ever smoked but – God – I needed a cigarette.

'OK. Let's sit down and work out what to do,' Eric said, for once taking control of a situation. 'And you had better tell us all about your boyfriend, so we know what to expect,' he added, turning to me.

'Well, first of all, he's not my boyfriend. I don't know why he's coming down; it's a complete waste of time. I told him how I felt when I last saw him – the day before I left for France.'

'I think it's fairly obvious why he's coming here. He doesn't want to lose you,' Miguel said bitterly, clearly struggling to contain his temper.

'No, it's not that; or at least that's only part of it. I think he's been encouraged by my mother. My mother and I don't get on very well and she's not very happy with me at the moment.

'I didn't tell you when I arrived because I thought you might harm me in some way if you knew; or at least, it would influence the way you and Eric dealt with me; but I've come here to live – permanently.

'I broke up with Robert a few weeks ago, having lived with him for four years. There was nothing to keep me in England any more, once I had finished with him.

'When I told my mother that I wanted to move to France, she went ballistic. I still don't understand why, but she was dead against it. We argued about it for two days, but in the end I thought she had accepted it. I have a feeling that she's encouraged Robert to come down, to bring me back. For some reason she doesn't like me being here. She even said that I could go anywhere in the world – why did I have to come here?

'But it was only natural for me to chose this place to

get my life back together. I'm half French; it's the house where my mother was born and it's now mine.'

While I had been speaking, Miguel had been repeatedly combing his hair back off his face with his fingers. I saw a muscle flexing on his jawbone. He was either frustrated or still annoyed. 'Tell me about your boyfriend,' he now snapped at me.

'He's your age,' I said, looking at him. 'And he runs an advertising agency in London. I ought to tell you that he's very conservative. He'd be shocked by the way you live; he wouldn't understand it at all. He would think that you are both degenerates.'

I had to tell them this, since they seemed to be oblivious to the fact that they lived without any moral code. What I didn't add was that Robert would blow a gasket if he found me in this strange three-way relationship. He would wonder how they had manipulated their way into my house, and if he discovered the circumstances he would, of course, report them to the police. Then he would drag me back to England, kicking and screaming if need be.

'Well, he'd be right. We are!' Eric said laughingly, picking up on my last comment. I looked up at him sharply, my eyes narrowing; it was hardly a laughing matter. But amazingly, he was taking all this far better than Miguel. I had expected it to be the other way around.

Hearing Eric's dismissive comment, Miguel looked up at him too. Suddenly he began to smile. Then he shook his head and began to chuckle. Thank God he is snapping out of his mood, I thought to myself.

But when his eyes returned to my face, they narrowed again. 'So when is your knight in shining armour coming to rescue you from this bed of corruption?'

I ignored his sarcasm and answered, 'Well, I imagine if he's driving from St Malo, the way I came, he could be here any time between eleven a.m. and one p.m. If he's driving his Porsche –'

'– Why did you leave him then? It sounds like you had everything going for you,' Miguel quipped, interrupting me.

'Money isn't everything. But then you wouldn't know that, would you? You just see what other people have got and want it for yourself, without making any effort to earn it. Unlike you, I'm not comfortable living in a place that isn't mine –'

'Hold on. You've got it wrong. We've got every –' Eric said, interrupting me to defend Miguel.

'Leave it, Eric. It's not worth it. Let's decide what we're going to do and quickly, before he gets here. We've probably only got a couple of hours,' Miguel cut in.

I heard the tone of indifference in Miguel's voice and suddenly panicked. He was going to leave and I would never see him again.

'What if you two were to just disappear for a while? I could talk to Robert – tell him that I want to stay here. He won't hang around when he sees that I won't change my mind. He doesn't need to know that you've even been here.'

'You still haven't told me why you left him,' Miguel said quietly.

'Initially, because I found out that he was seeing someone else. I think it had been going on for some time, but I never found out who it was. He admitted that he had been seeing someone, but it was over. I couldn't accept that. If he could do it once, then he could do it again. I was hurt and felt that I would never be able to trust him. But once I had left him, I realised that I didn't feel that much for him anyway. Certainly not enough to go back to him – despite all his money,' I threw in at the end, for Miguel's benefit.

'Come on, Eric. Let's pack up and get out of here. I don't want to get involved with all this shit. This guy is coming down here because he wants her back. I'm not going to hang around and watch.'

Miguel stood up and motioned for Eric to follow him. I got up, went up to him and put my hand on his arm. He looked down at me but his eyes were expressionless, as if he were looking at a stranger.

'Miguel, please – don't go. I want you to stay with me. I don't want to live here on my own now. Let me get rid of him. I promise you that he won't even know you exist. Please?'

He looked into my eyes for a moment. Perhaps he saw the pleading in them. He shrugged his shoulders and turned to Eric. 'It's up to you. You're part of the reason we're here, so you decide.'

'Well, even if he found out about us, he would have to go out to make some phone calls. He wouldn't take us on alone. And if he was going to cause trouble, we'd be on our bikes and long gone, before it even started. We may as well stick around.'

'OK, we'll stay. But if what you say is true, that you don't want him any more, then it should make no difference to you that I'm here. Eric and I can go down to the barn, out of your way, while you say your bit to him in private, but I expect to sleep in your bed tonight. You'd better figure out how you're going to manage it. He's coming an awful long way not to get what he wants.'

We sat there in silence while I worked out how to play this. Miguel smoked a cigarette, obviously still angry with me. His eyes smouldered as he watched me.

It was going to look very strange, if Robert insisted on staying, to find me sharing my bedroom with two men he had never even heard of. Equally, Miguel wouldn't hang around if I didn't spend the night with him.

This was a test, I realised. I wanted Miguel desperately, but I had to prove it to him.

'I think it would look better if Robert didn't know you two were staying here. I can introduce you to him as my boyfriend, and Eric as your friend or an old family friend, I don't care which, and he might just accept that without question. But anyone walking in here now would tell just by looking around that I'm not living here alone. I've lived with him for four years so he would know we had only met in the last few days. He would never believe that I've let you move in in such a short space of time; he knows I'm not that impetuous –'

'He doesn't know you very well then, does he?' Miguel butted in facetiously.

I ignored his remark and continued. 'So perhaps, if we took some of your stuff down to the barn, he wouldn't read any more into things than what I tell him.'

'Miguel, what she says makes sense. And if Katie can lose him as she promises to do, without spilling the beans, then we owe her an explanation.'

I owed Eric – again. This was the second time in less than half an hour that he had argued my corner.

Miguel stubbed out his cigarette impatiently. 'OK, let's get on with it then. We'll shift our gear out to the barn and then take some lunch down. I've got a feeling we'll be there for some time,' he added, looking me up and down.

He thinks I've dressed this way for Robert's benefit, I suddenly realised. But that had been the last thing on my mind.

They went backwards and forwards to the barn, carrying stuff from the house. It was amazing what they had accumulated since they'd arrived. It looked as if they had been here years rather than months. Certainly, they would never have got all their gear on the back of a motor bike and made a quick exit.

They had a pile of bike magazines about three feet tall, a dead give-away that men were staying in the house; not to mention beers in the kitchen, packets of cigarettes, books that had come out after my grandfather's death, but not exactly my cup of tea; crash helmets, boxer shorts, razors and aftershave. The list was endless. In every room I spotted stuff that most definitely would not have belonged to me.

At one point, Eric was clearing out the bathroom, Miguel was in the barn and I was carrying a pile of clean clothes. Miguel passed me in the doorway, intent on going back up to the house without talking to me. I stopped him.

'Miguel, can I speak to you in private for a moment?'

The bastard actually sighed with exasperation. He had been avoiding my eyes but now he was forced to look at me. He did so with a pained expression on his face. 'What is it? I'm listening.'

'Come into the barn and sit down for a moment. I don't want to say this in front of Eric.'

I walked into the barn and put the clothes on a chair. Miguel followed me in and stood by the window, waiting for me to say something.

'I just wanted to explain why I couldn't tell you before. I really wanted to, but I was scared –'

'Scared that I'll see you still like him, and now that he's come grovelling, you'll want him back?'

'That's a load of crap, Miguel. Haven't you listened to what I've been saying? I have no feelings for him at all, other than wishing he'd stayed at home. If you hadn't interrupted me, I was going to explain. Ever since I've been here, you and Eric have kept me in the dark about why you're in my house. I've asked you to tell me but you won't. It's not my fault if I suspect the worse, not so much about you, but about Eric.

'When my mother told me Robert was on his way, I was scared of what Eric's reaction would be. Remember, the first time I saw him he was waving a gun in my face. You say that he isn't capable of shooting me, but I only have your word for that. I was also scared that when I told you, you would just up and leave – to protect yourself and Eric from any trouble – not knowing, of course, what you've done,' I slipped in bitterly. 'And when I told you today, I fully expected you to walk out.

I knew you would be angry that I hadn't told you earlier but, equally, I wanted to spend some more time with you before you left me. What can I do or say, to make you believe me?'

He grabbed me roughly by the arms and lifted me up so that my eyes were on a level with his. He put his mouth on mine and kissed me in an aggressive, almost spiteful way. He was biting my lips, hurting my arms, but still he set my heart pounding with lust for him.

Suddenly he dropped me down; I landed on my feet and almost fell backwards with the abruptness of it.

'That was very good. I almost believed you then. I only wish that *was* the reason why you didn't tell me yesterday. As far as I'm concerned, the delay in telling me just shows me that you needed time to think; to make up your mind whether you're going back with him or staying. I'll know tonight. I shall wait until then before I decide what to do.

'But if you think that what we've had is just a passing phase and you want to get back with your boyfriend, just tell me now. I promise you that I won't react.'

I realised then that he was intensely jealous of me; irrationally so. I knew then that he loved me, even though he had never said the actual words. I had thought it was just physical before, and that he would have lived with me for just that. Now I knew it went very deep – too deep. But I didn't care; I felt the same about him.

'All I want is to stay with you. I feel that we were meant to be together. Robert means nothing to me and I'm never going back to England.'

'I told you that I would never physically hurt you, but I swear to you now that if I find out you're lying to me, playing with me, you'll be sorry. If you're frightened of Eric, he's nothing compared to what I'm capable of.'

He seemed so angry, but it wasn't with me, it was with himself. He was frightened of what it would do to him if I left him. Better for him just to cut his losses and cut me out of his life than for me to do it to him. That would send him over the edge.

I reached up and put my hands on either side of his face. I pulled his head down and kissed him on the mouth gently. He didn't move a muscle. 'I'm not lying to you – I love you.'

I stepped back and, turning on my heel, walked out of the barn. I left him standing there to make what he would of my revelation.

I ate lunch alone. It felt very strange, not having been on my own for any length of time since I'd been here. The barn was several hundred yards away and had been built in a clearing on the outskirts of the wood. Thankfully it was all but obscured. Robert would never know that anyone was there, unless he walked down to it.

I heard a car approaching on the road above the house. I looked up nervously, but at the same time thinking it hadn't sounded like a Porsche. I heard it pull off the road and enter the drive.

Nothing could have looked less like a 911; it was a dusty van. I didn't know the man who got out, but he walked towards me smiling.

The penny dropped when he started to speak. He was from the electricity company and he wanted to see the meter. He had to change it over to a more up-to-date one before switching on the supply to the house.

And so I was intent on showing the man where the old meter was, in an outhouse, when Robert pulled up in the drive.

I heard the car door slam and walked back to the house. He was standing by the front door when I caught sight of him, obviously wondering whether to go in or not; not sure if he had the right place.

I shouted a hello and he turned around. Typically he was wearing chinos, a Ralph Lauren shirt, Ray Bans and a smarmy smile. Even when dressed casually and after a sixteen-hour journey, he couldn't have contrasted more with Miguel's scruffiness.

I walked towards him but I didn't respond to his smile. Actually, seeing him again made me feel angry that he had the audacity to come down here, confident in the knowledge that he would be able to charm me all the way back to England. It hadn't worked before I left and it certainly wasn't going to work now. His smooth good looks and character had been eclipsed by Miguel's more rugged beauty and intense personality.

'Katie, how are you? You look great,' he said, running his eyes all over me. He put his hands on my shoulders and kissed me quickly on the mouth. I let him do it.

'Well, now you're here, Robert, you may as well sit down and have something to eat. Do you want a coke or a cup of coffee?'

'Coffee, please. You don't seem very pleased to see me. I thought you would be pleasantly surprised. Your mother was worried about you being here; she said you were nervous on your own.'

'Did she? Well, I'm sorry, but you've been misinformed.'

I walked into the kitchen and put the kettle on to boil. I got out some salad, bread and cheese, then laid a place for him out on the terrace.

'Robert, come and sit out here.'

He wandered out of the salon, down the hallway, poking his head around the dining-room door, before coming through the kitchen and out on to the terrace.

'This place is charming; very quaint and so quiet. I can see why you like it here. But why are all your clothes in the dining room?'

The question was innocuous enough; he wouldn't have known that the men had kept all their stuff upstairs. 'There is only one bedroom, quite small. I'm on my own and obviously don't use the dining room. I can spread out a bit more in there without cluttering up the place.'

He accepted this.

'So, Robert, why did you come here? I told you that I didn't want to see you again,' I said after a moment.

'I remember everything you said before you left. I'm sorry that I hurt you and I hope that, in time, you'll forgive me. But I don't want you to stay away from everyone because of what I did. I don't want to be responsible for ruining your life, your career. Come back with me and I'll make it up to you. We'll put it behind us. We could get married – I'll do whatever you want, but I just can't bear the thought of you not being with me.'

'It's a pity you didn't think of that before you had your little fling. But it doesn't matter now. It may be difficult for you to accept this, but I'm over it. I don't love you any more. And you can go back to your bit on the side for all I care.'

He got up and walked around the table to my side. 'Katie. I know why you're saying these things. You're trying to punish me. And that's why you left – to punish me. I'm going to take a few days' break. I'll spend some time with you, then you'll see it was all a big mistake –'

He was interrupted by footsteps on the terrace behind him. His eyes narrowed at me, before he turned around to see who it was. It was the man from the electricity company, telling me that he had swapped over the meters and now they could connect the mains supply to the house. I nodded and returned my gaze to Robert.

'Who the hell was that?' he asked, not being able to speak a word of French.

'He's getting the electricity switched on. It was disconnected after my grandfather died. We didn't see the point of paying for something we weren't using.'

'You mean to tell me that you've been staying here all week without any lighting?'

'Yes, and no hot water. They should be delivering gas today too. I just haven't got around to it before. I quite liked washing in cold water; it seemed more natural.

But, of course, I can't get through the winter like that. That's why I decided to get organised.'

'You mean you can actually imagine yourself here, alone, through the winter?'

'Yes, of course. Well, I did. Things have changed somewhat. I've met someone. I want to spend the rest of my life with him.'

I waited for Robert's explosion of rage and was surprised when there wasn't one. He was smiling with a smart-arsed expression on his face. 'That often happens – meeting someone else on the rebound. But it won't last, you'll see. Especially if I stay here with you.'

I wanted to smack him right across his smirking, supercilious face.

'Well, I'm afraid there's no question of you staying here. Miguel will be here later and there's only one bedroom. I'm sorry, Robert; if I had known you intended to come all this way, I would have saved you the bother. And you should learn not to listen to my mother. I stopped telling her anything years ago.'

His face faltered for a split second before he could retrieve his grin.

He was about to say something else, when a huge wagon came off the road and pulled up outside the house. It was from the company delivering gas. I asked Robert to excuse me while I went to talk to the men. The gas tanks were in an outhouse and I had to show them where they were.

It was at this point that Miguel walked up to the house. He would have heard all the commotion with the wagon, the men trying to back into the drive to get it as near to the tanks as they could.

He walked up to me and stood beside me with a questioning frown on his face. I smiled at him reassuringly then, taking his hand, led him to the terrace where Robert was still seated.

I immediately felt the hostility between the two of

them. 'He doesn't speak any French so I'll have to speak English. Will you be able to understand us?'

'I think so.'

'Robert, this is Miguel. Miguel – Robert.'

I was surprised when Robert didn't offer his hand. He was so polite as a rule, even if he didn't like someone.

Miguel sat down and lit up a cigarette. 'Do you want one, Robert?' he asked, offering one to Robert, who shook his head and refused.

Miguel's voice sounded gorgeous. He had a deep voice anyway, but speaking English in such a heavy accent was so sexy. Now I could hear that Spanish was his first language by the emphasis he put on certain words, and the inflections.

The atmosphere could have been cut with a knife. My stomach was churning with nervous tension.

'So what do you do, Miguel?'

'He's an artist,' I replied before Miguel had a chance to answer.

Robert turned to me and said in a quiet voice, laced with sarcasm, 'So where did you find him, Katie?'

'We met in the town,' Miguel replied, his eyes challenging Robert.

Looking at them both, sitting at the same table, the contrast between them couldn't have been greater. Robert, with closely cropped hair, freshly shaven, and grey eyes; Miguel, with long black hair, dark stubble and brown eyes.

Both were good-looking, but while Robert looked typically English, Miguel looked the epitome of a Spanish Gypsy. However, Miguel was probably four inches taller than Robert and powerfully built with it. He would have stood out in any crowd whereas Robert would have faded into insignificance.

Miguel, at this moment, chose to stand up. Robert could not but have been intimidated by him. Miguel just turned to me and said, 'I'll check on the men to see if everything's OK. I'll be back in five minutes.'

I nodded and went inside to make him a coffee. Robert followed me in.

'Do you know anything about this guy, Katie? You've only known him a couple of days; you're living here on your own. Are you sure you know what you're doing?'

'I'm telling you this for your own good – Miguel's got a lethal temper, so don't wind him up. But in answer to your question, I feel perfectly safe with him.

'Let's forget Miguel for a moment. While we're on our own I want you to appreciate that it's over. I don't want you any more and I'm not going back to England. It won't do any good for you to hang around here either; there's nowhere for you to stay. You may as well get back in your car and hit the road.'

'How can you treat me like this after the years we've been together? I deserve better than this.'

'No, you don't. You were a total fucking bastard to me and you're lucky to be getting a coffee. As it is, be thankful that I'm just walking away from the house. Anyone else would be going for half of it – common-law wife and all that shit. But I don't want anything. You can take back the car too, for all I care.'

'Whatever you think of me, I wouldn't leave you stranded here without a car. Not when you're hanging around with the likes of him – he looks like a Gypsy.'

'Yes, he's beautiful, isn't he? The most beautiful man I've ever seen, in fact.'

'You wait until I tell your mother. She'll break her heart over you throwing yourself away on someone like him.'

'I don't give a shit what you or my mother think. I've spent my whole life worrying about other people. I want to do something for myself for a change. Just drink your coffee and fuck off out of my life; you've already taken up too much of it.'

He put his hand on my arm and spun me around. 'Katie. Please –'

'You heard what she said. Now fuck off!'

Miguel had walked into the kitchen from the salon. He had come in through the front door. I didn't know if he'd heard the comment about Gypsies, but he looked absolutely menacing; his eyes smouldered with barely contained rage.

Robert immediately backed off, completely changing tack. 'All right, Katie. I get the message. But the last thing I want to do is get back in the car now. I've been driving since yesterday evening to get here. Let me stay tonight and I will be out of your hair first thing tomorrow morning. Is that all right with you, Miguel?'

Miguel slackened his aggressive posture and looked at me. I spoke in French to Miguel. 'I think he could stay tonight. We could give him the mattress and he could sleep downstairs in the dining room. Eric will have to sleep downstairs too, for the sake of appearances. Remember, everything he sees and hears will get back to my mother.'

Miguel shrugged his shoulders but didn't reply. It was my call. 'OK, Robert. But just for tonight.'

I turned back to Miguel and asked in English how the men were getting on.

He answered me slowly, but I was impressed with the amount of English he knew. With a little practice he could be fluent. I wondered where he had picked up his language skills. Surely not on the road.

'They want you to light the boiler, to make sure everything is working properly before they leave. It hasn't been used for years.'

'I don't know how; do you?'

'Yes. I'll do it for you. Do you want to come with me so that you can see what to do if it should ever go out when you're on your own?'

I nodded and followed him into the utility room. He squatted down on the floor and opened up a little hatch. 'Give me some paper. I need a taper to light it.'

'Really? I thought these things had automatic ignition.'

He looked at me as if I were trying to be funny. I was,

in fact, being totally serious. Seeing this, he laughed. 'On second thoughts, don't ever go near this unless someone else is here . . .'

'I won't need to, if you're here, will I?'

He declined to answer. He took the paper I held out for him and lit it with his cigarette lighter. After a couple of attempts, the pilot light was lit.

When we stood up, we brushed against each other. It sent an electrical charge pulsing through me. He looked down fleetingly at my face. I held his eyes for just a fraction of a second.

I wished that he would kiss me like he had in the barn earlier. Anything rather than this current coolness between us.

He took a step away from me; maybe he felt we were too close for comfort. As he did so, I was sure his eyes glanced down to my breasts. I was breathless with anticipation.

It was like pouring cold water all over me when he began to show me how the old time clock above the boiler worked. He explained the various options and he watched while I set it to water only. At least I would get my first hot bath in days.

When we walked back into the kitchen, Robert was sitting outside drinking his coffee. He looked very uncomfortable and I didn't blame him, but he didn't look exactly heart-broken. I had suspected all along that I wasn't the love of his life. He just liked having a pretty blonde on his arm when he went out, and someone warm in his bed to come home to. I knew he would get over me.

The men came up to the house and told us that they had finished. The mains had been connected and we now had electricity.

Forgetting the tense situation for a moment, I jumped up and went into the kitchen. I flicked the light switch on and off. It would seem weird this evening: the first time this old house had working lights in three years.

I went back out on the terrace and sat down. Miguel had taken off his shirt; the heat was intense here as always.

I glanced across at Robert. He was gazing beyond me with the most peculiar expression on his face; almost as if he had seen a ghost. I turned my head the other way to see what he was looking at.

Eric was strolling up the lawn towards us. He had his shirt off too and was just wearing cut-off jeans. His hair was loose and he looked stunning, as always. Perhaps that was why Robert was gawking at him.

I laughed. 'That's Miguel's friend, Eric.'

Eric was looking at Miguel with a look of concern on his face. There was an unspoken communication between these two; he was asking Miguel if everything was all right.

I felt a pang of jealousy as I realised that this only came from knowing someone really well for a long time; and they were as close as any two men could be who weren't actually in love.

'Katie, it's incredible, don't you think?'

'What? What are you talking about? He often comes here.'

'No, I don't mean that. Look at him. You could be twins, for God's sake. Haven't you even noticed?'

I looked at him as if he had gone mad, then looked at Miguel to see if he was amused by Robert's obvious amazement. Miguel was looking decidedly uncomfortable.

I had never seen him so before; it made me feel uneasy. He wouldn't meet my eyes either which told me there was something going on.

For one awful moment, I thought that maybe Eric was bringing up their gun and he was going to threaten Robert – that's what all the silent communication had been about. Then I decided that I was being paranoid and dismissed the notion.

'Well, we're both tall and blond with blue eyes. So what? Most of Scandinavia would fit that description.'

'No. There's more to it than that. Your faces are identical. His is more masculine, of course, but the resemblance is uncanny.'

Miguel had said as much when I arrived; he had thought we looked like brother and sister. Perhaps other people were more aware of it than I was.

'Well, I assure you he isn't my brother. I've got two teenage ones at home, as you know full well. And they are dark like my dad was, anyway. And since my mum moved to England when she was eighteen, and I am older than Eric, it's impossible.'

'I know that, Katie. I've completely overreacted. But it startled me when I first saw him.'

Eric had probably caught some of the conversation. He didn't look too happy either. Again there was a long look between Miguel and him.

'Eric, this is my ex, Robert. Robert – Eric.'

Eric went and shook hands with him and I told Eric that as Robert couldn't speak French, we would have to speak English. He said it was all right; he could speak a little.

Miguel turned to Eric and they began to speak quietly and earnestly together in French. I tried to catch what they were saying without appearing to be earwigging. I got the gist of it. Miguel was telling him that Robert would be staying just for tonight, but Eric and he would both have to sleep downstairs.

When he had finished talking, Eric looked up at Robert and started to laugh. I was sure that he had given Robert the once-over.

He made a comment to Miguel which caused him to fall about laughing, in spite of the horrible atmosphere which prevailed. I could only imagine what they had been saying.

Robert would be mortified to know that he would be sleeping with a homosexual this evening. He would never get over it. Even I could see the funny side. But keeping my face straight, I asked Robert if he wanted to walk around the property. Relieved, he got up and left the table.

'You'll have to excuse them. They're artists and not used to mixing with people. They like their own company.'

'He's very good-looking, isn't he? Eric I mean. I'm surprised you wouldn't have wanted to go out with him instead.'

'No, he's not my type. I prefer dark men.' The fact that Eric wouldn't want to go out with me, because of his own sexual persuasion, was not for me to say, and certainly not to Robert.

We did a little tour of the property, avoiding the barn. I didn't want him to see that they had their stuff there. Then we made our way back to the house.

'It's several hours to go until dinner time, Robert. You may as well make yourself comfortable; sit in the sun, read a book, have a rest or something. Make the most of the weather; it's probably raining back home.'

'If you've got an English book, I might just do that. I'll sit on the other terrace and read, out of their way.'

I nodded, relieved. That's got rid of him for a couple of hours at least, I thought to myself.

I went into the dining room, picked up three or four books at random, and brought them out to him. I left him and went to find Miguel.

'Miguel, it's not very nice if you take the piss out of him. He knows the score; he knows where he stands with me and he's going in the morning. He feels very awkward being here and he doesn't speak a word of French. Imagine what it would be like if you were in his situation. You've only got to be civil to him for tonight and then that's it. I don't want him going home and stirring up my mother.'

Seeing that they were still smiling, I became irritated

and added, 'You look like losers; do you have to act like it too?'

Miguel's face became serious. 'So you don't like the way we look, now he's here?'

'No, I like the way you both look. Clothes aren't important; not here anyway. But you're on a completely different wavelength. If you emphasise it, you'll just alienate him and make him suspicious of you and your motives for being here. It's going to be hard for him to swallow as it is – me choosing to stay here and leave behind everything I had, back in England.'

'Well, we weren't taking the piss out of him, if it makes you feel any better. We were laughing because I told Eric he would be spending the night with him. Eric's very happy!' They both burst out laughing again.

I ignored this and said, 'Really? Why?'

'Because Eric fancies his chances!' Miguel answered, still laughing.

'You must be joking. He's the last man in the world to be that way inclined. I should know.'

I spun on my heel and stormed inside. They were still taking the piss and for some reason I didn't like it. Not because I felt any affection for Robert, but maybe I still had some sort of loyalty towards him. He was on his own in a hostile environment. Someone had to stick up for him.

Chapter Six

I ran up to the bedroom and slammed the door shut. I was furious.

Robert was his own worst enemy, Miguel was behaving like I was nothing more than a casual acquaintance and Eric, to top it all, was being Eric.

If there hadn't been this undercurrent of intrigue, I could just have been myself; the way I wanted to be with Miguel. But the truth of the matter was I didn't really know what was going on. One minute they were treating me like a good friend and the next it was all this cloak and dagger stuff with which I was somehow connected.

If I had been absolutely sure that everything was legitimate, I would have been far happier. What Robert thought of me being here with Miguel and Eric wouldn't have mattered; neither would the opinion of my mother. He was my choice, like it or lump it.

But if I took this attitude and Robert left this place concerned about my judgement, my safety, and the people I had allowed into my home without seeming to know very much about them, he would take it further. And Miguel didn't seem to be that bothered, which was the surprising part, knowing how paranoid he had been about me talking to anyone before Robert had arrived on the scene.

As I was thinking this the bedroom door was thrown open and Miguel walked in. He slammed the door shut again then walked towards me.

'Fuck off and leave me alone,' I said, putting my hands on his chest and pushing him away. I might as well have been pushing a brick wall; he didn't back off an inch.

'Go and do something constructive. Go and fuck your boyfriend,' I added, more for a reaction than anything else.

Amazingly, he still didn't bat an eyelid.

'What's the matter, Katie? Has seeing your boyfriend again brought everything rushing back?' he asked coldly. 'Why don't you do yourself, and me, a big favour. Go home. Eric and I will pack up and go too, if you're worried about us staying here once you've gone.'

'Step back, Miguel, or hit me. The way I feel now, I couldn't give a shit.'

'I don't want to hit you,' he said, looking as if I had slapped him in the face. 'But you obviously still feel something for this guy. You want to punish him and you're using me to do it. Why don't you just come clean and admit it? Then we'll all know where we stand and you'll get what you want.'

'You're so wrong. I'm angry because Robert will make trouble if he's suspicious. I'm suspicious of you now; I saw the way you and Eric looked at each other when he walked up. If I've got doubts about you, Robert's bound to have.

'I know who I want and it isn't Robert,' I added, putting my arms around his neck and pulling his head down to me.

I kissed him on the mouth, amazed that, by just being close to him, all my anger had been washed away. All I felt now was desire.

'I wish I could believe you,' he whispered brusquely.

I pressed my body into his, his naked chest against my barely covered breasts, and kissed him a little more demandingly.

He shut his eyes in resolution and placed his hands on my buttocks. As he pulled me against his crotch, I felt his erection inside his jeans. I rubbed myself against it almost frantically.

I was panting with lust for him. Being around him all the time, this was all I wanted to do. I wished the other two would just disappear so that we could be alone.

Suddenly, he pulled his mouth away from mine. 'Did you mean what you said in the barn? I want the truth.'

'I would never say a thing like that if it wasn't true. And now that I know what it feels like, I realise that I never loved Robert. That's why I feel a little sorry for him.'

'Well, don't feel too sorry for him. I think Robert's luck is about to change for the better.'

'You see? There you go again,' I said, pulling away from him. 'Why can't you just leave the guy alone. You've got me and he knows it. Just back off. He'll be gone in the morning.'

'Katie, in some ways you're very naive. I promise you that Eric and I aren't bent on upsetting him in any way. OK?'

I nodded but I didn't believe him. They had something up their sleeve.

Miguel was starting to unbutton my shorts. He pulled them down, my knickers with them, and I kicked them off. He pushed me backwards against the wall and lifted my vest up over my head. I was now naked.

He pinned me to the wall with his body, pushing his crotch into mine, and he kissed me savagely. God, how I wanted him inside me.

I felt for the buttons on his jeans and started to undo them frantically; I felt the damp patch on them which had just rubbed off me. I pulled out his cock and started to move my hand up and down his shaft while he was still kissing me, his hands on my arse.

Suddenly he lifted me up. I wrapped my legs around him and manoeuvred myself so that he could enter me. As he did, he groaned.

He leant me back against the wall, his hands still holding me up, while he fucked me wildly. With each thrust my head hit the wall. It was like he was raping me, venting his pent-up emotions on my cunt. But I didn't care; I wanted it. I was a willing victim.

After a few minutes, he slowed down. He put his mouth against mine and kissed me hard, his tongue entering me, filling my mouth as his cock filled my pussy. I was being taken at both ends.

I felt his whole body spasm as he came. The groan muffled by the deepness of the kiss.

Gently he put me down. He pulled me away from the wall and ran his hand around my neck. He put his other hand under my chin and tilted my head upwards. He looked into my eyes for a long time. I felt the unspoken words. His eyes told me a lot of things, more than he could, or would, say. Then he kissed me softly.

Miguel left me while I ran a bath. I poured wonderfully scented bath oil into the running hot water and when it was filled to the top, I sank into the bubbles, relishing this luxury.

Eric was sitting alone, reading a bike magazine, when I came out on to the terrace later.

'Where's Miguel?'

'He's gone to make peace with your boyfriend,' Eric replied with a twinkle in his eye.

'Oh, great!' My mind boggled at what Miguel could be saying to Robert.

'There's more to Miguel than what you see here, you know. Just because he chooses not to mix with people, doesn't mean he can't. You underestimate him. He's extremely intelligent and he's had a good education. He wouldn't tell you this because he doesn't give a shit about such things; money's not important to him; but he's a very successful artist.'

'I've never thought for one moment that he wasn't intelligent, but he just doesn't make any effort, that's obvious. And most people would make a success out of selling the odd painting if they were living with virtually no outgoings. It's all relative.

'Look, don't get me wrong; I like the way he is. I like the fact that he doesn't give a shit about the things the rest of us spend our whole lives worrying about. If you and he can survive like that, then that's great. As long as it doesn't hurt anyone else,' I added, as an afterthought.

Miguel came over to us and, placing his hand on my shoulder, said, 'I've taken your advice and talked to the guy. Told him a little bit about us so that he doesn't think we're the losers you say we appear to be. He's quite relaxed about the whole thing. He says you have a lot of arty friends and he can see why someone like me would appeal to you.

'I'll start heating up the barbecue now. Eric, give us a hand.'

Eric stubbed out his cigarette and they strolled round to the back of the house. I decided to see Robert, to find out if he really was 'relaxed about the whole thing'. I walked round the front of the house, so Miguel wouldn't see me and think I was being nosy, and found Robert still sunbathing on the other terrace, buried in *The Beach*.

'Do you want a drink, Robert?'

'No, thanks. Miguel just gave me a beer.'

Then his face erupted into a smile, his eyes twinkling with merriment. 'Why didn't you tell me he was Miguel Gómez? I got the wrong impression when I first saw him.'

'Well, er ... I didn't think the name would mean anything to you,' I said, floundering. His words had taken me completely by surprise and, of course, I didn't know what he was talking about; or what Miguel had told him.

'Don't be silly. Don't you remember the article about him in the Sunday papers a few months ago? You didn't read it, but you said that you thought he was very good-looking when you saw the picture. It was all about him – a Spanish artist living in France, totally reclusive. He had a big exhibition in London but refused to attend. They were reviewing his work, debating whether it was pornography or not. He's worth a lot of money but you wouldn't think so to look at him, would you? Don't worry, I apologised for my earlier rudeness.'

I was gobsmacked. Not only by what Robert had told me, but because now that he mentioned it, I did remember being struck by a photo of a man in the magazine. I had thought him incredibly attractive. I was in a hurry to get out and hadn't read the article, but when I went to look for it on my return, Robert had thrown it out. I had been annoyed; for some strange reason I had wanted to cut out the photo and keep it. But that was nearly a year ago.

Since then, a lot of my fantasies had been based on that one photo. But Miguel's beauty, in the flesh, far exceeded the photo's. That was probably why I hadn't recognised him. In real life he was intense, vital, sensual. The photo hadn't captured any of that from what I recalled.

Robert's piece of information now started to turn the wheels of my sometimes slow brain. If Miguel was an extremely well-known artist, who sought solitude and privacy, no wonder he would pick a place like this to live; 'keeping a low profile' as he called it.

And all this time, I thought he was in hiding because he or Eric had done something illegal. He was in hiding because he was famous.

I suddenly felt very stupid. If I had listened to the little bits of information he had given me from the very beginning, I could have worked out most of it for myself.

He had even sworn to me that he had not done anything wrong, except stay in my house. And Eric had practically told me what Robert had, not five minutes beforehand, and still I hadn't cottoned on.

But why couldn't he have bought his own place; why did he have to come here? This part was still a mystery, but since I seemed to be discovering more and more about them with each passing day, I felt sure that I would know everything in the fullness of time.

The evening meal was not quite as stressful as I had expected it to be. I hadn't drunk quite so much in months and even Robert appeared to be a little worse for wear. Miguel and Eric, who both seemed to drink like fish anyway, or at least they were used to consuming large quantities of the local produce, were just laid back and amusing. And by the end of the evening, I had to acknowledge that it was one of the most entertaining meals I'd had in years.

I also felt relaxed now, because of what Robert had told me. He was obviously impressed with Miguel and, if anything, was ingratiating himself into his good books. It was evident that he thought the exact opposite of his earlier estimation of the situation. And at least he would carry home good tidings about me.

The language barrier between Robert and us was not as awkward as I had thought it would be. Eric spoke in stilted English, but if he got stuck on a word, we translated it for him.

At one point, Miguel asked me where I had met Robert.

'Robert's art director is a friend of mine from college. She started using me and that's how we met. Although I was freelance, I did a lot of work for Robert's agency.'

'Katie, what do you intend to do about your career – if you stay here?' Robert asked me later, as we carried the plates through to the kitchen.

'Well, I certainly won't be travelling backwards and

forwards to England. Actually, I'd like to start doing fine art photography – seriously. I think this place lends itself to . . .'

I didn't quite know how to finish my sentence, but since I was currently gazing at the backs of two perfectly proportioned men, naked to the waist, he might have got my drift.

'Well, I've got the *Erotic Print Society* catalogue at home somewhere. Would you like me to send it to you? You could get in touch with them. I mean, it's a starting point, isn't it?'

'Yes, please. That's a good idea,' I answered, smiling. He'd obviously got my drift.

The sun was setting; the sky was turning pink and orange and we continued to sit outside talking until it was very nearly dark. Then I remembered that the electricity was now on. I went into the kitchen and turned on the light overhanging the terrace. It was a cold, white light rather than the warm, orange glow of candles.

On second thoughts, I grabbed a few candles, lit them and carried them out to the table.

Eric got up and opened yet another bottle of wine. I got the impression that they were hell bent on getting pissed this evening.

And looking across at Robert, I couldn't remember the last time I had seen him so relaxed. He was unusually animated and, for once in his life, not talking about work.

The current topic of conversation was surfing. Robert would have found this interesting because he loved windsurfing and back in England belonged to a windsurfing club.

By eleven o'clock, I could barely keep my eyes open. I asked Miguel to carry the mattress downstairs for me, while I brought down some fresh sheets. I made up a bed in the middle of the salon for Robert, then another one for Eric, with cushions off the settee.

'What time will you be leaving tomorrow, Robert?' I asked.

'Well, hopefully I'll be able to catch the overnight ferry from St Malo, so I won't need to leave here before about lunchtime. Is that all right?'

I nodded and wished them all good night.

Several hours after I had gone to bed I heard them talking in quiet voices, broken now and again by sudden peals of laughter. At first I was curious to know what they found so amusing, but eventually their hushed voices sent me off to sleep.

Much later, maybe three o'clock in the morning, I felt Miguel slide into bed beside me. I turned towards him half asleep and he gently leant over and kissed me.

'Are you drunk?' I murmured.

'No, I'm not at all drunk. I have a high metabolism and alcohol doesn't seem to affect me. But Eric is well on the way and so is Robert. I've left them outside. You know, Robert seems to like him.'

'That's nice,' I said sleepily. Then I woke myself up, realising what he was inferring. 'I hope Eric doesn't try anything on. Robert will go crazy. You had better go down and warn him.'

'No, I'm going to mind my own business. They are both old enough to take care of themselves. Just because you lived with him doesn't mean to say that he can't find men attractive.'

'I know that. But he's always been so homophobic. And he slept with me for four years. If he was gay, he wouldn't be able to touch me, would he?'

'But I'm not gay. You thought I was because you saw me with Eric. And in my experience, the men who shy away from people with dubious sexuality are the ones with the most doubts about themselves. Like I told you before, I can fuck Eric just for the release; and I am completely comfortable with where my inclinations lie.'

'Miguel, I think you are the exception rather than the rule. I've never heard of anyone else carrying on like you and Eric and, if they did, they certainly wouldn't admit to it.'

'Maybe that's why I don't like mixing with other people then. They're so full of bullshit. I just want people to be themselves. Like you – you aren't frightened of expressing yourself sexually. I have seen you take pleasure from any sort of situation that you find erotic. You're a very sensual person; your mind in tune with what your body wants. I like that. And I'm so lucky to have found a woman like you.'

'Well, let's face it. You didn't have to put much effort into finding me. As I seem to recall, I found you. Naked in bed with another man! How long would you have gone on like that? Could you have lived like that with Eric indefinitely, or would you eventually have gone looking for a partner?'

'I wouldn't have gone looking for anyone. I was waiting for you.'

I was going to contradict him, point out the fact that it was by pure chance that we had met; but I decided against it. He was intense, romantic, I supposed, and lived in another world. What was the point in spoiling it for him? He was happy there.

'I wanted to ask you something. You know this morning, when you grabbed the knife? Would you have stabbed me?' he asked after a while.

'I don't know. Just thinking about it, I can hardly believe that I would do such a thing. But I guess that if it came to it . . . I'm sorry, Miguel. You were angry with me and I just saw red.'

'Shit! I'll have to bear that in mind, next time we have a row!' he replied, chuckling.

Then he sighed. 'I'm not proud of the way I am, Katie, but I just don't know how to control my feelings. The idea that you might have had feelings for Robert and that you weren't being honest with me about them . . . This morning I was overwhelmed with jealousy.'

'Well, it doesn't make any difference to me. The fact

that you are so intense and unpredictable – as far as I'm concerned, it's part of your attraction.'

While we had been talking, it had gone very quiet downstairs. Eric and Robert had obviously decided to call it a night. I listened in the darkness and could hear them whispering in the salon, at the bottom of the stairs.

'What do you think they're doing?' I asked Miguel.

'If you're so interested, why don't you go and have a look? I'm sure you'll find it stimulating.'

I got out of bed because I didn't believe him. I wanted to prove him wrong. I crept down the first few rungs of the stairs, but didn't dare go any further.

My eyes confirmed what my ears would have denied.

Robert and Eric were lying on the mattress together, naked. Eric was lying flat on his back and Robert was leaning over him, playing with Eric's erect cock, whispering to him.

I went back to the bedroom. I climbed into bed beside Miguel and whispered to him, 'You were right.'

He groaned in response and rolled on to his back – fast asleep.

Seeing Miguel with Eric had turned me on; they looked beautiful together. But seeing Robert with Eric . . . I was just shocked.

Robert had been a total hypocrite. He had denied this part of himself and, in doing so, had picked an overtly feminine-looking girl to bolster his image. If no one else doubted his sexuality, then how could he have doubts about himself?

Strangely, I wasn't annoyed with him; I felt sorry for him. We had both of us wasted all those years together when we could have found happiness with other people. Luckily I had found Miguel. That he was the man I had fantasised about for months was the strangest part of all. It was as if I had been destined to meet him.

I must have been really pissed last night, I mused, as visions of Robert with Eric flashed across my still groggy brain. Then I realised that it did actually happen. I had watched Robert almost lovingly fondle Eric.

Still feeling incredulous, I sat up and looked at my watch. It was 11 a.m. Miguel had left me to sleep in. I got up quickly and went to the bathroom to get washed in – hot water! I'd forgotten this when I turned on the taps and nearly scalded myself. Then I remembered that Robert would be leaving shortly to catch the ferry.

I tiptoed downstairs, thinking that they would both be still asleep with the amount they'd had to drink; but I was surprised to find the salon empty, the sheets folded up, the cushions back on the settees, and the smell of coffee and cigarettes wafting in from outside.

'I suppose you ought to make a move in a minute, Robert,' I said, noticing that he was wearing a T-shirt and shorts – quite out of character.

He looked a little uncomfortable and Miguel spoke to me in French. 'Eric has asked him if he wants to stay down here for a day or two – if it's all right with you?'

I was surprised, but I turned to Robert and said, 'What about the company? You can't phone them on your mobile from here. Won't they be expecting you back?'

'Well, I had planned to stay down here with you for a couple of days anyway. I've booked the time off; I haven't had a break for ages. But if it makes you feel awkward, I can go.'

'No, it's OK. As long as you're comfortable sleeping on the floor. There isn't a lot of room.'

Robert seemed relieved, almost happy. 'No, that's fine. It will make a nice break. Eric has been telling me about the surfing. I thought I might give it a try while I'm down here.'

'We'll go this afternoon, unless you prefer to stay here? They can go on their own,' Miguel said, turning to me.

'No, I'd like to go. But we'll have to go shopping this morning. The fridge is being delivered and we've got no food left.'

'Well, finish your breakfast and we'll get going. Eric can wait for the fridge.'

'Miguel, why didn't you tell me you were a famous artist? I mean, it wouldn't have made any difference to me, but it would have explained why you don't like mixing with other people,' I asked him, as soon as we had pulled on to the road.

I had taken the 911, since I was still covered to drive it on Robert's insurance.

'You knew I was an artist. You saw my work; although, I have to be honest – the first time you walked into the barn, I was worried in case you recognised it.' He gave me a Gallic shrug, then he added, 'I so desperately wanted you to like me for what I am, rather than who I am.'

'I knew you had money when I saw the bikes for the first time. I even thought that you and Eric might be bank robbers – they were obviously expensive.'

He laughed. 'Just boys' toys. My Bimota is the Ferrari of motorbikes, so I do allow myself some luxuries. But the money's not important to me, Katie, or the publicity. I do what I do because I love it.'

'Miguel, shall I tell you something very strange? A while back now, I saw a picture of a man in a magazine that really appealed to me. At the time I even commented on it to Robert; he reminded me yesterday. I thought he was very beautiful. I remember wanting to cut it out and keep it, but Robert had thrown it away and I was really annoyed. I often used to daydream about the man in this picture, because to me he was the epitome of what I found attractive.

'When I saw you for the first time, I knew you were like the man I fantasised about, but I never realised you were one and the same. Robert told me yesterday. Don't you think that's weird? Like I was drawn to you or something?'

I looked at Miguel for a moment, but he was staring

out of the window. I wondered if I had somehow upset him.

'No. I don't think that's weird at all. I believe in fate. You and I were obviously meant to meet,' he answered, after a pause.

'By the way, you were right about Robert; I saw them together. I was really shocked. I would never have believed it of him.'

'I know. And I knew almost straight away; so did Eric. Robert's eyes lit up when he first saw him. Besides, he accepted you and me together too easily. I would have gone ballistic if I had found you shacked up with another man after a matter of days. I'm sure he loved you, probably still loves you, but not in the right way. You said that he was unfaithful to you? Did you ever ask him about it?'

'No. I didn't want to know. I assumed it was a client. He assured me it was over by the time I had suspected anything anyway. But now I'm glad. If I hadn't left him, I would never have met you.'

'Katie, would you pull over, please?'

Surprised by the seriousness of his tone, I pulled up to a stop.

'What's the matter?' I asked, wondering why he was looking at me so intently.

'Could you get out of the car, please?'

I did as he asked, my stomach beginning to churn with anxiety. It crossed my mind that he might have something to tell me, something that could well upset me.

As I walked round to the passenger door, Miguel opened it and took my hand. He swung his legs out of the car but continued to sit in the seat. He pulled me to him and leant his face against my stomach. He let go of my hand and ran his hands up the back of my legs, under my dress, to my arse. I felt his hot breath on my skin, even through the thin cotton layer of my dress, as he kissed my stomach and pelvis.

He slid his hands to the top of my knickers and eased them slowly down my legs.

'Give them to me,' he said brusquely.

I stepped out of them and handed them to him, with a questioning frown on my brow.

As he stuffed them in his pocket, I noticed his erection, confined within his jeans.

'Thank you, Katie, for humouring me. I like the fact that you do whatever I wish. This morning, I want you to walk around the town with no knickers on. I want to know that you are accessible to me at all times; that if I want to touch you, if I want to fuck you, there is nothing in the way. Like I told you the other day; I want you to belong to me.'

'Is that all?' I cried out indignantly. 'Honestly, Miguel! All you had to do was ask. I thought you were going to tell me something awful, like you didn't want me any more, or that you and Eric were leaving or something.'

'You don't know me at all, do you?' he said, lifting up my dress so that I was exposed at the front but not at the back.

'I want to eat you –,' he whispered, lapping at the juices seeping out of me, '– live you and breathe you,' he finished, burying his face in my pussy.

I stood on the side of the road while this beautiful man sucked my clitoris. I didn't care that someone might see; he'd taken me past that point. All I could think about was his tongue, giving me such exquisite sensations.

My legs started to tremble with the oncoming orgasm. Miguel noticing this, pulled me on to his lap.

I sat astride him; my damp pussy covering the bulge in his jeans. Feeling incredibly frustrated, I unbuttoned his flies and pulled out his cock. I wanted him inside me – desperately.

'There's no room in the car, but I want you to fuck me. I can't wait until we get home.'

He laughed, then putting his hands under my arse, he

lifted me up, out of the car. He walked round to the front of the car and laid me down on Robert's bonnet.

He pulled his jeans down a little, just enough to expose his arse, and started to thrust in and out of me. I wrapped my legs around his back and used them to pull him in. I wanted him to fuck me quick and hard.

With one hand supporting his weight, he used his other hand to undo the buttons on the front of my dress. Within a couple of seconds, I was completely exposed.

I didn't care. It added to the fervour. I liked my flesh being exposed to the hot sun above me and the cold bonnet beneath me. I liked my breasts and my pussy being exposed to anyone that passed us by; and I liked the fact that if I wanted him to fuck me, then he would fuck me anywhere.

Still supporting himself with one hand, his other hand moved down to my pussy. As he thrust into me, he rubbed my clitoris. As his movements became harder and faster, so did his fingers. I was coming.

As my body shuddered the last couple of times, Miguel slowed right down. He plunged into me deep and hard, groaning as he released himself. We had come simultaneously and very quickly. We had satisfied our lust.

Some of my friends had talked about spur of the moment sex, but I had never fancied it. What was the point when we had a nice comfortable bed at home? But I was twenty-seven years old and now experiencing these incredible desires for the first time. They were making me do things I would never have entertained back in England. Miguel and I had just fucked in broad daylight, on the side of the road. I had loved every minute of it and I had never felt so alive.

He withdrew from me, then buttoned up his jeans. I sat on the edge of the bonnet, Robert's bonnet, and, laughing at our recklessness, I fastened up my dress.

* * *

Miguel told me that he wanted to buy me a crash helmet. He knew where there was a bike shop in the town and that was our first stop. While we were there, he bought me a leather jacket too.

A lorry had already delivered the fridge by the time we got back. We unpacked the car, stocked the fridge, then made some lunch.

At two o'clock, we got on the bikes. Robert, wearing the spare crash helmet, rode pillion with Eric and I went with Miguel.

When we got to Hossegor, Eric and Miguel went off to hire the surf boards while I stayed on the beach with Robert. I took this opportunity of being alone with him, to find out exactly what was going on. I had no choice but to state the obvious, as a way of broaching the subject. No doubt it was all terribly sensitive to Robert.

'Robert, you know that Eric's gay?'

'Yes, he told me.'

'And it doesn't bother you? You always shied away from people like that.'

Robert sighed and was silent for a couple of minutes. He was probably selecting the words he wanted to use before he could even begin to open up to me.

After a while, he took a deep breath and answered, 'Katie, I have a confession to make. When you suspected that I was having an affair, I thought it was easier for us both if I let you carry on believing that, rather than knowing the truth. I have battled with these feelings for years, suppressed them if you like, because I didn't want to acknowledge the fact that I was different – not like other men. I did love you – I still do – but having seen Eric . . .

'I just can't help it. Physically, I'm drawn to other men.'

'Robert, what are you telling me? That you never had an affair?' I demanded, genuinely stunned.

'No, Katie. There was never anyone else. At least, there was never anyone that would have threatened our relationship. I love you and nothing would have changed that. But I did have a couple of one-night stands in the last year that we were together. I just never let it go any further because I didn't want to lose you. I was sure that I would, if I admitted my inclinations.'

'So the one-night stands were – with men?' I asked, my brain trying to absorb what he'd been telling me.

'Yes, with men. But they didn't mean anything to me.'

'You idiot! Why the hell didn't you just tell me? Christ, I would have accepted you being gay, far more easily than I could you sleeping with another woman. You put me through all that pain. The suspicion, the bitterness and jealousy I felt, for weeks, when all along . . . Fuck, Robert! There was never any competition anyway. How could I have competed? I'm not a man!'

I was actually smiling; but perhaps, if I hadn't met Miguel, I would have been boiling.

Now it just seemed totally ludicrous that Robert had allowed me to believe he'd been shagging another woman, rather than admit he was gay – in case he hurt me. Only a man could be so obtuse, I secretly mused.

'You should have told me, Robert. I would have understood,' I whispered, squeezing his hand.

'God, if you had any idea how many times I tried to tell you. At the end of the day I just couldn't bring myself to do it. But I'm so sick of having to deny what I'm really about.

'Strangely, I feel different about it here. Miguel and Eric are so open about these things. Just talking to them, it's as if they've given me a green light to go forward in a direction that would make me happy. And the ambience of the place; Eric's and Miguel's laid-back attitudes . . . I guess I just feel more positive about myself now. Do you know what I mean?'

'Yes I do. I feel exactly the same way about Miguel – and the house. It's strange because it doesn't belong to them, it belongs to me; but they seem to be part of its aura. I don't mind if you want to stay here for a while,

Robert. If you want to see where your relationship with Eric leads.'

'Thanks, Katie – for the last four years and for being so understanding.'

We saw Miguel and Eric coming back, each with a surfboard under either arm. We stopped talking and I called out to Miguel, 'Why have you got four? You're not going to get me on a board.'

'It's Eric's idea. He wants to teach you.'

They all laughed, including me, somewhat dubiously.

So we all stripped out of our jeans and T-shirts. I had barely sat down on my towel when Eric grabbed hold of my hand and pulled me up. He ignored my protests, insisting that I go down to the water with him and he would show me what to do.

Embarrassed in front of all the surfers on the beach, I waded out into the water.

He was very nice, very patient – loath as I was to admit it – and, within about ten minutes, he had me trying to catch a wave. Of course I was completely hopeless and fell straight off and underneath. He pulled me up, coughing and spluttering, and made me do it again. He went on and on at me but, within another half hour, I had managed to stay on sufficiently for him to allow me a break.

I didn't admit it but by then, I was determined to be a 'surfer' by the end of the day. And I was getting personal tuition from the best. I rated my chances.

I dropped down on my towel, breathless, and Miguel handed me a Coke. Eric said that he would take Robert out for a while, then he would come back for me.

I watched them together. Despite the language barrier they got on really well. I had to acknowledge this to Miguel.

'Yes, it's a coincidence, don't you think, that your ex-partner gets on with my ex-partner? Very fortunate.'

'Or very awkward. I don't think it can go anywhere. Robert's got a big agency back in England; Eric's a surfer. The most this can be is a holiday romance. They don't have much in common, do they?'

'Do you think that about us, too?'

I looked at him, genuinely shocked. 'Of course I don't. I would drop, and have dropped, everything and everyone to stay with you. I could never imagine you living in England; you just wouldn't fit in. So I shall have to fit in with you.'

'I am very lucky.'

He lay down on top of me and kissed me passionately, regardless of the people all around us. I felt his erection inside his trunks and laughed. 'Please Miguel, do me a favour. Don't roll on to your back for a few minutes; you'll make Eric's friends very jealous!'

He moved off me, laughing, but stayed on his stomach.

'I would fuck you right now, if you wanted me to. I don't care what other people think.'

'I know you don't. And I want you to fuck me, but I don't think I would want such a big audience.'

'What about a little audience?'

I looked at him puzzled, not knowing what to make of this last comment, so I changed the subject.

'I'm going to get back on the surfboard and practise, while Eric's still busy with Robert. Do you want to come?'

'No, I'll stay here and watch until Eric's back with you. And be careful; he makes it seem easy, but it can be dangerous. You're only a beginner, so don't try and get too clever.'

I decided to move away from all the other surfers and practise on my own. I walked up the beach a little way and started to wade out.

Suddenly I felt a hand on my shoulder. I spun around and Miguel was beside me. He seemed angry.

'Didn't you hear what I said? I'm watching you in case you get into trouble. How can I help you if you walk away?'

'Oh, sorry; I didn't realise. Well, could you stay here for a little while then? I want to be away from all the other boards. I don't know why they all have to be together like that; it's dangerous. They've got the whole sodding beach.'

Miguel sighed with exasperation. 'The whole idea is to get the best waves. The pull on the tide varies up and down the beach and Eric's in the best spot. But go ahead. I don't think you need to worry about the "tubes" and the "peaks" for this afternoon. I'll stay here to pull you out, when I need to.'

I gave him the most withering look I could muster and swam out with my board. He didn't have much confidence in me, evidently.

Stubbornly I battled with my board for half an hour. Miguel sat in the breaking waves, watching me with an amused expression on his face. When I had managed to stay on the board for as long as I had before, under Eric's supervision, I decided to have a break.

When we sat down, Miguel lit a cigarette and looked across at me.'You're tenacious, aren't you?'

'I am if I think it's achievable. If I think something's beyond my capabilities, I'm afraid I don't even try.'

I looked towards Robert. He seemed to be doing quite well. I supposed that he would have already had a head start, being a good windsurfer. They were different sports, but he would have picked up a certain empathy with the waves which I was yet to master.

Miguel stubbed out his cigarette and said that he was going out too.

Robert had been left to his own devices; Eric and Miguel were riding the waves and looking absolutely brilliant. Like on the last occasion, they were pulling crowds just to watch them.

I wished that I had my camera with me. They would have made fantastic photographs. And Eric looked like an advert for Old Spice – he had the looks as well as the skill.

The three of them came out after a while. Miguel dropped down next to me, combing his wet hair back off his face. The rivulets ran down his face, down his body; he looked beautiful.

We left the beach at about seven o'clock, laughing and joking about our afternoon's accomplishments. All things considered, I thought that I'd done rather well. I felt that, with practice, I could hold my own against fifty per cent of those supposedly experienced surfers on the beach with us.

Thanks to Eric. He had given me a solid hour just before we had called it a day.

It was almost dark by the time we had left the pizza restaurant and got back on the bikes. Miguel took it slow going home. Eric arrived ten minutes ahead of us and had put all the lights on. There was a bottle of wine already waiting on the terrace.

I excused myself, wanting to have a bath and wash my hair before I could relax. At least I could now use my hair dryer.

We stayed outside until about midnight, then we all decided to go to bed. Miguel and Eric went up ahead, wanting to use the bathroom first, while Robert and I tidied up the kitchen and turned off the outside lights.

When I came upstairs, Miguel and Eric were talking in the bathroom, hushed whispers in fast French which I couldn't hear. The door was ajar so I popped my head in to say good night.

Eric was sitting in the bath; Miguel was shaving. Both of them were naked and I found it hard not to stare.

Eric stood up, completely uninhibited by me standing there, and without thinking I passed him a towel.

He stepped out of the bath, at which point I turned away, but not before Miguel had seen my – curiosity. I supposed that was what it had to be.

I found it fascinating, living with these two so natural men; unlike any others I had ever known, they were oblivious to their own physical attributes, but very aware of each other's.

And Miguel, having seen me give Eric the once-over, seemed to be neither jealous nor irritated; yet he had gone absolutely ballistic at the prospect of me having feelings for Robert.

It was still hard for me to understand and even accept the peculiar relationship they had shared, especially now that one of them was my lover.

Eric went downstairs and Miguel and I went to bed.

We could hear Robert humming and splashing about in the bath; we heard him pull out the plug and turn off the light.

If he had popped in to say good night, he would have been met with an interesting scenario. Me, lying back on the pillows, thighs wide apart, with this gorgeous-looking man giving me oral pleasure. The exhibitionist within me liked the idea of Robert watching. The sordidness appealed to me, as always – of late.

When we heard Robert go downstairs, Miguel moved up the bed and lay down beside me on the pillow.

'Do you want to come?' he asked, stroking my hair.

'Of course I do. Stop playing around and finish it.'

'I will, but on my terms. Stand up.'

I got out of bed and stood up. He climbed out of bed, took something out of the bedside cabinet and led me to the door.

He pushed me against the wall in the hallway, then he kissed me. I felt his hands go to my head. I felt something soft brush against my cheek. I knew, before I saw the blindfold, what he was going to do next.

He bound the scarf tight over my eyes and ears. I couldn't see a thing and could hear little more.

I was so wet, the juices were seeping out of me. I didn't think that I had ever been so aroused; knowing that I was standing blindfolded and naked at the top of the stairs, with two other people at the bottom, oblivious to our activities. I felt very vulnerable – ecstatically so.

I took his cock in my hand and rubbed it against me, pushing my pelvis out to meet it. I tried to put him inside me but he drew back from me. 'On my terms, remember? I don't want to fuck you yet.'

He came towards me again and slipped his hand down between my legs. He rubbed my clitoris gently while he kissed me. 'You like being submissive, don't you, Katie?' he whispered.

I just nodded; there was no need for words. He could feel how turned on I was.

I had never felt so disorientated – and so frustrated. I had his huge erect cock just inches from me, but he wouldn't satisfy me.

'Please, Miguel. Let's just do it. Stop playing games,' I whispered to him.

'But we've only just begun. If you want it then you'll have to come downstairs with me. I want to fuck you in the dining room.'

'We can't,' I said, giggling quietly. 'They're sleeping downstairs. They might hear us.'

'Well, you'll just have to be quiet then, won't you?'

He took my hand and led me down the stairs. I could hardly believe that I was letting him do this; that I wanted to do this. My heart was pounding with excitement, my pussy pulsing with desire.

We got to the bottom of the stairs and I felt him manoeuvre me to the left, into the salon, rather than right, towards the dining room.

Of course I couldn't say a word. The chances were Eric or Robert might have still been awake and I didn't want to draw their attention to us.

Despite feeling mortified, I was incredibly exhilarated.

With his arm around my waist, Miguel guided me into what must have been the centre of the salon, where two settees were positioned.

Still holding me, he must have sat down, because I felt myself being pulled on to his lap. I felt his hands on my thighs, forcing them apart.

I was now in such an abandoned, degrading position, that I prayed Eric and Robert were fast asleep.

Thankfully, we had come in and sat down without making any noise, although I was panting with anticipation as to Miguel's next move.

I felt his hands go to my head. In a second he had pulled off the blindfold.

I was stunned to find myself greeted with an almost mirror image of what Miguel and I had been engaged in upstairs, not twenty minutes earlier. And very reminiscent of the other evening, when I had seen Miguel in the same situation with Eric. But this time, Eric was the recipient of Robert's lovingly bestowed attentions.

With something like shock, I looked up at Eric's face to find him watching me intently. I could see everything clearly by the light of a candle placed on the mantelpiece.

And like the other evening, Eric continued to receive oral pleasure, while Robert remained completely oblivious to our presence.

I had almost forgotten why Miguel and I had come downstairs, so taken was I with this erotic, almost surreal scenario.

As if to remind me, Miguel put one hand between my legs while the other stroked my breasts. Eric just continued to lie back, watching us – actually, me.

I felt dirty, perverted – a degenerate. But at the same time, I was so aroused that I thought I would literally erupt in orgasm at any moment, simply because my lover was touching me in front of another man. A man who seemed to be as interested in my body as my lover was.

Suddenly Eric put his hands on Robert's head and told him to stop. Eric stood up and walked towards us. My heart was pounding fit to burst, but I didn't like to think about the reason why.

Robert turned around and gasped with shock. He was probably mortified that we had been watching them but, at the same time, had to appreciate that I was in an equally compromising situation.

But I was past caring. I was in another place, where it was perfectly all right for people to admire beauty – male or female – and perfectly natural to relish the pleasures of the flesh – amongst good friends.

Eric just said two words to Miguel. 'Can I?'

Miguel didn't answer.

I knew what he meant and gasped. Not with shock, although I was surprised by his obvious intention, but with relief. Thank God someone was going to fuck me. And if not Miguel, then why not Eric? Miguel loved him and he was so beautiful.

As Eric ran his hand over me, I felt as if Miguel were offering me to him, and he was checking the goods first; examining every last bit of me, before he made the decision whether or not to go ahead. And, Jesus, he was taking his time.

It suddenly occurred to me that perhaps they had planned this. Maybe Eric had been waiting for me. But how could they have predicted that I would be on board with this? How could they have assumed that I was up for being passed around like a cheap whore? Amazingly, this last thought sent another thrill rushing through me.

I bit my lips, shuddering with anticipation, while Eric's fingers trailed down from my breast to my pussy. He was studying me so intently, I felt as if I were some weird and wonderful creature he had just discovered; and he was making mental notes, taking mental photographs, for future reference and study.

As if to assist in his exploration, Miguel held my thighs wide apart, while Eric cupped my pussy in his hand. His hand would have come away very wet.

I felt as if I were little more than chattel, but it just made it even more exciting for me. If Eric didn't hurry up, I was going to have to beg for it; and at this moment Eric was the one I wanted most, to put me out of my misery.

At long last, he pressed himself against me. His cock automatically slipped inside me, I was that wet; and my body almost arched backwards in welcome, I was that desperate for him to fuck me.

As he entered me, his eyes locked mine. He wanted to see my reaction to him, and to what we were doing. He must have seen that I was almost overcome with lust, and relief, that he had taken this step.

And as I felt him taking me, filling me, I felt Miguel's cock pushing against my anus. Miguel just held me, his arms tight around me, while he stroked my clitoris and my breasts. But the whole time I was aware of this other sensation, this extremely tempting pressure, between my buttocks.

Eric was watching me; Miguel was watching Eric while he slowly fucked me. It was the strangest, most bizarre – and the most intensely erotic – situation in which I had ever been.

Robert had been lying on the floor watching us, absolutely spellbound. Now he got up and moved behind Eric. I knew what was going to happen before Eric did.

Robert penetrated him. As he pushed into him, so Eric penetrated me. And as Eric pushed me back on Miguel's cock, so he penetrated me too, just a little, in my most private place.

It was the most exquisite feeling; the nearest I had ever come to ecstasy without orgasm, coupled with the realisation that this was the best, the most incredible, sex I was ever going to experience.

I had two gorgeous men taking me, touching me, filling me and fulfilling me. And they were getting pleasure too – Eric from me, Miguel from me and Robert from Eric.

I was coming in big long waves, crashing over me, picking me up and throwing me higher. They were relentless; Miguel and Eric were relentless; I was breaking up. Going on and on until, at last, I felt Eric groan, and with great long shudders, he came too.

He stayed still inside me for a moment, then withdrew.

He was followed by Miguel who stopped touching me, lifted me up, turned me over and penetrated my pussy from behind. With my face buried in the settee, he thrust into me quick and hard, until I felt his body tense. Then he released himself, groaning softly, almost under his breath.

I lay curved over the settee with my arms stretched out. Miguel was still lying on top of me, but now he was kissing my neck, my shoulders, my back. He put his mouth to my ear and whispered, 'We did that for you; I thought you would like it. Did you like it?'

I didn't answer him. I was still in another place. I'd just had this incredible fantasy about me having sex with two, no, three men. It had to have been a fantasy because I could never have done anything like that for real.

I closed my eyes, painfully aware that Robert was fucking Eric.

And then it dawned on me the depths of depravity to which our lust had sunk us – actually, me.

I was well aware of the fact that as far as Miguel and Eric were concerned, there were no limits; therefore in all fairness, I could only reproach myself for my behaviour. Yet I couldn't deny that what we had done together had been mind-blowingly erotic.

I pushed Miguel off and stood up. Without turning around I left the salon and climbed the stairs. I went to the bathroom, washed myself under running water and climbed into bed.

After five minutes Miguel joined me. We didn't speak – to be honest, I didn't know what to say – and after a while I fell asleep.

I opened my eyes to find Miguel lying on the bed beside me, dressed in jeans and a T-shirt. He had been watching me sleep.

'What time is it?' I asked, stretching.

'It's ten o'clock. Eric and Robert have gone to the beach for the day. I wanted to spend some time alone with you.'

I blushed as the pictures of last night's orgy came to mind. In the cold light of day, I felt very uncomfortable with what had happened.

While it had been dark, the house lit by candles, a strange mood seemed to take hold of the house – and us. It was like a transformation: some magical force coming into being, lifting away the cloaks of morality which we all wore. We had escaped to a place where fulfilling one's basic instincts and natural inclinations was permitted – encouraged.

But by morning that feeling had dissipated. Not for the first time, I wondered whether it was the house, or Miguel, that had created this strange phenomenon.

'I'm glad they've gone out. I don't think I could have faced them after what happened last night. I can hardly believe what we did.'

'Why should you feel ashamed? We all enjoyed it. It wouldn't have happened otherwise.'

'I wish I could have your attitude, Miguel. I dread to think what's going through Robert's mind at the moment. He probably thinks this place is nothing more than a den of iniquity, corrupting all of us, him included. We would never have done anything like that in a million years, back in England.'

'Only because you've never met anyone like us. I knew, that first evening you arrived, and you stood at the bottom of the stairs and watched Eric and me together, that you were exactly like us. Eric took a little persuading but, after a day or two, he saw it in you too. And I honestly wouldn't worry about Robert. He loved every minute of it.'

'But I don't know what to say to them when they get back. I feel so awkward about it.'

'Don't say anything at all, unless you want to. We all

did it, Katie; not just you. But it was only fucking. Interesting, because it was different, but still only fucking.'

'You sound like you didn't enjoy it that much.'

'Eric had asked me earlier if he could; and I said yes, only because I believed that it was what you wanted too. But I would have preferred to have waited until Robert left. Robert doesn't belong with us.'

I nodded but said nothing. What could I say? Miguel's perceptiveness was spookily accurate. He seemed to know me better than I knew myself. He had an extraordinary knack of visualising my every fantasy; even the ones I would have emphatically denied on a conscious level.

'But Eric's gay. Why should he want to have sex with me?' I asked him after a while.

'He told me that he finds you attractive. But he's never been interested in women before. Actually, he's never been that interested in anyone; simply using men as and when, without giving them any kind of commitment. But we've led a strange life. Eric and I have been on our own for years and I probably wasn't the best role model for a teenage boy – a man with ambiguous sexuality who spends all his time painting erotica. I wouldn't be surprised if Eric had simply jumped to the wrong conclusions. He's probably bisexual, finding both men and women attractive, and perfectly capable of having a fulfilling relationship with either. He may have just assumed he was gay because up until now, he'd never met a woman who appealed to him.

'Robert, while we are on the subject, says that meeting Eric, and seeing how relaxed we both were about anyone's sexuality, has helped him come to terms with himself. I am sure he will be a different person when he goes home.'

I declined to answer, not believing for one minute that Robert would come out of the closet. He still cared too much about what other people thought.

So different from Miguel and Eric.

And Miguel, whilst describing himself as someone with ambiguous sexuality, seemed to me to be the most masculine guy I had ever met. He didn't feel the need to prove anything. He was so comfortable with his own sexuality that he didn't care to put a label on it.

Chapter Seven

Miguel wanted to paint that morning, so we strolled down to the barn together.

I made myself comfortable on a chair with my feet up, resting on a window sill, then opened Joanna Trollope's aptly titled *A Spanish Lover*.

Two days ago, Robert had arrived. This was the day I realised that Miguel loved me and Eric liked me, which gave me the excuse I needed to throw caution to the wind – along with *Sense and Sensibility*.

'Are you hungry, Miguel? Would you like me to bring you down some lunch?' I asked him after a couple of hours.

'No, I'll come up with you, if you could just hang on a minute.'

It occurred to me that I hadn't seen what he was currently working on, although he had been busy with the same picture since I had arrived.

I walked over to him, aware of his eyes studying my face as I looked down at the painting, perhaps to gauge my reaction.

I found myself suddenly shivering and yet I wasn't cold. I felt as if someone had just stepped over my grave.

On his canvas was a picture that could have easily

been painted by my grandfather. It was of me. My face was so like how my grandfather had portrayed it, but as I was now – a woman.

I was lying in a bed, the bed upstairs, I thought. The sheets were crumpled; there was a dent in the pillow next to where my head lay, and I was asleep with my hair falling all about me. The sheets just about covered me, but my bare shoulders and legs suggested that I was naked underneath.

The sun was shining through the window on to my hair, lighting me up like a halo. My mouth was slightly open, my hand underneath my face.

I seemed almost innocent, like a child, but the sheets moulding my curves showed that I was, in fact, a woman.

Once I got over the shock, I saw that it was a beautiful, sensual picture. It suggested many things without being overtly erotic: that I had been sleeping with someone else; that we had just made love; that I seemed content, fulfilled, in love.

'It's beautiful. I don't know how you could have done it without me sitting for you. It's very – suggestive, but totally inoffensive.'

'It was easy. The first morning Eric and I woke up before you, we found you like that. You looked so naive, so trusting, but at the same time completely irresistible. All I wanted to do was lie down next to you and wake you up, but I had to be patient; you didn't know me at all.'

He shrugged his shoulders, then added, 'I just carry pictures in my head.'

'It's startled me though, because my grandfather used to paint me a lot; often when I was asleep. But not like that – as a child.'

He looked as if he were going to say something more, but then changed his mind. 'Come on. Let's get some lunch.'

* * *

Later in the afternoon, we decided to go for a walk. After three quarters of an hour, we had left the woods behind us and had climbed to the top of another hill.

'Let's stop here for a while. The grass is soft and the views are wonderful. We can start to head back once we've had a break,' I said, sitting down.

Miguel dropped down beside me on the grass and we lay on our backs, watching the clouds pass swiftly by, giving us occasional relief from the sun's intense rays.

After a while, Miguel rolled on to his side and looked at me. He started to stroke my hair, my face, as if he were miles away.

'I've waited too long for you and me to be like this,' he said brusquely, completely out of the blue.

'Yes, it's been a long week!' I answered, trying to lighten his intensity.

'No. I've been waiting years for you to come down here so we could meet each other. I've loved you nearly all your life, but you never even knew of my existence.

'And when we met, I was so frightened that you would just up and leave again, without ever coming back. That's why I went crazy when you told me Robert was coming down. I would have been devastated.'

He had lost me completely, but he continued. 'I wanted to tell you on several occasions. Even yesterday when you were telling me about seeing my photo in the press, and how you had felt drawn to me, that's exactly how I felt about you.

'I've known you since you were little. I've watched you grow up. But I was never allowed to speak to you. I used to see your grandfather's paintings, marvel at how lovely you were, but whenever you came down to stay, he sent me away. He said I was too wild, and you were too innocent, to mix with the likes of me. Sometimes, I couldn't stay away. As a boy, I cycled over here; and when I was older, I'd come by motorbike. I used to watch you walking around, talking to your grandfather. Once or twice you went into the woods by yourself and

I was tempted to speak to you. But I always got cold feet and walked away. I never imagined that I would have to wait three years after he died for you to come back.'

'What are you saying? You knew who I was when I walked in the other day? So why the threats? Why the gun?'

'It's like I told you – I wanted you to stay. I wanted you to get to know me. I didn't know what else to do to keep you from running away. I didn't expect you to fall instantly in love with me.'

'And yet I did. How did you come to know my grandfather? I still don't understand.'

'There's not much more I can tell you at the moment. I will, once Robert's gone home. But basically, I've known him since I was a child. He taught me to paint. I spent most of my time working in his studio.

'But he wanted to keep me away from you. I think it was to do with your mother. She wouldn't have approved of her daughter consorting with Gypsy kids, and would have stopped your visits, if you had.'

'So you've been staying in the house since he died?'

'Yes, the last three years. Waiting for you. I didn't attend my biggest exhibition to date in case you showed up while I was away.'

'That's so intense, it's – unhealthy,' I said, as I absorbed what he'd been telling me.

He rolled on to his back and sighed. 'I know!'

We were silent for a few minutes, then he took my hand and laid it on his chest. I could feel his heart pounding.

'That's what happens whenever I see you; whenever I'm with you. That's why you can't ever leave me. I have lived my whole life thinking about you.'

'Miguel, it's incredible. To think, all these years you knew about me; you knew my grandfather; and yet we'd never met. I feel that I've wasted so much time.

The years with Robert when I could have been with you.'

As we walked slowly back to the house, I remembered all the times I had strolled through these woods, thinking I was alone when, in fact, he was there, somewhere; watching me grow up.

The last time I had been to France was a few months before my grandfather had died. I was then twenty-three years old and had just started living with Robert. Miguel would have been about twenty-seven.

I didn't attend the funeral. My mother had come down and arranged everything; she didn't tell me until it was all over. I never forgave her for that and I never understood why. Perhaps it had something to do with Miguel. Maybe she knew him and didn't want me to get involved.

Slowly the fog was lifting. When Miguel told me the rest, I was sure the picture would become as clear as day.

When we reached the house, we could hear laughter from the terrace. Eric and Robert were back from the beach and had obviously had a good time.

They chatted away to us, as if last night had never happened. Maybe Miguel was right. I had read too much into what, at the end of the day, was just a good fuck.

I glanced at Eric. He was looking at me in a most peculiar way, as if he were miles away. Robert asked him a question and he was visibly startled.

Several times throughout the afternoon, I met Eric's eyes and he smiled. I began to feel a little uncomfortable.

Although the weather had been scorching for days, a wind had picked up making it too chilly to sit outside this evening. And clouds were beginning to gather in the sky. I knew the weather was about to change. Once the rain had been and gone, it would be as hot and sunny as it ever was. But in the meantime, we would be in for a day or two of cloudy weather.

After dinner we sat in the salon drinking wine. We

talked about books, something we all had in common, then cars. By the time they got on to bikes, I stifled a yawn and said that I would go to bed.

Miguel laughed. 'Well, what would you do in England in the evening, if you didn't have a television?'

'Well, if I were on my own, I'd read; but if I were with other people, and we knew each other too well to make polite conversation, we'd probably play a game.'

'Yes like *Sexual Pursuits* or some other silly trivia game,' Robert added.

'But we haven't got anything like that here. I've only seen a pack of cards in the dining-room sideboard,' I said, turning to him.

'Well, we could play strip poker?' Robert suggested, laughing.

Miguel looked questioningly towards me and I shrugged my shoulders. I was far too pissed to feel inhibited, but not too pissed to forget that I wasn't a dab hand at cards.

The person who lost their hand had to take something off; that was the rule. I soon discovered that I had the advantage here, wearing earrings, a watch, a couple of gold chains and rings on my fingers. Eric was down to his boxer shorts before I'd even started on my clothes. Miguel and Robert had removed their T-shirts.

Then I lost again. Having run out of jewellery, I chose to remove my bra. Thankfully I was wearing one. It was easy for me to undo the clasp and slip it off my shoulders without exposing myself in any way. Miguel seemed to be disappointed but I just laughed.

I was determined to keep the rest of my clothes on. The prospect of playing cards with three naked men definitely appealed.

Eric stood up and removed his boxer shorts, completely unabashed, and sat down again naked. Robert lost next and removed his jeans. He only had his Calvin Klein underpants to go, I noticed, greatly amused.

And then unfortunately, I had to remove something

else. It was a toss-up between my shorts and my T-shirt. I didn't fancy sitting there with my breasts on display so I removed my shorts. I was kicking myself for having put on a G-string instead of my other, less skimpy knickers. They laughed as I stood up, probably because my irritation showed on my face.

'Katie, it's only a game,' Robert said, to another bout of laughter.

I was delighted when Miguel lost his hand. He stood up and made a great show of slowly unzipping his jeans. We were all surprised when he pulled them down to find that he had nothing on underneath. If he had been wearing underpants, he would still have been in the game.

So now it was down to Robert and me.

My heart was beating with tension; I really didn't want to lose. But then the inevitable happened; something had to go. It was my T-shirt or my G-string and I opted for the T-shirt. I consoled myself with the thought that if we had been on a beach, I wouldn't have looked anything out of the ordinary.

But I did feel embarrassed, as all eyes turned to me while I removed my top. As an afterthought, I undid my plait, shook my hair loose and hid underneath it.

Eric laughed. 'I could do that, but it wouldn't make any difference!'

I laughed at myself too, and was glad I had thought of it.

Then Robert lost and had to remove his underpants. I had won the game; and being the only one with a stitch of clothing on, felt suddenly very superior to these naked, supposedly skilled card players. Certainly it was the first time I had ever beaten Robert.

'Imagine, Robert, if my mother could see us now. She'd have a fit!'

'Yes, and if she'd seen us last night, she would have had heart failure!'

It was the first time any mention had been made of

last night but, because we were all so drunk, we burst out laughing. And I could just imagine my mother's face, which made it all the funnier for me.

Eric poured out yet another bottle of wine and my head was swimming. I stood up to go to the toilet and couldn't even walk in a straight line to the stairs.

I came down after a couple of minutes to find Miguel stretched out on one settee, Eric on another, both of them smoking. Robert was lying full length on the carpet and looking as if he were about to fall asleep.

The candles had been lit, the overhead light was off; it was as if the strange phenomenon were upon us again.

Perhaps it was something in the candles. Some drug in the wax, that when they burnt, they created this languid, sensual aura. It certainly hadn't been there five minutes ago.

I had to say something. I wanted to know whether the others felt it. 'Don't you think there's something funny about this house? The minute the candles are lit, it's like it takes on a completely different mood.'

'Do you think the place is haunted?' Robert asked, half asleep.

'No, I'm not saying that at all. It's not a creepy feeling. It's something else; warm, earthy. I can't really describe it and if you don't feel it then you won't know what I'm talking about.'

Robert didn't reply; he had dozed off.

'I know what you mean,' Miguel said quietly. 'I used to sleep here before your grandfather died. I felt it then, even if I was on my own. Your grandfather thought it was to do with the woods. The trees are very old; the timber that was used to build the house had been taken from the woods. He said that, a long time ago, people inhabited the woodlands around here. These people practised the ancient religions – I think you call them Druids in England. He believed, along with many of the locals, that the woods may have absorbed some of the power that these people evoked. I'm sure the trees aren't that old, but it could be something in the earth.'

Probably because I was pissed, this seemed very logical to me. And since I couldn't think of any other explanation for something that I had been aware of from the first moment I arrived, I accepted it.

'Where did you sleep, Miguel, when you stayed here?'

He looked over to Robert, and satisfied that he was fast asleep, he answered quietly, 'Upstairs in the bed. Your grandfather slept in the barn.'

'So every time I came down, you would have to give up the bed for me? It's amazing that I slept here, completely unaware of your presence.'

'But I was aware of yours. And the last time you came here, I think it was shortly before he died, I didn't change the sheets for weeks. I liked the smell of you on the pillows.'

'That's true,' Eric cut in, whispering too. 'He often thrust a pillow under my nose and asked me if I could smell you. I thought he'd lost it completely.'

The three of us giggled.

'But he's right. You do smell different. I'm not used to women, but your hair, your skin, has a scent that men just don't have – it's nice,' Eric added, as if he thought that he ought to qualify it or I would take offence.

We were silent for a while, then I asked Eric a question. 'What's happening between you and Robert? Have you made any plans?'

Eric hesitated for a moment, looking towards Miguel for support or permission, I wasn't sure which, then he replied, 'He's going back to England the day after tomorrow. He says there's someone back home that he met this year who wanted a relationship. At the time he was involved with you and didn't want to blow it. He says he'll give him a call when he gets back.'

'So that's it. You've talked about it and you don't want it to go any further?'

'I feel more for you guys than I do for him. What else

can I say?' Eric retorted, giving a Gallic shrug which said far more than his words.

I got the picture. Robert would be gone and we would be back to a threesome. For some reason I felt pleased – or relieved. I wasn't sure which and I didn't like to analyse my reaction.

I was sitting on the settee with Miguel. He had pulled me down so that I was lying in his arms and he was almost absent-mindedly stroking my hair, my shoulders, my breasts. It was nearly two in the morning, we were all very tired, and I got the feeling he was beginning to doze off.

His hands had slowed down to the point were they had stopped moving altogether, and hearing that he was breathing rather deeply, I realised he was fast asleep.

I looked across at Eric. He seemed strangely alert. He didn't say a word but his eyes never left me. I felt as if he were studying me in a detached way; perhaps weighing me up.

It suddenly occurred to me that I was lying on the settee, virtually naked, with three naked men lying around me. And, more to the point, Eric had been leisurely watching Miguel stroke my breasts for the best part of half an hour.

I had been too pissed and too sleepy to have received any sexual pleasure from Miguel's caresses, but now that I was sobering up, I realised that I had been displaying a complete lack of modesty.

Still watching me intently, Eric suddenly flicked his cigarette lighter. He must have been holding it in his hands for ages before deciding to light another cigarette. He saw me jump, but he didn't smile. He didn't even blink. His eyes continued to bore into mine as he took a drag on his cigarette.

I decided to go to bed, feeling suddenly uneasy in Eric's company.

I was to be sleeping alone. It reminded me of the other night, when the Gypsies had been here. But so much had happened in a matter of days that everything was completely different now. I knew exactly where I stood with Miguel, and I liked to think that, even if Eric didn't like me, he certainly tolerated my presence.

When I had finished in the bathroom, I walked through to my bedroom. I turned the bedroom light off, then leaving the door ajar, I went to climb into bed.

Suddenly, I felt someone's hand on my shoulder. I didn't jump or scream because I knew who it was, even before I turned round.

'What are you doing here?' I whispered nervously.

Eric didn't answer me. Instead, he reached out his hand and combed the hair back off my face.

Incredibly, I felt breathless; my heart beginning to pound with excitement.

He leant over and kissed me, very gently, almost tentatively. I opened my mouth to protest and, as I did so, his tongue entered my mouth.

A moment later, he slid his arms around my waist and pressed his erect cock against my pussy.

Although I was stunned, his action aroused me. And I had neither the strength or the inclination to move away.

Sliding one hand down to my buttocks, he continued to press himself hard into me, his cock lying down, almost curving round underneath my pussy.

Cupping my face with his other hand, he continued to kiss me, so softly, so gently. The whole time his prick rubbed against my pussy, sometimes actually nudging at my clitoris.

I found myself responding to his kisses, even returning them, though I didn't like to think about what I was doing or why.

It was as if we were dancing, naked, his hands pressing me to him, his pelvis moving in time to a silent beat. And I found my hips swaying, my pelvis arching, desperately trying to accommodate him.

I could feel the juices running out of me, I was so wet.

I wanted him to throw me down on the bed, slide his shaft inside me and fuck me senseless. I needed to be senseless, to come to terms with what we were doing.

And then, all of a sudden, he stopped kissing me and broke away.

Totally frustrated, yet overwhelmed with relief, I sat down on the bed and tried to gather my wits.

'Eric, why did you come in here?' I whispered, when my heart rate had returned to normal. 'I don't think Miguel would like it, do you?'

He walked towards me and, when his erect cock was only inches from my mouth, he began to stroke my hair almost reverently.

It was almost too inviting to resist, but I managed to quash the desire to run my tongue over the end of it.

'I've never kissed a girl before. It feels really nice. But I think it's because it's you. I'll leave you alone now. I'd never want to hurt Miguel.'

He walked out of the room, leaving me sitting on the end of the bed, with my jaw on my chest.

Was that what we were doing? Kissing? I would have called it major league, heavy petting. And had he not restrained himself, I would have gone all the way.

I was only aroused because the whole thing was so illicit, so dangerous, I told myself firmly. This has nothing to do with Eric; it has more to do with Miguel. Playing with fire can be a huge turn-on.

Still, I found my reaction to Eric very unsettling. In a moment of passion, I had lost my head. I had temporarily dismissed my overwhelming love – my obsession for Miguel – and focused on Eric.

I climbed into bed and tried to sleep; it was impossible. My mind was churning with this latest development. And I was just as baffled by Eric's complete change in attitude towards me.

When I arrived, he had hated me to the point where I thought he was capable of killing me. Now he wanted to be close to me, kiss me, even though he was supposedly gay. But I was beginning to have my doubts about that, too.

When I woke up in the morning, the three of them were still asleep downstairs. Miguel as I had left him, stretched out on the settee; Robert on the carpet and Eric lying next to him on the cushions.

I sat in the kitchen because it was overcast outside, and I began to think about living here, seriously. I had to set this place up to suit me and the way I wanted to live. And I needed a darkroom.

The house was quaint, I loved it as it was, but nothing had changed in perhaps forty years. I had to bring it up to date somehow without sacrificing its refreshing simplicity.

When Miguel wandered into the kitchen twenty minutes later, I told him of my intentions. He agreed that I should renovate rather than modernise.

'First and foremost,' I said, 'we need another bathroom and bedroom, although God knows there's no room upstairs. And I'd like a telephone, satellite TV, a beautiful garden and, one day, if I can afford it, a swimming pool!'

'Well, don't worry about the money. I can give you everything you need to make the house as you want. The only thing I don't like the sound of is the satellite TV.'

'I know why you wouldn't like a TV, but while I can live cut off from the outside world for the odd month or two, I feel that I have a moral obligation to follow the news, if nothing else. World War Three could have broken out this week for all I know.

'Anyway, the barn is yours. We'll leave it exactly as it is, if you like; but I need a darkroom set up somewhere. Perhaps we could convert one of the outhouses into one? I'd like to continue sleeping upstairs and I wouldn't want to change it; it reminds me of when I was little. But maybe we could knock through the outhouses behind the utility room, to give us a self-contained guest suite?'

'Next time we're in town, we'll arrange for an architect to come and check the place out,' Miguel answered.

Of course, these ideas would probably take a couple of years to realise, but the sooner we got started, the sooner things would be finished. There was something I could do now, though, without anyone's help: the garden.

Miguel had obviously kept the lawns cut and the grounds tidy, but it needed some time and money spent on it to transform it into the charming garden it had the potential to be.

We heard a car pulling up on the drive outside. This was surprising as we were off the beaten track and not expecting anybody. Miguel went out to see who it was.

He came back in almost immediately with a couple of letters. It had been the postman. One was addressed to me and the other to him. I opened mine; it was from the gas company, just confirming the monthly contract. Miguel was reading his with an irritated expression on his face.

'What's the matter?' I asked, as he folded it up and stuck it in his pocket.

'It's from my agent. He's coming down here to collect some of my paintings tomorrow. I have an exhibition next month in Barcelona, and he's going to insist that I attend. Would you come with me?'

'I hope you don't think I'm being funny, but I'd rather stay here and wait for you. I've only been here a week and I just want to get settled. I'll go another time though – when I've been here for a while. OK?'

He nodded. 'I don't blame you. But I dread anything like this: having to talk to all those people, smiling sweetly, while they tell *me* why I've painted something the way I have. It's a farce. But they pay a lot of money for my work, so I just have to keep my mouth shut and go along with it. And I hate the publicity. The quieter I am, the more reserved I am, the more famous I become. It's crazy, but my agent loves it.'

'You can't blame them, Miguel. Look at you. If you're stand-offish, women will say you're intense and brooding. Coupled with the fact that you look like a tormented Heathcliff, of course you're going to get a lot of publicity. Even I noticed you, and I don't read the papers!'

He laughed and ruffled my hair affectionately.

Eric walked into the kitchen stark bollock naked and put the kettle on. I steeled my eyes to remain on his face.

'It's Robert's last day and the weather is crap. What shall we do?' he asked Miguel.

'We could go to Mont de Marsan for lunch. The festival's on, so we might run into my sister.'

'What festival's that, Miguel?' I enquired, curious.

'Every July in Mont de Marsan, they hold a festival of Flamenco Arts. My sister and the others were on their way there, when they stopped off. We'll have to go in cars though. We don't have enough waterproofs for all of us and we'll get drenched if we go by bike,' Miguel added.

Miguel and I went in my MG; Eric went with Robert in his Porsche.

Miguel took us to a restaurant which overlooked one of the two rivers which flowed through the old town. We all chose to eat off one of the four set menus on offer, and I was greatly amused to watch Robert, with great gusto, tucking into blood sausage, jellied gizzards, wood pigeon . . .

If I had told him beforehand, he would have had a fit.

Towards the end of the meal, Miguel asked if we minded staying on for another coffee, while Eric and he went off to find his sister.

I was glad to be alone with Robert so we could talk.

'I'd appreciate it if you didn't tell my mum too much about Miguel and Eric. She won't like it that I'm not coming back and I don't want her getting the wrong end of the stick. In her eyes they would be drifters – drop-outs.'

'Don't worry. You can trust me not to say anything at all, other than that I've met Miguel, he's a really nice guy and he's a well-known artist. Besides, he may be unconventional, but he's hardly a drifter. He must be wealthy.'

'I don't know and I don't care,' I replied flippantly.

'Now I know where you are, would you mind if I came down from time to time? I've really enjoyed being here. It's a nice place to be, to relax and let my hair down, without worrying about what other people think.'

'Yes, of course. It would be lovely to see you. You can bring me all the news from home. But, Robert, aren't you upset that things didn't work out with Eric? I mean, you seemed to really like each other.'

'No. Eric has been completely up front with me from the word go. He likes me, but not enough for it to lead anywhere. Besides, he's feeling a little confused. I think he's going through a little identity crisis at the moment,' he added, smiling. 'Not that I'm in any position to pass comment, having been going through the same thing for the past ten years. But, with Eric, he may not be what he thought he was. And, as if you hadn't guessed, it has something to do with you!'

I swallowed, feeling a little uncomfortable. 'Has he said that to you?'

'No, but he doesn't have to; it's fairly obvious. And Miguel must be blind if he hasn't noticed Eric's more than passing interest in you. I picked it up almost immediately. He might be able to get it up for a man, but he's thinking about you while he does it!'

'God, that's disgusting, Robert! But I know for a fact that you're wrong. Miguel told me that Eric's never been with a woman before I came along. He's only ever been attracted to men. I'm sure he finds it strange suddenly to have a girl around, when he's only ever lived with

Miguel. He's probably just curious about our relationship,' I said, trying to convince myself as well as Robert.

'No, you're wrong. Trust me on this one: he's not gay. But I don't understand why he's never even tried it with a woman. I accept that heterosexual people living in an all-male environment will sometimes have homosexual relationships. You just have to look at what goes on at public school, prison and the armed services to see that. But, with Eric, it's a completely different story. He knows loads of people; he's really popular. Every time he goes to the beach he creates a stir. He's had plenty of opportunities with girls, but has never wanted to take advantage of them.

'I think he's either bisexual, not particularly drawn one way or the other; or, for some reason, he's fought shy of women in the past. Perhaps he's scared of them. Either way, you have come crashing into his personal life without any warning while his barriers were down. You're beautiful, sexy; but more to the point, you're not unlike Miguel and Eric – totally laid back about everything. It had to be someone like you, to have made an impact. Strong enough for him to explore it further, in spite of his love for Miguel; strong enough to overcome any fears or phobias he might have had about the female sex. Miguel had better watch out!'

'Eric couldn't possibly come between us – there's no question of it. I love Miguel more than anything,' I answered, more than a little irritated.

Not wishing to delve any deeper into why I was feeling quite so irritated, I abruptly changed the subject.

Miguel and Eric rejoined us after about half an hour. They had located his sister and their friends, and they had invited all four of us to join them later for a party. Miguel asked us if we would like to go.

Robert was all for it; I tentatively agreed. The prospect of meeting Miguel's sister again, after our last encounter, made me cringe.

I kept thinking about Robert's comments. He had

obviously noticed Eric giving me attention, which only made me more aware of it. Even when they had returned to the table, I was conscious of both Miguel and Eric looking at me before they directed their attention to Robert. For Miguel to do so was perfectly understandable; he loved me and his eyes told me so. But Eric; why did he seek me out in preference to anyone else? There was nothing between us.

We spent a couple of hours in one of the town's museums, which was devoted to modern figurative sculpture. It had works by over a hundred different artists on display. My favourites, perhaps predictably, were the works of Charles Despiau – a series of nudes, including Apollo and Eve.

We strolled through the old town, back to the cars. There was a bullfight taking place in the town arena which I didn't care to watch, although Miguel assured me that the bull would not be harmed.

So, as it was going to be several hours before the party was underway, we decided to go back to the house to get changed.

I wanted to make an effort this evening. I had virtually lived in a T-shirt since I had been here and I did have a lot of nice dresses.

I washed and dried my hair, then put on a silk shift dress, light blue in colour and almost matching my eyes. It was well cut, accentuating my curves, and, finishing just half way down my thighs, it showed off my long legs.

I left my hair loose, then put on a pair of high-heeled mules. They made me taller than a lot of men, but not *my* men. By the time I had finished, even I could see that I looked striking.

I sat in the salon and waited for the others to come down; they were taking turns in the bathroom.

Miguel came down first. He was wearing black jeans and a silver grey T-shirt. It was tight, accentuating his biceps, hard chest and stomach. His hair was tied back into a pony tail. He looked drop-dead gorgeous.

He sat down beside me. 'You look absolutely stunning,' he said quietly.

Eric walked into the room, lit a cigarette and sat down opposite us. His eyes ran over me too but, of course, he didn't say anything. He was wearing faded jeans, a denim shirt and his blond hair loose. He reminded me of Brad Pitt in *Legends of the Fall*.

When Robert came into the salon, we all stood up to go. We decided to take just one car, the Porsche, as it had four seats, even though it would be a tight fit in the back. Miguel would have to sit in the front, being the biggest, and, as Robert would obviously be driving, Eric and I would have to sit in the back.

It was getting dark as we set off. As well as the onset of night, grey storm clouds were gathering in the sky. We were in for some torrential rain; I just hoped that it wouldn't spoil the party.

Eric and I climbed into the back seat. I had nowhere to put my legs, so I had to sit at an angle facing Eric. He was six feet tall and looked totally cramped with his legs half across my seat. I had no choice but to put my legs on top of his, but he didn't seem to mind. I was glad that it would only take about half an hour to Mont de Marsan.

When we neared the town, Miguel directed Robert to a campsite. There were hundreds of people milling around, far more than had come to my place. I realised that they had joined up with other travellers.

Miguel virtually had to pull me out of the car; there was no room to manoeuvre myself off Eric's lap and he couldn't budge until I was off him.

Once on my feet, I felt the ground actually pulsing with the music, sounding more like rave than flamenco. Miguel put his arm around me and we followed the sound.

The atmosphere was fantastic. So many young people,

bent on having a good time.There were tables laid out with bottles of wine and Miguel handed us some glasses. Equipped with our drinks, we walked into the throng.

Robert and I danced for about two hours while Miguel and Eric just went around talking to people. I was really sweating, even though it wasn't that hot, and I was relieved when they stopped the music and cleared a space in the middle of the dancing area.

A Spanish band, *mariachis* I supposed, started to play; and a stunning woman in a long red dress started to dance flamenco. It was Miguel's sister.

She danced for about twenty minutes, simply because every time she stopped, they cheered, clapped and whistled for her to continue. She was dripping with sweat and completely breathless, but she went on and on. She was fantastic and they all loved her.

I had to admire the way in which all these young people had become suddenly subdued and appreciative of their own culture and heritage, obviously enjoying every minute of what had to be the antithesis of rave.

The moment she had finished, and she walked away from the centre, the music started up again.

I had seen Miguel go to his sister, and I saw him bringing her towards me. I smiled, thankful that it was quite dark and she wouldn't see my blushes, and she returned my smile. When she reached my side, she took my hands and kissed me warmly on both cheeks.

She spoke to Miguel in Spanish and he translated it for me. 'My sister is happy that you have made me happy. I've talked about you for years and she was worried about me living a fantasy, waiting for you. She is relieved that you are no longer a figment of my imagination!'

I laughed. 'Why don't you tell her that you weren't the only one with the fantasies? She won't believe it if you say that I became fixated with your photograph, long before we ever met.'

He relayed my words, but she didn't laugh; she just

nodded her head and said something more in Spanish. 'She's not at all surprised. We were meant to be together. Gypsies believe in fate and that our lives are mapped out for us from the very beginning. You seeing my picture was all part of the plan. When you saw me in the flesh you felt drawn to me; you felt you knew me although we'd never met. It was destiny.'

'And you believe that too, do you, Miguel?'

'Yes, I do.The first time I ever saw your face, I knew that when you grew up, you would be mine. Do you honestly think I would have waited around for you all these years, if I hadn't known our meeting was inevitable?'

'I don't know. And I don't know whether I believe it or not. I just know that I felt very strange when I met you. But what about Eric? Where does he fit in?'

'Eric's destiny is linked with ours. But he will have to decide whether to follow it or choose another path. He may not be satisfied with what fate has allotted him,' he answered, his brow furrowed into a frown.

A little bit spooked by his words, I left Miguel with his sister and went to find Robert. Sometimes Miguel was so intense he frightened me.

Robert was dancing in the midst of a crowd probably ten years younger than him. He didn't care; he was having a brilliant time. I could tell by his face.

I wandered off, initially looking for some wine, but seeing that I had come into the actual camp site, where all the caravans had parked up, I strolled around, just being nosy.

Suddenly a hand was placed on my shoulder. It was a strange man between twenty-five and thirty-five years of age. He spoke to me in Spanish so I didn't understand him, but I did understand the look in his eyes.

He then spoke to me in a French dialect which I just about grasped. 'Are you looking for something or someone?'

'Neither,' I replied quickly. 'My boyfriend's over there.'

I nodded in the direction of the crowds, but he must have seen the panic in my eyes.

'Well, let's move away from him then, shall we?' he said, laughing.

He took my wrist and pulled me behind one of the caravans. I tried to pull his fingers off me but I couldn't. He just laughed again, holding me even tighter.

All I could think about was if Miguel could see this he would go ballistic. And I didn't want any trouble, or to cause him any trouble, with his people.

Looking at the man's face, he was obviously drunk. I supposed that he was not unattractive, in a dark way like Miguel, but this man was no taller than me, although he was built like a brick shit house.

He pushed me against the side of the caravan and attempted to kiss me. I just turned my face away, which only made him more excited. He slipped his hand behind my back and grabbed hold of my arse.

I didn't believe that I was in any real danger at this point; certainly I didn't think he would go as far as raping me, with all these people milling around. But when he began to feel my breasts roughly with his other hand, it suddenly occurred to me that he was probably too drunk to care. I decided that I had no choice but to kick him in the balls and make a run for it.

Then I saw Eric, nonchalantly strolling along in my direction. Our eyes met. I knew he had taken in the situation and I silently pleaded with him to help me. I hoped that he would rush up to the guy, pull him off me and beat him up; I was sure Miguel would have done. But what he did took me by complete surprise, and was probably far more effective.

'There you are! I've been looking for you everywhere. I'm sorry, has my sister been leading you on? She's a fucking cock-teaser. She does this all the time,' Eric said to the man, with feigned irritation. 'Come on. Dad's waiting for you. He wants you to help us pack up. We're going.'

The man, having been surprised by the interruption, had taken a step back at the mention of the word 'sister'. He looked at Eric, then back to me again; our uncanny likeness apparent to him even in his drunken state. He mumbled an apology, probably thinking I was actually younger than I looked, and walked quickly away.

I was overwhelmed with relief and genuine gratitude. 'Eric, thank you. That was really quick thinking of you. How did you know I was here?'

'Miguel asked me to keep an eye on you. I saw him take you away and I knew what was on the cards. It's not exactly quick thinking though; I just know the way their minds work. If I had said I was a boyfriend, it would have turned into something. But anything to do with family, they respect; it's very important to them. He would have been happier to force himself on someone's girlfriend than on someone's sister because he would have had to suffer the consequences – most of us having very large families.'

Understanding what he had said, I nodded. 'But you don't think he was really going to harm me, do you? I mean, he was pissed out of his head.'

'So what? Come on, Katie; look at them. You and I are the only blond people here out of, what, maybe two hundred people? You stand out a mile because you look so different. Of course he was going to "harm" you; not deliberately, but he wouldn't have taken "no" for an answer. Lots of men here would be doing the same thing given half a chance. So, no more wandering off. Stick close to Miguel or me.'

I fell in step beside him as we made our way back to the party. I stayed within several feet of Miguel for the rest of the evening, having taken on board what Eric had said.

But I was glad that it had been Eric and not Miguel who had got me out of the situation. He had been cool, calm and collected, because he was not emotionally involved.

I couldn't help but feel that if Miguel had come across me, with that man, his hands touching me, all hell would have been let loose and someone would have been seriously hurt. Miguel, as he had already admitted to me, could not control his feelings.

I looked across at Eric talking to Robert, both completely laid back with glasses in their hands, and realised that, like me, Eric stood out a mile.

It was strange because, in England, Miguel would have caused a stir anywhere, with his Latin lover looks that English girls dreamt about but seldom saw except at the cinema.

Eric and I would be by no means out of the ordinary; most of my friends were some shade of blond. But here, among all these swarthy dark people, with his flaxen hair, his piercing blue eyes and his height, Eric *was* a Viking!

I wondered how he came by his looks. I took mine from my mother; my father had been dark. But Miguel had told me that Eric was a Gypsy. He couldn't have looked less like one.

And as I was thinking this, Eric looked up and ran his eyes over the crowd until they landed on me. He didn't smile at me, but his eyes stayed with me, while he chatted to Robert almost inattentively.

I felt my heart quickening under his gaze and, almost petulantly, I turned my back on him.

Just after one o'clock in the morning, the heavens opened. Within seconds everyone was absolutely drenched. There was a mass exodus to the caravans and vehicles, and I presumed it was the end of the party.

Miguel grabbed my hand and we ran towards Robert's car. Eric and he were already there. We all looked like drowned rats.

Robert wasn't particularly keen for us to get in on to his leather seats soaking wet. 'For fuck's sake, Robert.

What do you expect us to do? Stand here all night until the sun comes up and dries our clothes off?' I snapped angrily although I could see his point; we were going to wreck a couple of grands' worth of leather.

'No. You can do what I'm going to do or get yourself another ride,' he answered, just as cross with me.

He peeled off his shirt and jeans, threw them into the boot of the car and jumped into the driver's side.

Eric and Miguel did the same, leaving me standing there like a lemon. I had to do likewise or Robert would leave me behind. I knew what he was like when he was in a mood.

I quickly unzipped my dress, dropped it into the boot and closed it. Miguel got out of the car so I could squeeze into the back, feeling very self-conscious in just my bra and knickers.

Thank God it was dark, and I couldn't see their amused expressions.

As before, I had no choice but to lay my bare legs across Eric's. I was glad he was wearing boxer shorts though; I didn't fancy being so close to him if he were naked.

Miguel directed Robert back on to the main road, and I sat back in the seat with my eyes closed.

About ten minutes into the journey, Eric rested a hand on my leg. I couldn't read too much into that; he had to put his hands somewhere. But then he started to slowly run them up and down my thighs, actually stroking them.

I couldn't say anything, not with Miguel sitting in the front, totally oblivious to what was happening. I just had to bite my lip and look out of the window.

His hand crept up to the top of my thigh and waited. I willed myself to breathe steadily, quietly; it was impossible. And by then Eric knew I wasn't going to stop him.

His fingers crept inside my knickers and felt my

pussy. Although I was still looking out of the window, I was now panting with excitement.

Of course, the moment he touched me, he would have known how aroused I was . . . I had never been so wet. His finger located my clitoris and he began to tease it, even as he began to chat to Miguel about people I didn't know, whom they had met that night.

His boldness amazed me. The way he was nonchalantly fingering me while he was discussing the time of day with my lover. But it turned me on – incredibly.

I began to squirm in my seat, then I parted my thighs as best I could, allowing him better access. I was going to come.

A car passed us on the other side of the road, its headlights momentarily lighting the car interior. Eric was looking at me with a mocking smile on his face.

My body gave in to what my head would have denied. I was coming in great long shudders. I pushed myself hard back into the seat and groaned quietly, just under my breath, but Eric heard me. He pulled his hand out of my knickers and returned it to his lap.

And then, a few moments later, I felt the regular movement that his hand was making as his fist grazed against my calf. I couldn't see but I sensed that he was masturbating. The bastard was getting off on what he had just done to me.

His hand became quicker, his fist now banging against my leg. Suddenly he groaned; he had come very quickly.

'Are you OK, Eric?' Robert asked, looking in his rear-view mirror. Obviously he'd heard him.

'It's been a little frustrating being cramped in the back with Katie, but it's better now,' Eric replied innocently enough, but he was looking directly at me.

For the rest of the journey I looked out of the window, feeling decidedly uncomfortable in my damp, sticky knickers.

When we got back to the house, Robert took all the

clothes out of the boot and I hung them up to dry in the utility room.

'What time are you going tomorrow?' I asked Robert.

'I won't need to leave until lunchtime.'

'I'll see you in the morning then. Good night.'

Robert wished me good night; Eric gave me an impudent grin. I gave him the most withering look I could muster, then went up to bed.

Miguel was already under the sheets waiting for me.

'Did you know that Eric got me out of a horrible situation tonight? Some man dragged me off and Eric, believe it or not, saved me. He told the bloke to leave me alone because I was his sister, and the man backed off completely.'

Miguel sat up in an instant rage. 'Why the fuck didn't you tell me this before? I would have fucking killed him. Would you recognise him if you saw him again? We could go back in the morning and –'

'That's exactly why I didn't tell you earlier. Eric sorted it. There was no violence. He got me away without any incident – the best way.'

Miguel calmed down a little. 'Did the guy do anything? Did he hurt you?' he asked, almost as if he were afraid of the answer.

'No. Eric was there as soon as it started. He said he'd been watching me. I still enjoyed the party, even after that.'

'We both noticed that people were staring at you. That's why either Eric or I tried to keep an eye on you. A lot of these people don't mix with outsiders at all, and to see a girl like you walking around, with long blonde hair ... I was stupid to have taken you. Next time we go anywhere, I won't let you leave my side.'

'I think that's taking it a bit too far. It was a one-off, the guy was drunk. Anyway, it's over with. I just wanted you to know what Eric did for me.

'The other thing I wanted to say to you is that I think Eric likes me.'

'Of course he does. I knew he would when he got to know you better. He's like my brother. How can I love you so much and he not even like you?'

'No. I don't mean like that. I mean, I think he *really* likes me – physically,' I added, almost exasperated.

I was going to have to spell it out for him in a minute. For someone so intuitive, he could be incredibly obtuse.

'Yes, I know. But why shouldn't he find you attractive? We're complete opposites, but we tend to like the same things.'

'So you don't mind?' I asked, stunned by his lack of emotion.

'Does it affect the way you feel about me?'

'God, no. I feel more strongly about you than I've ever felt about anyone. I think he's attractive and I don't hate him any more. In fact, I've grown to like him. But he irritates me; I don't know why. He's laid back, but arrogant with it. Sometimes I feel like smacking him, he winds me up so much.'

Miguel laughed quietly. 'I'm glad you like each other and I'm glad you find each other attractive. It would be impossible for you to live together if you didn't. As long as it doesn't come between what we have together, I'm delighted. Good night.'

Miguel put his arms around me and kissed me. I fell asleep with his big strong arms around me and my head on his chest.

Chapter Eight

The sun was shining; it was a beautiful hot sunny day and the three of them were sitting on the terrace when I finally came down. It was Robert's last morning.

Robert got up and asked Eric to come with him; I sat alone with Miguel.

'Your agent is coming today, isn't he?'

'Yes. I'll need to talk to him about my work, so I hope it will be later, when Robert's gone.'

'Well, I'll keep out of your way. I want to make a start on the garden anyway.'

Robert and Eric were walking up from the outhouse, where they kept the bikes, with some huge boxes. Whatever was in them looked heavy.

'What are they up to, Miguel?'

'I have no idea.'

They carried the boxes into the house and I followed them in.

'Katie, I've bought you a present. I know how much you like music and it might be a while before I can come back down again with your things, so I've chosen some new stuff for you.'

He handed me a plastic bag. Inside were about twenty CDs. A lot of them were ones that I'd had in England –

Madonna's *Ray of Light*, George Michael's *Older*, Portishead's *Dummy* . . . Robert had obviously remembered my favourites and found them here. I was over the moon.

'Thanks, Robert. But you shouldn't have,' I said, smiling.

'Don't be silly. It will make you feel more at home here.'

It took Eric and Robert about half an hour to set up all my new hifi. When it was ready, Robert selected one of my all-time favourite tracks and put it on. It was Seal's 'Kiss from a Rose' and it sounded fantastic and almost unearthly after the silence we had all become accustomed to.

Miguel came in to listen. 'That's a beautiful track. I've never heard it before.'

'I bet there's loads of stuff you haven't heard, if you've cut yourself off from everything for years. I'll play some more for you later.'

We left the Seal album on and went back out to the terrace.

'It's a really good idea, Robert. I hadn't thought about getting a hifi, it wasn't on my list of priorities. But now you've bought it, I've realised how much I miss listening to music and it doesn't detract from our surroundings.'

'That would depend on what it is,' Eric said, smiling at Miguel.

It was almost a foregone conclusion that Miguel wouldn't be too keen on having the tranquillity broken. But then, if he felt like that, he could escape to his studio.

About 11.30 a.m. Robert collected his things together and packed up the car.

He shook hands with Miguel, cuddled Eric and kissed me. He seemed to be a little choked up. 'There's no point in asking if you've changed your mind and want to come back with me?' he asked quietly.

'No way. But come back soon. I'll miss you.'

Strangely enough, although I had dreaded him coming, now he was leaving I felt a lump come to my throat. It was like the final cut-off from my old life. I had severed all the ties, Robert being the biggest one.

Once Robert had left, I went back inside to play 'Kiss from a Rose' again.

I sat on a settee, shut my eyes, caressed by Seal's beautiful, rich voice. I got goose bumps every time I listened to this song anyway, but today I was vaguely aroused by it. It could have been the heat, or maybe the atmosphere; perhaps it was a combination of both.

It was almost perfect timing when two hands were placed on either side of my face and my head was tipped back. As a mouth closed over mine, I didn't want to open my eyes and spoil the moment.

As Miguel's tongue entered my mouth so tentatively, almost exploring my lips, my tongue, my teeth, I opened my eyes in surprise. His kiss seemed so different. Equally sensual, but not one of his aggressive, passionate kisses.

I was shocked to find Eric kissing me, but I didn't push him away. I was mesmerised by his piercing blue eyes, searing into mine.

He took my hand and pulled me up. In an instant, he had wrapped his arms around me and was dancing with me, slowly, sensually, rubbing himself against me in time to the music. I felt his erection inside his jeans.

My pussy was on fire, even though my brain kept trying to dampen the flames. What would Miguel make of this?

I turned around almost guiltily, to find Miguel standing in the doorway, leaning against the frame, a strange far-away expression on his face.

I could see that he wasn't unhappy about what we were doing. If anything he was aroused by it, judging by the bulge in his jeans. He found Eric and me attractive and, perhaps, with his artist's eye, he was studying the picture that we made together.

I was again struck by the unconventionality of these two men, and the relationship that we shared.

We continued to dance to the end of the track. Eric, placing his hand on my buttocks, was pushing me into him. His other hand had slipped up to my breast and was cupping it. His fingers stroked my nipple rhythmically in time to the music.

I was bursting with lust; I could feel myself getting wetter and wetter by the second. He was still kissing me, his tongue entering me more confidently now. How I wished it was his prick.

Suddenly Miguel straightened himself and came towards us. He had obviously had enough of watching and now wanted to take part. He stood behind me and, putting one hand on my shoulder, he slipped his other hand down to the bottom of my T-shirt. He lifted it up, exposing my breasts.

Eric now cupped both my breasts in his hands, almost as if Miguel had offered them to him.

I was panting with lust and prayed that one of them would take me – quickly! Miguel's hand moved down to my skirt. It was a loose, thin cotton skirt. He bundled it up in one hand so that I was exposed to my hips. Eric put his hand down, hooked his fingers inside my knickers and ripped them off.

Now Miguel held me by the shoulders, while Eric unbuttoned his fly and took out his prick.

It was as if they had rehearsed this, the way these two were working together. But I knew it was because they had been lovers; they knew what the other wanted, almost instinctively. Today Eric wanted to fuck me, and today Miguel wanted to watch.

Was it for art's sake? He obviously expressed his desires in his paintings. Mine were expressed in my fantasies. But my fantasies were fast becoming a reality. I suspected that his were too.

Miguel held me tight, pulling me backwards so that I was supported by his arms underneath mine. Eric put his hands on my hips and entered me quickly. It was easy for him; I was dripping wet and desperate for it.

No words were exchanged; no looks. We were following our basic instincts. I had a desire to be taken frantically; these men wanted to take me. But they would take turns.

They didn't fit into society; they didn't uphold any morals. They wanted to be themselves, as nature intended them to be. They wanted to carry out whatever they felt inclined to do, with no holds barred. I understood this now.

Eric slammed into me while Miguel held me for him. I was being ravaged by these men, carried away by their lust.

As if I were in a dream, I heard my voice filtering through the fog, groaning with relief and pleasure; wanting to be used and abused. They were bringing me close to ecstasy.

When Eric came, he withdrew from me and, without a word, took my hands. He pulled me forward, away from Miguel and kissed me on the mouth. Even while he was kissing me so gently, in stark contrast to his act of violence seconds earlier, I heard Miguel unzipping his jeans.

When Eric pulled me against him, so that my breasts were crushed against his chest and his face was buried in my hair, I felt Miguel's hands on my thighs, lifting my skirt up again; but this time to expose my arse.

I cried out in surprise as Miguel took me another way; a way I was unaccustomed to, but which felt good just the same. As he entered me, it was a fulfilling sort of pain. And with the pain came a new kind of ecstasy. Eric stifled my groans with kisses. He was being so gentle now, while it was Miguel's turn to be rough.

Eric slipped a hand down to my pussy while he kissed me. I was on the verge of orgasm anyway, without stimulation. That they were both taking me this way, so selfishly, was enough to take me to the edge.

In seconds, Eric's fingers took me over the brink. I cried out as I plunged into the deepest, longest orgasm I'd ever had. I felt Miguel shuddering, as he came too, even while I was still quivering with the aftershocks.

The three of us sat on the terrace drinking cokes. Now it was like before Robert's visit, only much better. Eric's attitude towards me had altered drastically since I had first arrived.

'OK, Miguel. Now you owe me an explanation. I want you to tell me everything you didn't tell me before. You promised.'

Eric stood up to go. Miguel put his hand on his arm to stop him. 'Sit down, Eric. It mainly concerns you, so you should be here.'

Eric sat down again, looking decidedly uncomfortable, and I wondered why.

'I told you that I have known Eric all his life, and that I had known your grandfather since I was little?'

I nodded in agreement and for him to continue.

'Well, my parents were Spanish Gypsies; they died in an accident when I was four. Eric's mother, also Spanish, had recently married a Frenchman. She decided to adopt my sister and me because my mother had been her best friend. I was seven years old when Eric came along.'

'So what does this have to do with me?' I asked.

'Well, jumping back another thirty years or so – Eric's paternal grandmother. She fell in love with an artist. He wasn't a Gypsy; they had met in a place, like yesterday – a festival.'

My blood was turning icy cold. 'My grandfather.'

'Yes, that's right.'

'When did my grandfather meet Eric's grandmother?'

'About three years after yours had died. But he didn't have a conventional relationship with Eric's grandmother. She used to come and go, preferring to live on the open road, rather than be tied to this house. She got pregnant and had a little boy, about six years younger than your mother. Your grandfather sent your mother away to boarding school so they never met. When she was old enough to understand, he told her about her brother. But she refused to accept it; it was a big shock for her. And she has resented her father ever since, for mixing with Gypsies.

'Sending your mother to boarding school didn't do him any favours. It gave her delusions of grandeur that he couldn't possibly live up to and so they drifted apart. The point of telling you all this is that your mother has a half-brother – Eric's father.'

'But that makes Eric my cousin. How the hell could you have let him come anywhere near me, put his cock anywhere near me, if you had known that? It's disgusting – it's incest . . .'

Words failed me. I felt so indignant.

But even as his words sank in, I realised that I had known all the time, deep down. Robert knew; anyone who had ever seen us together had known we were related. And I had disregarded the little alarm bells that had rung in my head from time to time.

Eric was listening to my reaction, but his face was turned away from me. I didn't know how he felt about it.

'Half cousin. It makes a difference and it's not incest. First cousins can marry legally. The thing that's incredible is that you two look so alike. You look like your mother; Eric looks like his father. It's amazing that, for all Eric's Gypsy blood and Spanish blood, he is an exact replica of his grandfather. As you are.'

'I think I need about a week to digest all this. So what happened to the Gypsies? Eric's mother and father and grandmother?'

'Eric's grandmother died years before your grandfather did. He was very sad and lonely towards the end of his life. You, Eric and I meant so much to him. Your mother had all but deserted him.

'Eric's mother and father are alive and well. They've

just turned fifty and are still on the road. We see them maybe once a year. I'm afraid I was a bad influence on Eric; I always did what I wanted as a child and he followed suit. He is not close to his family, even now, preferring to spend his time with me. But he was very fond of his grandfather. We lived with him rather than move around with the rest of Eric's family. As a consequence, we both got a good education without any disruptions.'

I looked across at Eric. He was listening intently, but his face was still turned away.

'Now I can see why you and Eric are so close. You are virtually brothers. Eric's father adopted you before he was born and you've never been separated since. And Eric hasn't had much parental influence; you and my – I mean, our – grandfather brought him up.'

And that's why he has or had an aversion to women; he never had anything to do with them, I added to myself.

'Yes, but don't get me wrong; Eric's parents were very good to my sister and me. They became our family. I was just a bit too wild for them and they left me to my own devices. But your grandfather channelled that. He saw that I was artistic and he showed me how to develop it. I loved him very much.'

'So if you have both lived with my grandfather since you were kids, how is it I never saw either of you, or he never told me about you? He must have loved you both.'

'Of course he did. But he loved you too. Your mother knew she had a Gypsy brother, but she didn't know that she had a nephew, and that Eric and his adopted brother lived here. If she had known that, she would never have allowed you to come and visit. We always knew when you were coming down; you used to write and tell him. He would pack us off to join Eric's parents for the summer. But like I told you, I often used to stay behind, hide out in the woods, just to catch a glimpse of you.'

'So does my mother know about Eric now?'

'Yes, she had a rather rude awakening at the funeral. She met Eric and her brother. She was absolutely furious that we were all there. And particularly when they read the will. Your grandfather had cut her out completely, which you couldn't blame him for, after the way she had neglected him. But he left the house to you. He told us that he was going to do this, because he wanted you to live here. As an adult, you could make your own decisions and you would want to make this your home. He was convinced of this. He felt that deep down, you were like us.

'Eric was the only one who didn't believe it and felt bitter about what he thought was his grandfather's misguided faith in you. Particularly as the years went by and you didn't show up. He thought you or your mother would turn up one day, with an estate agent and solicitor on each arm, to sell what has been his home for most of his life.

'But you've changed your mind now, haven't you, Eric?' Miguel asked him, trying to draw him into the conversation.

Eric just shrugged his shoulders.

'And your grandfather left all his money to Eric. Your mother went absolutely ballistic. He was worth a considerable amount, being a successful artist.'

'And what about you, Miguel? What did you get?'

'I got an education. He paid for me to go to art college and supported me at university. And he gave me – you. He knew I had a thing for you, even though we'd never met. And he believed in fate too. He told me to be patient and to concentrate on my work. If I became a successful artist, then the stigma of being a Gypsy wouldn't matter much as far as you were concerned.

'He was right about everything. I'm very proud of my roots, and everyone who knows my work knows I'm a Gypsy. But your mother could never turn around and say I'm freeloading; a "loser", I think, is the term you used. I have financial independence; I can look after you for the rest of your life, if you will let me. I only stayed here because your grandfather wanted me to stay. Then later, because of Eric and you.

'But I'm not surprised your mother didn't want you to come down here. She must have been worried that you would meet us sooner or later; although she doesn't know we've been living in your house.

'I have been staying here, waiting for you. Eric has been staying here, because it has been his home for most of his life, and he feels that he has a right to be here. That about sums it up, doesn't it, Eric?' Eric nodded, a little sad.

I now understood why Miguel had been so angry with me when I had made disparaging remarks about his Gypsy friends. He must have thought I was just like my mother.

But I wasn't. I was like my grandfather, drawn to Miguel's exotic, wild looks as he must have been to Eric's grandmother.

'So you aren't criminals? You aren't hiding away because you've done something awful?'

'No, I told you before – the worst thing we've ever done is continue to live in this house which isn't ours any more. And we wanted to be careful as far as you were concerned, in case you tried to kick us out before you got to know us – and the truth.

'If I had come clean with you when we first met, how was I to know that you wouldn't be horrified, as your mother clearly is, about the "Gypsy connection"? You had to be given time to grow into the relationship we now share. You would have rejected us both if we had told you straight away. There was no other way we could have drawn you into our world, except in the way we did.

'Your grandfather would have wanted it to be as it is now. The three of us – together.'

'Thank you for telling me, Miguel. But now I'd like to

be on my own for a while. I want to sort it all out in my head.'

I got up and strolled down the lawn into the trees. I sat on a fallen tree trunk for a long time, just mulling everything over.

The house was as much theirs as mine, I realised. But then, I had always felt that to be the case. My grandfather had evidently wanted me to live here; and in doing so, he would have known that I would meet Miguel and my cousin. But what sort of relationship did he imagine the three of us would share?

I was attracted to Eric – almost as much as I was to Miguel – and yet it was wrong; we were related.

I was obviously going to have to distance myself from Eric. Not because of Miguel; he would welcome any closeness between us; but because of me. I felt that it was unhealthy harbouring any thoughts about Eric, other than platonic ones. But being around him all the time, it was hard not to look at him in any other way than as an extremely fuckable young man.

Eric had not looked at me once since Miguel had begun to tell me the truth. He obviously felt uncomfortable with me knowing our connection. Maybe he was harbouring thoughts about me, in the same way as I was about him. Perhaps he, too, found them distasteful, although nobody had picked up his cock and fucked me with it. He had done that all by himself.

There was no denying that the situation was going to be very awkward, unless we kept contact to a minimum. But, on the other hand, I would not have wanted him to leave. My grandfather had evidently wanted us to live together.

The whole thing was totally bizarre. But then, so was my grandfather.

I walked slowly back to the house. I believed everything that I had been told. Just looking at Eric was enough to confirm his connection to me and the house. But I had a desire to phone my mother. I wanted to hear her reaction to the things which had been revealed to me.

I got my car keys and told Miguel I was going out for a drive. He looked up from his book, alarmed.

'I'm not going anywhere. I'll be back in an hour. I won't even take my purse if you think I'm leaving.'

'No, that's OK. I believe you. But don't be too long. I can't come with you because my agent's coming.'

I drove to the town, parked in a side street and switched on the phone. 'Hi, Mum. Robert left this morning; he will be home tomorrow.'

'You're not coming back with him?' she asked tentatively.

'No. How many times do I have to tell you? I want to live here. Besides, I've met somebody. He's moved in with me. Robert met him and they got on like a house on fire.'

'Well, if Robert likes him, he must be nice,' my mum replied, sounding relieved.

'Yes. We did lots of things – Robert, myself, Miguel and Eric.'

After my mother gasped, there was a long pause.

'Who's Eric?' she asked, eventually.

'Why don't you tell me who he is?' I retorted, in an unmistakably caustic tone of voice.

She sighed, as if with resignation. 'I suppose you must be talking about my bastard brother's son,' she retorted icily.

Wow! My mother using the B word; this was obviously a touchy subejct for her.

'So why didn't you tell me about them?'

'What should I have told you, Katie? That my father went crazy after my mother died; that he had an affair with some horrible Gypsy woman and there was a baby? Come on; you thought the world of my father; I didn't want to shatter your illusions and the whole thing was so bloody sordid that –'

' Mum, it wasn't sordid. It was love. He fell in love

with her. Can't you understand that?' I snapped, interrupting her.

'Don't talk to me about love,' my mother retorted, now snarling down the phone at me. 'I grew up knowing that my father loved his Gypsy bastard more than he ever loved me.'

She paused again, as if to recover her composure, then she went on in a more controlled voice, 'Why do you think I didn't tell you about the funeral? Because the whole clan were there, the whole time; it was awful. I found out that he had a grandson; and that he and another boy had actually lived with him for years. He must have been round the twist, bringing up a boy that wasn't even related to him and . . .

'Have they been bothering you, Katie?' my mum now demanded, sounding distinctly agitated. 'You could take out an injunction if they are. The house is legally yours. They have no claim on it; my father never married the Gypsy woman.'

'I wish you'd told me before, Mum. It would have made everything so much easier. Miguel and Eric are living with me. They may be Gypsies, but they're educated men who just want to lead a normal life.'

'Are you mad? They're just scruffy layabouts; I've seen them, don't forget. Get them out of the house; go to the police if you have to. You don't have to get mixed up with them. They only took advantage of my father because he wasn't mentally equipped to deal with them.'

There was a pregnant pause, then she spoke again, even more agitated. 'Did Robert really see them? Please God, tell me he didn't. I'd be so ashamed if he thought there was any connection.'

'For fuck's sake, Mum. What is your problem? Robert spent the whole time with them. He loves them and can't wait to get back here. Instead of spending your life worrying about what other people think of *you*, why don't you start thinking about other people for a change?

I want to spend the rest of my life here, with Miguel and Eric. I feel like I've come home.'

I disconnected the call, glad to have got it off my chest. What I had said was only how I felt; I didn't want to stay in the house without one or both of them.

My mother had verified everything that Miguel had told me, in a couple of short sentences. Not that I disbelieved him, but I had to hear for myself that my mother was aware of all the facts.

She had now dropped in my estimation to an all-time low. She hadn't even told me about my grandfather's funeral because she was ashamed of his family.

I drove back to the house. I parked the car next to a new Jeep, and walked round to the back. Miguel was on his way down to the barn with his agent. He looked back and waved at me. I was glad that he had seen me.

Eric looked up at me too, but when I didn't speak to him he turned his eyes away. I detected something in them, a flicker of a sadness or hurt, I wasn't sure which. So the cocky bastard does feel some things, I thought to myself.

Then I remembered how he had hated me when I arrived. I couldn't blame him. If he'd had the pleasure of meeting my mother, then it would not have been inconceivable for me to have been like her – a hypocrite and a snob. And he must also have felt a little jealous of me coming between him and Miguel; all those years on their own together. He knew what Miguel's intentions were, as far as I was concerned, even before we had met.

Miguel was in the barn with his agent for a couple of hours. Eventually they came out carrying pieces of work and loaded it into the jeep.They walked up and down several times, until I imagined that they had cleared out the whole studio.

'I've told him about you being a photographer, Katie. He's very interested to have a look at some of your work,' Miguel said, as soon as his agent had left.

'Really? That's great. Thanks, Miguel. So what do you do now?'

'I carry on. All I have to do is paint. I'm no good at selling myself. He does that for me. But I definitely have to go away in a few weeks' time. I'll go by bike; it will be quicker. But I hate the idea of having to leave you, now that I've just found you.'

'Well, since I love you madly and want to spend the rest of my life with you ... I'll be here when you get back!' I added, ending on a flippant note to lighten the intensity of what I was feeling inside.

The next three weeks passed swiftly by. Miguel spent much of his time painting, Eric went to Hossegor every day to teach at the surf school and, when I wasn't working on the garden, I took photographs.

Close-ups of Miguel's beautiful, expressive face: when his eyes were closed and his long black eyelashes cast shadows on his cheeks, or when his brows were knitted together into a frown of irritation ... he didn't like me taking his photo; Eric, looking like a god, riding the waves on his surfboard; Miguel, stripped to the waist, a cigarette dangling from his mouth, messing around on his motorbike.

But my favourite photos were of Eric, naked, the day I spotted him sunbathing on the terracotta-tiled roof over the kitchen. Close-ups of Eric's face – his chiselled jaw covered in corn-coloured stubble. Close-ups of Eric's body – the beads of sweat trickling down his biceps, his toffee-coloured pelvis glinting with golden hair. I'd shot off two rolls of film while he'd been asleep that morning.

Eric continued to sleep downstairs, as he had done every night, since Robert had arrived.

I hadn't said anything to Miguel, but I thought Eric and I both felt, in the light of our 'relationship', that it would be better not to put ourselves in the way of temptation. We were both aroused by one or other of us engaged in erotic, abandoned sex, and Miguel and I indulged every night in such games.

For my part, if Eric were to have laid a hand on me, I could not have guaranteed that I would not respond or even welcome his attention. Since it didn't seem right, it was easier to simply avoid him.

It was the night before Miguel had to leave to attend his exhibition and I was going to miss him terribly. But he had assured me that he was only going to be away ten days. The exhibition was being held for a week, then I had to allow two days either end for him to travel by bike. He hated flying and wouldn't even consider it.

After dinner, he surprised me by giving me an envelope. 'There's some money in here, just in case anything should go wrong with the house while I'm away.'

I thanked him, glancing inside. It looked to be about £5,000 in French francs. 'If you need anything else, Eric will help you and I'll sort it with him when I get back. I've told him he's to look after you. He's not to go to the surf school until I get back. You're miles from anywhere and if you fell down the stairs and broke your leg, or cut yourself on one of your gardening tools, there would be no one to help you. I trust Eric implicitly.'

Miguel and I had a bath together, then went into the bedroom. I asked him to close his eyes and stay standing. I got out the pair of handcuffs that we used sometimes and walked towards him. He still had his eyes shut, so I took his wrist and put it behind his back. I slapped the handcuff on quickly and, as he opened his eyes in surprise, I secured the other one.

'I don't want you to leave me so I'm going to keep you here.'

'You can't. I don't want to go, you know that; but they're expecting me.'

'Stop talking, Miguel. I've made up my mind.'

He sighed, but his erection spoke all the words I needed to hear. I pulled his head down to me and kissed him on the mouth. His tongue searched mine, hungry for more.

I ran my fingers all over him, committing every muscle, every sinew to memory. I stroked his beautiful face, lit up by the nearby candle, before I knelt on the floor in front of him.

I ran my tongue over the end of his cock while my fingers stroked his balls.

He groaned, flexing his pelvis forward, for me to take him in my mouth. But I didn't; not then anyway.

My tongue continued to dart back and forth over the end of his prick for several minutes. I tasted his sweet nectar, like a glistening pearl on the tip of his cock; then I took it in my mouth, all the way.

I moved my head backwards and forwards, working over every inch of his shaft. He was groaning softly as he plunged deeper and deeper into my mouth.

I felt the tip of his prick change shape, becoming thicker, more engorged, as he was coming close to orgasm.

I heard him trying to pull his wrists out of his handcuffs, to no avail. I knew he wanted to grab hold of my head, to control it and guide my movements like he had on other occasions. But tonight he would not be allowed; I was in control.

I felt his muscles spasming, so I slowed down, my lips grasping and feeling every contour of his shaft. I took him in as far as I could. He was hitting the back of my throat as he came.

The salty sweet liquid in my mouth was his leaving present to me. I savoured the taste, as I savoured everything about him. This would have to satisfy my thirst until he came back. Then I let him go.

Although it was a hot sultry night, he held me all night long.

He woke me up early and said he was leaving. I got up too and went downstairs with him.

He was dressed in black bike leathers with his hair in

a ponytail. He looked stunning and I imagined all the women that would be lusting after him while he was away. But I wasn't worried. He was too intense, too focused on me, to even notice anyone else.

He kicked Eric in the arse to wake him up. They gave each other a brotherly hug, then a Gallic kiss on both cheeks. Then he left.

I watched him pull away on his Bimota. He didn't wave; he just nodded his head in acknowledgement.

I went back into the kitchen. Eric was filling the kettle, wearing just a pair of jeans. 'So, Katie. What are we going to do without Miguel for a whole week?'

His tone had been heavy with innuendo, so I gave him the most withering look I could muster.

I worked in the garden; he sat on the terrace reading Bernard Werber's *Empire of the Ants*. Lunchtime, we ate together, mainly in silence.

Whenever I looked at him, he was smirking, as if he were enjoying some private joke. He was irritating me without having to say a word.

In the evening I had a bath and afterwards, wearing a T-shirt and pair of knickers, I came back downstairs to sit in the salon. I played some CDs while we both read our books. I had now read every book that I had brought with me, bar one – *Women On Top*. I kept it on my lap, so he couldn't see the cover; he could speak English so more than likely he could read it too. Eric smoked the occasional cigarette, but we still didn't talk.

About ten o'clock I announced that I was going up to bed. He got up too and said he would lock up, then have a bath. I just nodded and said good night.

Alone in the room, I was overwhelmed with longing for Miguel. We had been together every night for weeks.

I was just falling asleep when Eric opened the bedroom door and turned on the overhead light.

'For fuck's sake, Eric. Did you have to do that?' I said, covering my eyes until they were accustomed to the light.

I sat up in bed, wondering what was the matter. As I did so, the sheet fell away, revealing my breasts. I pulled the sheet up around me and looked at him questioningly.

His eyes looked me over, then caught sight of the handcuffs on the bedside cabinet. He laughed, turned the hall light on, then turned the bedroom light off.

'Sorry. I didn't think you'd be asleep already.'

Instead of leaving the room, he came to my side of the bed. He dropped the towel that was wrapped around him to the floor, then he pulled back the sheets to get in beside me. As he did so, I saw his huge erection.

'Eric, what on earth do you think you're doing? You sleep downstairs now, remember?'

'No, not any more. Miguel gave me strict instructions that I was not to leave your side. And he didn't want you to sleep up here on your own. Perhaps he was worried about fire or something, I don't know,' he added sarcastically. 'Anyway, I'm only doing what he asked me to do and I wouldn't dream of provoking him. Would you?'

I didn't answer him, but moved over so that he could lie down beside me. I could well believe that Miguel had asked him to sleep with me. But I was irritated that he had taken my side of the bed – although they were probably not the thoughts I should have been having, at this particular moment.

He lay on his back. I was on my side facing him. I felt like smacking him, but I didn't know why.

He shut his eyes so I thought he was trying to sleep. I started to relax, my eyelids began to get heavier and, minutes later, I dozed off.

I was woken up by a hand between my legs. I didn't know how long it had been there, but I had obviously rolled on to my back in my sleep. For a moment I didn't react, but I could feel that Eric was now on his side, leaning over me. He was busy running his hands over my thighs, my breasts; he was even exploring my pussy.

'Eric, for fuck's sake get your hands off me. What are you playing at?' I demanded angrily.

He seemed startled that I had woken up, because he jumped almost guiltily. But he answered me in a husky voice that I'd never heard before. 'I want you so much it hurts. Can I fuck you?'

His words aroused me even as his hands had made me angry. 'Forget it. We're cousins. We can't be like that together. Not now. And besides, there's Miguel. I love him.'

'I love him too, but I think he wants this to happen or he wouldn't have asked me to sleep with you. He's not stupid; he would have known this was on the cards.'

'Eric, I can't. Leave me alone and go to sleep.'

'No. I can't either.'

He leant across the bed and, before I realised what he was about, he had slapped the handcuff on my wrist. 'It was so thoughtful of you to leave these out for me. They're going to come in useful,' he quipped sarcastically.

He rolled on top of me and took hold of my other hand. I tried to break free from him but I couldn't. He was too strong for me. He handcuffed my other wrist and now I was restrained with my hands in front of me.

I continued to try to wriggle out from under him, getting more and more aroused with each moment that passed. 'I hate you, Eric. Just leave me alone.'

Even as I spoke, he had pulled my legs apart with his hands and had pushed his prick between my thighs. I tried hitting him with my two fists, bound together, but he just laughed.

And then he felt my pussy. It was dripping wet with excitement. And then he knew. I wanted him. At that moment, more than anything.

He took his cock in his hand and pushed himself inside me. I was still struggling, God knows why, and he just laughed at my futile efforts.

He slipped his hands underneath me and grabbed me by the buttocks. He held me still while he plunged into me, deeper and deeper with every thrust. I heard myself groaning with relief or pleasure, I didn't know which, and he kissed me on the mouth very roughly.

He was just using me, I realised, like he used men.

But then he spoke to me; and when he spoke, I knew it was different. 'I love you, Katie. I used to hate you but now I love you. I wish you could be as nice to me as you are to Miguel. I wish you could just give me a little of your love. Then I'd be happy too.'

He squeezed my arse so tight that it hurt. He plunged deep and hard, shuddering with his climax. When it was over, he didn't get off me and he didn't let go of my arse.

'Get off me, you bastard. You've done what you wanted so now let me sleep.'

'You wanted it as much as I did. But now I just want to lie on you and smell your hair, your skin . . . It's the first time I've been totally alone with you and I want to relish the moment.'

'So – how do I rate compared with the others?' I couldn't resist asking.

'Far more exciting. Far more beautiful. I find men a little boring. With you, it's hard work; a challenge. I want you to love me. I want you to feel about me as I do about you.'

'Eric, that's not going to happen. And what we've just done is immoral, so it won't happen again,' I answered resolutely, as much for my benefit as his.

'That's OK. I know you want me even if you don't like me. And how long do you think you can wear those handcuffs for? They're staying on until you're nice to me.'

He withdrew from me and rolled to one side.

'And I know for a fact you would do anything when you're in bondage. You get a kick out of it. I watched you in the barn that day, with Miguel. Do you know that, if I hadn't walked out, he was going to tell you to give me a blow job? You would have done it too. We both know it. So don't lay down rules for me, someone who loves you, when you've probably shagged complete strangers before now.'

'Do you mind? I've never slept with anyone other than Robert, before I met Miguel and you,' I retorted, somewhat primly.

He burst out laughing. 'Well, you're very broad-minded, for someone so – so virginal! But I guess that when you've had Robert, a latent homosexual, Miguel, a deviant, and now me –'

'– Yes? And what about you?' I snapped, interrupting him. 'You hadn't even been with a girl before I came along.'

I noticed that Miguel's sister hadn't been added to my small, but nonetheless diversifying list. Miguel evidently didn't share everything with him.

'I guess you could say I was suffering from a delusion. But I'm much better now.'

'Well, I'm pleased to hear it. I'd hate to think that you put me through all that for nothing.'

He rolled away from me and sighed with exasperation. I hoped that my last comment had hit him where it hurt.

But I couldn't help wishing that he had made me come, like he had in Robert's car a few weeks ago. Lying next to him in the bed was very frustrating.

I was rudely awakened in the morning when he stood up, selfishly taking the sheets with him. 'Jesus, you look beautiful,' he said, quite seriously.

'So now take these fucking things off me; they're hurting me. I've got no blood going to my hands.'

'No, I'll take them off you when you beg for me to fuck you. Not before. Get up and I'll make you some breakfast.'

Sighing with irritation, I sat up in the bed, swung my

legs over the side and stood up. I went to the bathroom and he followed me in. He watched me nonchalantly while I sat on the toilet.

'If you climb into the bath, I'll wash you,' he said, with a wry smile.

I needed a wash anyway, so I did what he said. But instead of filling up the bath, he slid me down to the running water, washed me between my legs and splashed my face for good measure. He was taking the piss out of me and thoroughly enjoying every minute of it.

'Now, if you get out, I'll help you clean your teeth.'

Without a word I stood up. He helped me out of the bath, wrapped a towel round me and spread some toothpaste on to my toothbrush. Like a baby, I opened my mouth for him to clean my teeth. When I spat it out, I spat it in his face.

He just laughed and washed it off with tap water.

He took the towel away from me, washed his prick in the sink and cleaned his teeth. His familiarity was almost insulting.

He took my arm and led me downstairs. 'I don't want you to fall down and hurt yourself, so that you moan about it for the rest of the week,' he said, by way of explanation. He led me out to the kitchen.

'Would you mind getting me some clothes? I'm not going to sit here all day with nothing on.'

'Yes, you are. There's only you and me here. I've seen it all before so what's the big deal?'

I shrugged my shoulders but declined to answer. I didn't want him to know that he was making me very, very angry.

He walked me out to the terrace and sat me on a chair. 'Wait there and I'll bring you out some coffee.'

A few minutes later he came out with a couple of mugs. He sat down next to me and lit a cigarette. After a couple of minutes he held up my cup for me to drink from it. My hair fell forward as I bent towards it and he stroked it back off my shoulders, almost absent-mindedly.

I glanced down and saw his prick, huge and throbbing with lust, then looked back to his face. He wasn't absent-minded at all.

We finished the coffees and he finished his cigarette. 'What shall we do today?' he asked, smiling. 'It's a pity you've got the handcuffs on, otherwise I could have taken you to the beach.'

I ignored him.

He reached over and slid his hands underneath my arms. He stood me up then pulled me on to his lap.

'Just leave me alone. I don't want you. Can't you get that into your thick skull?'

He put his mouth against my ear and whispered, 'Shut the fuck up!'

Then he placed his hands on my breasts and started to stroke my nipples gently. They became erect within seconds and, of course, he noticed.

'Spread your legs!'

I parted my thighs, my breathing becoming unusually rapid and my heart beating way too fast. His touch and his words had set my pussy on fire.

Still stroking my nipple with one hand, he dropped his other between my legs. He started to stroke me down there very gently, obviously feeling how wet I was.

He played with me for about ten minutes. I knew I was nearly coming. Then he stopped, just like that, and took his hands off me. He nonchalantly leant forward, got a cigarette and lit it, as if he were suddenly bored with me; as if it meant nothing at all to have a naked woman sitting on his lap, desperately wanting him.

I groaned with frustration and, squirming in his lap, hoped that I could somehow capture his prick and force it inside me. I dropped my cuffed hands down between our legs, but they just touched his balls; his cock was lying against my back. I would have to stand up to put him inside me, and even that would be difficult without full use of my hands.

'Do you want me to fuck you? You act as if you do,' he asked in an offhand manner.

'Yes, just do it now. Stop pissing about.'

'But you said you didn't want this – that you didn't want me?'

'Well, I've changed my mind. I want you to fuck me even though I hate you.'

'Well, that's a good start. Stand up!'

I stood up and he pushed me down so that I was lying across the table, bent at the waist. My arms were stretched out above my head, my breasts squashed against the cold tabletop, my buttocks – an open invitation.

Oh God, now he's going to sodomise me, I thought to myself.

But he didn't. He leant down over me and put his mouth against my ear. 'Now repeat the magic words – "Please, Eric, I'm begging you to fuck me."'

I groaned with despair. I was going to have to swallow what was left of my pride and do this for him, or he wouldn't put me out of my misery; and this sick, infuriating little game of his would go on all morning.

I repeated the words he wanted to hear, through gritted teeth. To have said that I sounded ungracious would have been an understatement. But a moment after I had said the words, he lifted me up by my hips to gain access to my pussy, then rammed his prick into me.

He fucked me violently, half lifting me on to the table with the force of it. But I was just sighing with the relief.

He ran his hand underneath me to my pussy and his fingers rubbed my clitoris while he thrust into me. I started to groan as my muscles spasmed in orgasm.

He was coming too; I felt his body shuddering as he leant over me. His mouth went down to the back of my neck and bit me spitefully as he released himself. Even as I was coming, I squealed with the pain.

'That was to get you back for spitting at me,' he said casually, withdrawing from me. 'Maybe you hate me, but you sure as hell want to fuck me.'

He was so flippant, so unromantic – so different from Miguel.

He helped me inside and back up the stairs. He got the keys to the handcuffs and removed them for me. I massaged my wrists; they were bruised.

'I'll let you explain these to Miguel,' I said, holding them up for him to see.

He shrugged his shoulders.'They will have faded by the time he gets back, but even if he were to see them I'd just say that you were being unco-operative. It's the truth and he'll understand,' he answered dismissively. 'Get dressed and we'll go to the beach. I'm going to teach you how to surf.'

Chapter Nine

I met him outside. He had brought his bike up to the house and had got out the leather jacket and crash helmet that Miguel had bought for me. Eric fastened the clasp on my helmet, then I got on the back.

I went with him to the surf school to borrow some boards because he didn't want to leave me alone on the beach. Not because he wanted my company, I realised, but because of Miguel. Miguel would never forgive him if anything were to happen to me and he knew it.

Eric was extremely patient and very attentive – while he was in the sea with me; as he was on the other occasion, in fact. But after an hour he told me to get out of the water and sit on the beach with him for a while.

I lay down on my towel and was rudely pushed to one side so he could share it with me. 'Help yourself,' I retorted.

'I think I will.'

He dropped his mouth down on top of mine and kissed me.

'How come you are so mean to me and not to Miguel?'

'Because I hate you and I love Miguel. That's the difference.'

He got off me and, sitting up, lit a cigarette. 'Be

careful. I'm more easy-going than Miguel, but you can't push me too far.'

I closed my eyes and sunbathed, trying to forget that he was beside me, his leg against mine, his hair stroking my shoulders. It was difficult.

I must have dozed off. When I woke up I was alone. I panicked for a moment, thinking the bastard had taken offence and left me.

But then I spotted him surfing; the crowd watching him was a dead giveaway. And I felt a sudden flutter of pride as I thought to myself, I've got him too. He's mine; he's not interested in anyone else and he's fucking gorgeous.

I knew that I was being greedy.

And then it suddenly occurred to me how lucky I was, to be loved in different ways, by two men. Both young, big and strong. One or both of them could be around me for the rest of my life, looking after me. Incredibly good-looking and incredible in bed.

What more could I want, any woman want, come to that, out of life? They both had money, more than we would probably ever need; and I had the house.

What a team we could make, if this were permitted. If we allowed ourselves to go through life in this bizarre threesome.

It was what my grandfather wished for, I had no doubt. And if it was all right by him, who knew the circumstances, then surely it had to be all right by me?

Eric came out of the water and dropped down beside me.

'When I woke up, I thought you'd left me,' I said reproachfully.

'Why would I want to do that?' he answered, frowning.

'I don't know. I thought I'd pissed you off.'

'You do piss me off – all the time.'

He didn't say any more, so I rolled on to my stomach to sunbathe.

After about half an hour, he said, 'Let's get some lunch. There's a bar near the surf school we could go to, then before we go home this evening we could eat at the Italian place.'

I slipped my jeans on over my bikini, but stuffed my T-shirt into my bag. It was too hot to wear it. We walked off the beach and into the town.

I couldn't help thinking that, if Miguel had been with me, we would have held hands walking along.

Eric needed only a sexual relationship and any physical contact we had reflected this. His kiss was just foreplay. He didn't want to belong to me; he didn't want me to belong to him.

I had seen his underlying passion, but it was masked by this off-hand, couldn't-care-less attitude. I realised that we treated each other almost like brother and sister and that was part of the problem. We were too familiar, too inattentive, because we felt comfortable with each other. We felt – related.

Miguel, on the other hand, was openly affectionate and incredibly possessive in public. Anyone watching us would have had no doubt that we were lovers.

Eric took me to a café bar full of young people. Judging by their appearance, they were mainly surfers.

Eric greeted practically everybody there. They all knew him. We sat down at a table and he introduced me to a couple of his acquaintances. They joined us for lunch.

'There are a lot of girls here who are going to be really pissed off with you. They make a beeline for Eric because he makes out like he's gay and not interested. If he's got you at home, I don't blame him,' one of his friends said.

I smiled and thanked him for the compliment.

Eric has a big mouth, I thought to myself. God knows what he's told his friends. They obviously think we're together. But then, if we're sleeping together, we *are* together.

I had a tuna salad; Eric had a baguette. He spared me little attention, talking animatedly to his friends. And, as Robert had already pointed out to me, he was obviously very popular.

So different from Miguel, I mused. Eric, although content to live in peace and quiet with Miguel, needed other people. Miguel avoided contact with anyone, if he could.

I remembered Robert's thoughts on Eric's sexuality. He was right about one thing: he'd certainly had plenty of opportunities to have relationships with girls, judging by the hostile glances I was getting.

Towards the end of the meal, a good-looking boy walked into the café. I saw him look at Eric, then at me. His eyes narrowed – obviously he disliked me for some reason – then he turned away.

Eric paid the bill, then told me to wait while he went to the toilet. The boy looked up, saw Eric walking into the loo and followed him in.

I realised that something was going on. I had the urge to go to the toilet myself, just to spy on them, then thought better of it.

They were in there some time. Eric came out first, nonchalantly walked over to me and picked up our stuff. 'Let's go,' he said flippantly.

As I stood up, the boy came out of the toilet. He looked actually distressed, as if he'd been crying. I was completely baffled.

Outside I asked Eric what had gone on. 'The guy's a complete pain in the arse. He used to follow me around like a lovesick schoolboy. He's upset that I've come in here with you.'

'Why? Is he gay?'

'Yes.'

'Did you ever . . .?'

'Yes. Just to get him off my back. But it had the opposite effect.'

'Eric, that's awful. How can you use people like that?'

'Because some people want to be used.'

'And do you enjoy it? I mean, Miguel said that you've been with several men. Do you prefer it with men or women?'

He looked at me for a moment, slightly irritated by my directness, I thought. 'I prefer it with you and Miguel. Does that answer your question?'

'Not really.'

He took my hand and we crossed the road, declining to make any further comment.

On the way to the beach, we passed Quiksilver. Apart from the surf boards in the window, they had some really nice T-shirts and shorts. I asked Eric if we could go inside.

The shop was equally divided into men's and women's clothes. I picked up a couple of T-shirts, a pair of dungarees and some Lycra shorts that I wanted to try on.

'Eric, will you wait while I try this lot on?'

He nodded, looking through the men's T-shirts.

I went into a changing cubicle and took off my jeans. I was going through each item that I'd picked up, when Eric stuck his head over the door to watch me. I ignored him and continued to try everything on.

'I like all of it. Which ones do you think I should buy?' I thought that I may as well ask him since he'd seen them all on me.

'Buy the lot. If you're staying here, you'll use them.'

'I can't buy everything, silly.They're quite expensive and I can't afford it. I haven't got all my money over from England yet.'

'I'll buy them for you.'

'No, you don't have to do that. I'll just take this T-shirt, these shorts and –'

Eric opened the cubicle door and scooped up the lot. 'Get dressed. I'll go and pay for them. I want to buy some stuff anyway.'

I couldn't argue with him because he had already

walked up to the counter. I slipped on my jeans and joined him. 'Thanks, Eric,' I said, as he handed me the bag. 'How are we going to carry it home on the bike?'

'We'll manage.'

We spent several more hours on the beach and, at about six o'clock, we packed up all our things. Eric had stuffed our clothes into each of our backpacks, and had discarded the thick carrier bags we had been given in Quiksilver.

He picked up both the surf boards and we dropped them off at the school before we headed for the restaurant. I had been here a couple of times now, with Miguel, Eric and Robert too; but never alone with Eric.

We sat out on the terrace overlooking the beach as usual, and watched everyone having a good time while we waited for our pizzas.

Something on the beach suddenly caught my eye. There seemed to be a commotion going on. One of the lifeguards, who seemed to spend every day flexing his biceps and sunbathing, was currently leaping around and blowing his whistle.

'Look over there, Eric. What do you think's happening?'

He looked in the direction that I was pointing, then suddenly jumped up. 'Wait here; I'll be back in a minute.'

He raced across the road, ran down to the beach and talked to the lifeguard, who was now pointing out to sea.

I watched in absolute amazement as Eric ripped off his T-shirt and jeans, then dived into the huge breaking waves and disappeared from view.

I began to get quite concerned. Not only because he hadn't come up for air, but because, if he drowned, I would be all on my own. I was shocked at my selfishness.

And then I saw him. He seemed to shoot up out of

the water and go back down again, under another wave. I had to acknowledge that he was an excellent swimmer.

The lifeguard was still blowing his whistle, getting everyone out of the water. I hoped that there wasn't a shark or something. Eric was too beautiful to end up mauled and disfigured by some big monster. But I would have looked after him if he was.

I decided it was best not to analyse this reaction.

Then I realised that a group of people were consoling someone. It was a woman who looked to be absolutely hysterical. The lifeguard was now going into the water too, obviously helping Eric to look for whoever.

A helicopter came over the beach and hovered, searching. The lifeguard must have called for help. I was now praying that Eric would be all right.

And then Eric's head appeared out of the water and I was overwhelmed with relief. As he strode unsteadily through the breaking waves, I saw that he had somebody in his arms. A couple of people rushed out to take the burden from him. It was a little boy. He had been under the water for maybe some time.

They laid him down on the beach and someone tried to give him mouth to mouth. Eric stood there for a moment watching, then he pushed the guy to one side.

Eric knelt down over the kid and I saw him massaging the child's heart, then giving him mouth to mouth resuscitation. Even from across the road, I saw the child suddenly shudder. Eric rolled him to one side and the child seemed to cough.

There was a cheer on the beach and a cheer outside the restaurant. I had been so absorbed in Eric that I hadn't even noticed the crowds and the traffic at a standstill.

At that moment some ambulance crew arrived on the beach. They patted Eric on the shoulder and he stood up, making way for them to take over.

The woman, whose child it obviously was, threw her

arms round Eric in gratitude. He removed them kindly but evidently embarrassed by the fuss.

I watched him as he shook his hair, put his jeans on over his wet body, picked up his T-shirt and ran up the beach, across the road to where I was sitting.

A waitress came out with a towel for him and congratulated him. The manager came out with a mug of coffee. As Eric lit a cigarette, I saw that his hands were shaking.

'Eric, you were fantastic. I really mean it. You've saved that little boy's life. But why didn't the lifeguard go in? What would they have done if you hadn't been there?'

'The kid would have drowned. All these inexperienced surfers go out on their boards. They don't look where they're going. The parents let their kids play in the waves, not keeping them away from the surfers. Sooner or later, one of them gets hit on the head. They go under, they get dragged out. The current's very strong. I just knew where to look for the kid, because I know the waves. The lifeguard can save someone from drowning but, in this particular instance, the child had to be found first, before he could be saved.'

People kept interrupting us to praise Eric. Several of them offered him free drinks.

'You must be exhausted. Do you want to stay in the town for a while, until you feel better?'

'No, I'm OK. I'd rather go home and relax. If we stay here, they won't leave us alone,' he answered, nodding at the people around us, who were still whispering about the afternoon's entertainment.

'Well, maybe we should go now, before the press get here!' I said, smiling.

A smile flickered on his face, but I could tell he was worn out.

I felt somehow maternal towards him at this moment. My usual irritation was replaced by a desire to look after him, nurture him. Very weird.

We carried all our gear to the bike. He fastened my

crash helmet for me, zipped up my jacket and put my backpack on my back. I could hardly move, weighed down with all this extra weight.

He slung his backpack over his shoulders, took the bike off its centre stand, then I climbed on the back. It wasn't dark, being only 6.30 p.m., but he took it slowly. We arrived back at the house at sunset.

We dropped all our stuff in the salon, then it occurred to me that Eric's hair was still wet.

'You must be really cold. Do you want me to run you a hot bath?'

He nodded and wheeled his bike down to the outhouse.

He came in, stripped off his clothes in the utility room because they were damp and salty, then walked slowly upstairs.

I heard him get in the bath, drain off some water because there was probably too much in it, then there was silence.

I went into the bathroom because I needed the toilet and found him lying back in the bath with his eyes closed. He looked like a little boy . . . an angel.

As I sat on the loo watching him, I remembered my feelings about him, not much more than a month ago. I had thought him arrogant beyond belief, laid back to the point where I wondered if he cared a damn about anything other than himself; and I had thought him dangerous – even capable of murder.

I couldn't have been more wrong.

Eric was extremely considerate, but in a very subtle way, almost as if he were embarrassed by it and didn't want to draw attention to it. He was laid back, certainly, but by no means lazy. He worked when he wanted to, because our grandfather had given him financial independence. But far from being a murderer, he was a life saver.

On the other hand, Miguel, whom I had at first thought to be the gentler one of the two, had turned out to be the one who was totally unpredictable and potentially dangerous when in a temper.

I wasn't complaining: Miguel was exciting; living with him made me feel like I was living on the edge. But considering they loved each other like the closest of brothers, you couldn't have got two men more different.

I got off the loo and walked quietly towards the door. Eric opened his eyes just before I left the bathroom.

'What are you thinking about, Katie?'

'I was wondering why you pointed a gun at me, when you saw me in the bedroom that morning. You must have known who I was.'

'Yes, I did, but I wouldn't have shot you. You took me by surprise and I was angry that you were there. I'm not as perceptive as Miguel. I thought he was stupid, the way he set such store by you coming here. I thought you would have gone ballistic, made threats, because we were in your house. I wanted to shut you up in case you hurt him – disillusioned him. I was wrong. You're not like your mother at all.'

I nodded, then went downstairs.

He came down after a while, just to tell me that he was going to bed.

I wished him a good night, read my book for about an hour, then decided to have an early night too.

I got into bed next to Eric. I didn't know if he was asleep or not, when suddenly he spoke. 'Why don't you make love to me like I've seen you do with Miguel? Why do I have to practically rape you? I haven't got the energy tonight and it would be so easy for you.'

I leant over him and stroked his face. 'You know why. We have an expression in England – "When the cat's away, the mice do play." And that's what we'd be doing. Why start something that can't go anywhere?'

'Because it's already started. It started when I first saw you and Miguel together; and when I touched you for the first time. I can't live like this, Katie. If you can't give me anything then I'm going to have to leave. And Miguel wouldn't like that.'

'I don't want you to leave, but whenever I'm with you I feel like I'm betraying Miguel. Can't we just be friends?'

I rolled on top of him and kissed him. I had meant it affectionately, rather than anything else, but he kissed me back, almost desperately.

I decided to move away from him before things got out of hand – again.

'I can't believe what I've been missing all these years. I never thought it would be like this,' he whispered, playing with my hair.

'Why did you think you were gay?'

'Because I never found girls attractive. Thinking about it, the men I fucked were quite feminine, but they weren't like you. And I never found it mindblowingly fulfilling. I could always come, of course, but only in the same way as I could having a wank. I never felt a strong desire for anyone, until I got to know you. And when I first saw you, I hated you ... your long hair, your smooth white skin, your curves. But then I realised that it wasn't distaste I was feeling, but fear. Fear of the unknown. I had never touched a girl, never wanted to touch a girl, because I hadn't met the right one.

'I'm not jealous of Miguel; you're all he ever wanted. But day after day I have to watch you and Miguel together. It's making me very unhappy. I know I'm not what you want, but I never expected to feel like this. I don't know what to do.'

I felt incredibly warm towards him at this moment; a lump had come to my throat just listening to him express his feelings. It was all I could do to stop myself from squeezing his hand and promising him life-long devotion. But of course, I kept myself in check.

Perhaps the darkness had helped him; it was easier for him to be honest when I wasn't watching his face.

He could drop that irritating act of his and let out the sensitive boy who was hiding inside.

And Miguel and Robert had been right. He wasn't gay; he was bisexual, with a fear of the unknown. And as Miguel's sexuality was governed by the eroticism of a situation rather than the sex of a person, so Eric's sexuality was governed by the emotions he felt for a particular person. What strange men they both were!

We didn't talk any more. I dropped to one side of him and we soon fell asleep.

In the morning, it was as if the previous night's conversation had never taken place. He sat up, shook me, thinking that I was asleep when in fact I was awake, and told me to get up.

'Leave me alone. I want to stay in bed for a while. How is it that, now Miguel's away, you're bursting with energy? You're usually the lazy fuck around the house.'

'Because Miguel's away and I'm on a mission. I've got to make you fall in love with me before the end of the week. And since you hate me so much, I've got a lot of work to do.'

He pulled the covers back and half dragged me out of the bed. He was being as irritating as ever and he irritated me.

'Well, you certainly know how to win a girl's heart. With these tactics, you'd stand more chance with your beach bums,' I retorted angrily.

He just laughed at me.

I pushed his hand off my arm and stood up. He followed me to the bathroom door. 'I'm quite capable of having a piss by myself, thank you. Go and put the kettle on or something.'

When I had finished in the bathroom, I put on my new Lycra shorts and matching T-shirt, then walked out to the terrace where Eric was sitting – naked as usual.

'You didn't have to dress on my account,' he quipped sarcastically.

'Don't worry, I didn't. I'm going to have to go into town and get some bread and stuff. I also want to get a telephone line installed. What are you going to do?'

'I'm coming with you, of course.'

'Not like that, you're not. Hurry up and get ready before all the decent bread has gone.'

I realised that I had spoken to him in much the same tone as I used with my brothers. I wouldn't have dared speak to Miguel like that. I wondered if it was because Eric was my cousin.

He came down wearing a tight grey T-shirt and jeans. He hadn't shaved, but he looked stunning.

We locked up and got in my car. It was the first time he had been in it and he talked about it for a good ten minutes. Then we talked about music, our favourite films and, in no time at all, we had reached the town.

He was on a completely different wavelength from Miguel. Eric was young, like me in some ways, with similar interests. Miguel was in his own private erotic world, yanked out occasionally by one of us talking to him. I was kind of in the middle, hovering from one plane to the next, understanding where both of them were coming from.

Later in the morning, when we were on our way home, I noticed a sign on the edge of the road – PICK YOUR OWN STRAWBERRIES. I fancied some and asked Eric if he would help me pick them. He agreed, so I turned the car round and pulled up on the verge. The old woman on the stall gave us a couple of punnets and directed us on to the path, through a field of sunflowers, to the strawberry field. It was totally deserted. And scorching hot.

Eric took off his T-shirt and jeans straight away, folding them up and putting them on my handbag. At least he's wearing boxer shorts, I thought to myself.

The strawberries were beautiful, much bigger than English ones, and very ripe. Since my hands had become stained in seconds, I decided that I would follow suit and take off my new clothes too. There was nobody about and, if someone were to come, I was sure that we would see them before they saw us.

I undressed carefully and put my clothes on top of Eric's. Thankfully I had a bra on today, as well as my knickers.

We knelt down together and slowly filled our punnets. Of course, we were eating as many as we were saving. When I picked an enormous strawberry, the size of an apple and the biggest I'd ever seen, I showed it to Eric.

As I held it up, it disintegrated, covering my fingers with its red, sticky flesh. Eric immediately grabbed my hand and began to eat what was left of the strawberry.

I was stunned, actually shocked by the overtly sexual imagery. I wondered if he knew what he was doing.

I sat on my heels and watched him, mesmerised, while I felt his warm mouth repeatedly close over my palm. He had closed his eyes and I could not but imagine him eating something else – not too far away from him and equally wet with juice.

Then he put my fingers to his mouth and licked them clean, sucking the tips as he went through each finger.

Something that had started out as quite spontaneous had now become incredibly exciting. He was being so wonderfully sensual that . . . he knew exactly what he was doing to me.

I snatched my hand away and went back to picking strawberries.

A few minutes later, he stopped and said, 'Look at your legs! How could you have got in such a mess? You won't be able to get dressed or sit in your car.'

I had been kneeling down, totally absorbed in what I was doing. I looked down at myself to see what he was on about, and perceived my red-stained thighs.

I attempted to stand up but my legs had gone numb, having been sitting on them for so long. I lost my balance and fell backwards on to a strawberry plant. I felt the splats all over my back – evidently exploding strawberries; and Eric burst out laughing.

'Now look what you've made me do. I'm absolutely covered in the stuff,' I snapped, feeling a squashed strawberry dribbling down my back.

Half annoyed and half amused, I picked up a strawberry and crushed it into his chest. It had been a childish, thoughtless gesture, and I should have realised that he would retaliate.

He pushed me and I fell backwards again. This time he pinned me to the ground by my shoulders. 'Now you can lick it off or I swear I'll cover you in them.'

Looking up and seeing his face above me, his blue eyes glittering with a mixture of irritation and desire, I knew he would.

I put my mouth against his smooth, golden chest and licked the strawberry off him. Actually it tasted very sweet.

He got off me, sat down again and crossed his legs; then suddenly he grabbed me by the arms and pulled me on to his lap, my back against his chest. Lifting my hair out of the way, he started to lick my strawberry-flavoured skin.

It felt really nice, almost affectionate rather than sensual. But when he put his hands to my bra and unclasped it, I grabbed the straps and tried to do it up again.

'You've got to take it off; it's covered in strawberry juice. You'll have to put your T-shirt on instead,' he said, by way of explanation.

He was only being sensible, I told myself. But when he swivelled me round to face him, he wasn't looking at my face.

Suddenly, he tipped me back so that I was almost lying in his outstretched arms. He bent his head down towards me and, as he did so, his long blond hair fell against my naked breasts. My nipples instantly reacted to such feather-light caresses and he noticed.

Within seconds, his tongue had traced a line down from my shoulder to my erect nipple. He proceeded to lick, then suck my nipple for several minutes before turning his attention to the other one.

I looked down and saw how hard and pink they had become: a combination of Eric's teasing mouth, being exposed to the sun and air, and they were pulsing with desire.

Giving me a wicked smile, he crushed another strawberry on my breast. It was all the excuse he needed, and I needed, to be honest, for him to lick the juice; which was conveniently running down to my nipple, anyway.

I was now actually panting with lust, but for reasons I could not comprehend, I felt that I had to distract him.

'Eric, strawberries don't grow on me! Let's carry on picking them before the woman comes down and sees what a mess we've made.'

I abruptly broke away from him, stood up and turned around.

'Keep still, Katie. There's more on you. I'll have to get it off you before you put your shorts back on.'

I put my hands behind me and felt the sticky mess on my buttocks. Oh no, I thought to myself; if he does what I think he's going to do, I won't be able to resist.

Even as I was thinking this, he grabbed me by the legs to stop me moving away and began to lick the tops of my thighs. Slowly he inched down my knickers, while his tongue covered every inch of my backside, even between my buttocks. 'Please, Eric. Don't . . .'

He grabbed my hips and spun me round and, before I could stop him, he almost reverently kissed my pussy. I just sighed in resignation when I looked down at his beautiful face. His eyes were shut and his long, golden eyelashes were glinting in the midday sun; so too was the stubble on his unshaved, chiselled jaw. His pink tongue was caressing me, almost washing me, like a cat washing its kitten, and I was so overwhelmed by the image of this gorgeous man going down on me that I actually groaned out loud with pleasure.

His hands were still holding my hips, pressing me hard to his face, while his teeth nibbled and his tongue grazed my clitoris; so gently, yet so very precisely.

'If you don't stop, I'm going to come!'

He ignored me and carried on teasing, sucking, licking my clitoris, as if his very life depended on it. My whole body was shaking with the sensations he was drawing from me.

I buried my fingers in his long thick hair, relishing the attention he was lavishing on me, forcing him to stay buried in my pussy after my orgasm, until every last lingering sensation had faded away.

When I was well and truly satiated, I pushed his hands off me and moved away from him. I certainly didn't want him to think he was getting anything in return. Much as I had enjoyed it, I hadn't asked for it.

I kicked my knickers off because they were covered in squashed strawberries, put my T-shirt back on and slipped on my shorts.

Eric watched me with a mocking smile on his face. He could see I was uncomfortable with what I had allowed him to do; especially in an open field in broad daylight. But this didn't change anything as far as I was concerned. I had simply given way to a moment of passion . . . I had temporarily lost my head.

'Have you had enough strawberries now?' he asked sarcastically, holding up his half empty punnet.

'I think so,' I said lamely, not meeting his eyes. I guessed that he was feeling frustrated; it had been very one-sided.

I tipped my punnet into his, and we walked back through the fields to the old lady. I handed her the empty punnet and she charged us for the other one. She was clearly irritated. Judging by the state of us, we'd squashed far more than we'd picked.

* * *

We'd had our lunch and I was sitting on the terrace drinking a coke, when Eric came out and stood behind me.

'What, Eric? What do you want?' I asked him after a minute; he was making me feel uncomfortable – again.

'I want you to finish what you started this morning.'

'I didn't start anything. It was you, remember?'

He grabbed my hand, pulled me up and dragged me inside. 'Why do you have to make this so difficult? Miguel can just click his fingers and you do it on the spot.'

'You're not Miguel,' I quipped, giving him a bitter-sweet smile.

He let go of my hand and placed his hands on either side of my face. 'And you're never going to let me forget that, are you?' he said brusquely, squeezing my head between his hands in frustration.

When he kissed me on the mouth, I turned my face away. He retaliated by pushing me backwards into a chair. Now I had nowhere to go.

'You're a bitch, do you know that? I could hate you so easily.'

'I'd rather you hate me than what you're doing now.'

'Just shut up. I don't want to hear any more of it.'

He picked up my T-shirt and pulled it off over my head. As he pinned me to the chair, he started undoing the buttons on my shorts. Once undone, he was able to remove them quickly and easily.

In seconds, I was naked, with my legs slightly apart and the bulge in his jeans pressing against me.

I was extremely turned on – again. I didn't wait for him to get himself out. I unbuttoned his flies and pulled out his cock.

I parted my legs and he rammed his prick into me, wanting me frantically. I took what he gave me, just as frantically.

He was pushing me over the back of the chair, he was taking me so roughly. I held on to him for dear life, my nails clawing into his back. 'I hate you, Eric, for making me do this.'

'I love you for letting me do this,' he answered in a brusque voice which ended in a groan.

He shuddered in climax, literally coming as he spoke. He must have been really wound up; not just sexually, but emotionally.

He got off me immediately and, after wiping the sweat off his forehead with the back of his hand, buttoned his flies. This time there were no words, no affection afterwards. I hadn't deserved any.

We didn't talk to each other for the rest of the day.

We hadn't fallen out exactly; I didn't know what it was. But I resented Eric for the way he was making me feel about him. I was being disloyal to Miguel, who I loved more than anything.

I cooked the dinner and we ate in silence. In the evening I played some CDs, then went to bed without a word.

I knew I was hurting him, but I couldn't help it. He made me want to hurt him; to punish him for the way I felt.

He came to bed after about an hour. He lay down beside me without a word and went to sleep. I listened to his steady breathing for a couple of hours before I fell asleep. I was worried about Miguel coming back to this awful, tense atmosphere.

When I woke up in the morning, I turned over carefully, to find him already wide awake and watching me.

'I can't go on like this, Katie. I can't live with you any more – like this.'

'Why not? You ignored me for days when I arrived. You weren't that bothered about it then.'

'It's different now and you know it. You want me as much as I want you. Why do you deny it? I'm not trying to take you away from Miguel. But we could share you. You could give us both what we each need from you.'

'Don't you think that's a little sick? I mean, what would Miguel make of that? He's extremely possessive. He nearly throttled me the day I told him that Robert was coming down here.'

'He feels differently about me; I know he does. He knows we both love him. And if he were worried about you and me together, he wouldn't have left us alone, would he? Trust me on this; I know him better than you and I've known him longer. As long as we're not doing anything without his knowledge, and as long as it didn't affect his relationship with you, he would share you with me.

'Let's be honest, he finds both of us sexually attractive. We both give him what he needs, in different ways. And the prospect of us living like this, long term, the three of us, would be so exotic, so fulfilling for him, for all of us that – he would love it.'

Even as Eric talked, I remembered a conversation that Miguel and I'd had, very much along the same lines. I knew that Eric was saying what he believed, and not what he thought would win the argument.

'And what about us being cousins?' I said after a while.

He punched the water off the bedside cabinet in a sudden burst of temper.

'That's a load of crap and you know it. You're just using it as an excuse.'

As soon as he had said it, I knew it was an excuse. I had clung to it as a means of denying the attraction he held for me; for Miguel's sake as well as my own. It wasn't incest, it was allowed; and we weren't even full cousins.

'All right then, I'll try and be as you want me to be.'

He looked at me sharply, as if he had misheard me; then seeing how serious I was, his eyes lit up and his face broke into a huge grin. He looked just like a little boy who had been given the toy he had always wanted. I couldn't but laugh at his expression.

'Do you mean it? You'll let me get close to you?'
'If you like. As much as I'm able to.'
He pulled me into his arms and whispered, 'I'd like it – very much.'
As he began to fuck me, he kissed me on the mouth, passionately, gratefully.

We spent the next week in bed, on the kitchen table, on the sofa, on the grass. Not like Miguel and I; ours was an intense relationship, almost perverted. Dabbling in domination and submission; worshipping each other; escaping the real world to Miguel's private kingdom where fantasies became reality; where his pictures came to life.
Eric and I laughed, teased and argued like brother and sister. We fucked quickly, frantically, when we felt the need. He, to make up for all his lost years, I supposed. Me, because I just wanted him, as soon as he laid a hand on me.
I knew that Miguel would be arriving home tomorrow or the day after. We weren't sure. I just hoped that everything would fall into place and we could survive together – the three of us.
Eric and I drank a bottle of wine with dinner. Slightly drunk, we played some of my dance albums which Miguel wouldn't have liked, and we danced.
Hot and sweaty, we fell back on the settee and I laid my head in his lap. He stroked my hair which fell across his legs.
'I failed my mission,' he said, looking down at me sadly.
'Excuse me?' I said, laughing. 'What did you say?'
'I failed. I wanted you to fall in love with me by the end of the week and it hasn't happened.'
He saw my incredulous expression.
'Oh, I know you want me. You've been very good to me. You've given me everything. But I wanted you to love me too. I don't know if I can stick around any

longer – watching you with Miguel. I won't be able to stand it.'

I was horrified. 'Eric, you're not thinking of leaving? I don't want you to go. I want you to stay with me – with us. We can work something out. We've got to try,' I said, my voice bordering on hysteria.

'What's the point? It won't work if you don't love me. Miguel will come back and you'll forget all about this week. I know when to call it a day.'

'Don't talk like that. It's not funny.'

But seeing the sadness, the resolute look in his eyes, I knew he meant it.

'Eric, I do love you.'

As I said the words, I knew they were the truth. And so I said them again. 'I've loved you from the very beginning, even as I fell in love with Miguel. I just never showed it because I thought you hated me. And when I realised that you loved me, I was scared. Scared because I didn't know where it could go.

'I don't know how I can love two men so much, but I do. I didn't think it was possible to feel so much for Miguel, and have enough left over to love you as much. But I do.'

He looked down at me, looked into my eyes and believed me.

'God, I love you so much,' he said. Then he added, 'I don't know if I could die for you, but that doesn't matter; I'm sure Miguel would!'

He laughed and I laughed too, but I felt extremely disconcerted.

Everything I had said, had come out without thinking. Incredibly, it was the truth. And I knew that having told Eric, I would have to tell Miguel. But I didn't want to lose either of them.

That night we undressed each other and made love tenderly, as if me confirming my feelings had made all the difference to him. I was no longer a challenge. His mission had been a complete success; he could relish in his victory.

I awoke in the morning, to feel the hot sun beating down through the window on to my head. I opened my eyes slowly.

Leaning against the wall next to the window was this giant of a man, simply watching me. He was beautiful. Long black hair, brooding dark eyes fringed with long black eyelashes, set in a tanned, unshaven face.

With dismay, I realised that Eric was sleeping naked beside me, his hand lying across my breast, almost possessively.

But Miguel, if he noticed, didn't seem to mind.

'God, you two look so fucking beautiful together,' he said, beginning to peel out of his T-shirt and leather trousers. 'I'm so glad to be home.'

BLACK LACE NEW BOOKS

Published in August

LIKE MOTHER, LIKE DAUGHTER

Georgina Brown
£5.99

Mother Liz and daughter Rachel are very alike, even down to sharing the same appetite for men. But while Rachel is keen on gaining sexual experience with older guys, her mother is busy seducing men half her age, including Rachel's boyfriend.

ISBN 0 352 33422 3

CONFESSIONAL

Judith Roycroft
£5.99

Faren Lonsdale is an ambitious young reporter. Her fascination with celibacy in the priesthood leads her to infiltrate St Peter's, a seminary for young men who are about to sacrifice earthly pleasures for a life of devotion and abstinence.

What she finds, however, is that the nocturnal shenanigans that take place in their cloistered world are anything but chaste. And the high proportion of good-looking young men makes her research all the more pleasurable.

ISBN 0 352 33421 5

Published in September

OUT OF BOUNDS

Mandy Dickinson
£5.99

When Katie decides to start a new life in a French farmhouse left to her by her grandfather, she is horrified to find two men are squatting in her property. But her horror quickly becomes curiosity as she realises how attracted she is to them, and how much illicit pleasure she can have. When her ex-boyfriend shows up, it isn't long before everyone is questioning their sexuality.

ISBN 0 352 33431 2

A DANGEROUS GAME
Lucinda Carrington
£5.99

Doctor Jacey Muldaire knows what she wants from the men in her life: good sex and plenty of it. And it looks like she's going to get plenty of it while working in an elite private hospital in South America. But Jacey isn't all she pretends to be. A woman of many guises, she is in fact working for British Intelligence. Her femme fatale persona gives her access to places other spies can't get to. Every day is full of risk and sexual adventure, and everyone around her is playing a dangerous game.

ISBN 0 352 33432 0

To be published in October

THE TIES THAT BIND
Tesni Morgan
£5.99

Kim Buckley is a beautiful but shy young woman who is married to a wealthy business consultant. When a charismatic young stranger dressed as the devil turns up at their Halloween party, Kim's life is set to change for ever. Claiming to be her lost half-brother, he's got his eye on her money and a gameplan for revenge. Things are further complicated by their mutual sexual attraction and a sizzling combination of secret and guilty passions threatens to overwhelm them.

ISBN 0 352 33438 X

IN THE DARK
Zoe le Verdier
£5.99

This second collection of Zoe's erotic short stories explores the most explicit female desires. There's something here for every reader who likes their erotica hot and a little bit rare. From anonymous sex to exhibitionism, phone sex and rubber fetishism, all these stories have great characterisation and a sting in the tail.

ISBN 0 352 33439 8

If you would like a complete list of plot summaries of Black Lace titles, or would like to receive information on other publications available, please send a stamped addressed envelope to:

Black Lace, Thames Wharf Studios,
Rainville Road, London W6 9HT

BLACK LACE BOOKLIST

All books are priced £4.99 unless another price is given.

Black Lace books with a contemporary setting

PALAZZO	Jan Smith ISBN 0 352 33156 9	☐
THE GALLERY	Fredrica Alleyn ISBN 0 352 33148 8	☐
AVENGING ANGELS	Roxanne Carr ISBN 0 352 33147 X	☐
COUNTRY MATTERS	Tesni Morgan ISBN 0 352 33174 7	☐
GINGER ROOT	Robyn Russell ISBN 0 352 33152 6	☐
DANGEROUS CONSEQUENCES	Pamela Rochford ISBN 0 352 33185 2	☐
THE NAME OF AN ANGEL £6.99	Laura Thornton ISBN 0 352 33205 0	☐
SILENT SEDUCTION	Tanya Bishop ISBN 0 352 33193 3	☐
BONDED	Fleur Reynolds ISBN 0 352 33192 5	☐
THE STRANGER	Portia Da Costa ISBN 0 352 33211 5	☐
CONTEST OF WILLS £5.99	Louisa Francis ISBN 0 352 33223 9	☐
THE SUCCUBUS £5.99	Zoe le Verdier ISBN 0 352 33230 1	☐
FEMININE WILES £7.99	Karina Moore ISBN 0 352 33235 2	☐
AN ACT OF LOVE £5.99	Ella Broussard ISBN 0 352 33240 9	☐
DRAMATIC AFFAIRS £5.99	Fredrica Alleyn ISBN 0 352 33289 1	☐
DARK OBSESSION £7.99	Fredrica Alleyn ISBN 0 352 33281 6	☐
COOKING UP A STORM £7.99	Emma Holly ISBN 0 352 33258 1	☐

SEARCHING FOR VENUS — Ella Broussard ☐
£5.99 — ISBN 0 352 33284 0

A PRIVATE VIEW — Crystalle Valentino ☐
£5.99 — ISBN 0 352 33308 1

A SECRET PLACE — Ella Broussard ☐
£5.99 — ISBN 0 352 33307 3

THE TRANSFORMATION — Natasha Rostova ☐
£5.99 — ISBN 0 352 33311 1

SHADOWPLAY — Portia Da Costa ☐
£5.99 — ISBN 0 352 33313 8

MIXED DOUBLES — Zoe le Verdier ☐
£5.99 — ISBN 0 352 33312 X

RAW SILK — Lisabet Sarai ☐
£5.99 — ISBN 0 352 33336 7

THE TOP OF HER GAME — Emma Holly ☐
£5.99 — ISBN 0 352 33337 5

HAUNTED — Laura Thornton ☐
£5.99 — ISBN 0 352 33341 3

VILLAGE OF SECRETS — Mercedes Kelly ☐
£5.99 — ISBN 0 352 33344 8

INSOMNIA — Zoe le Verdier ☐
£5.99 — ISBN 0 352 33345 6

PACKING HEAT — Karina Moore ☐
£5.99 — ISBN 0 352 33356 1

TAKING LIBERTIES — Susie Raymond ☐
£5.99 — ISBN 0 352 33357 X

LIKE MOTHER, LIKE DAUGHTER — Georgina Brown ☐
ISBN 0 352 33422 3
£5.99

CONFESSIONAL — Judith Roycroft ☐
£5.99 — ISBN 0 352 33421 5

ASKING FOR TROUBLE — Kristina Lloyd ☐
£5.99 — ISBN 0 352 33362 6

Black Lace books with an historical setting

THE SENSES BEJEWELLED — Cleo Cordell ☐
ISBN 0 352 32904 1

HANDMAIDEN OF PALMYRA — Fleur Reynolds ☐
ISBN 0 352 32919 X

THE INTIMATE EYE — Georgia Angelis ☐
ISBN 0 352 33004 X

CONQUERED — Fleur Reynolds ☐
ISBN 0 352 33025 2

FORBIDDEN CRUSADE — Juliet Hastings ☐
ISBN 0 352 33079 1